FINAL SHOWDOWN

THE BLACK SPECTRE retraced his path through the large doors and into the spacious gambling room. Big Jack's office, where he expected to find the notorious mobster, was just in the back.

The casino was a picture of contrasts from his first visit. The lights all out, the tables quiet, and the room devoid of people.

There was only one sign of life. A sliver of light coming from the slightly ajar office door.

The Spectre hadn't noticed the pineapple motif when he was there before. Carved into the doors and wooden trim. Repeated in the wallpaper. The symbol for hospitality.

He was about to move to the office when he spotted one more. A ceramic pineapple that had previously been on the mantle.

Only now it was smashed on the floor below.

THE BLACK SPECTRE

BOOK THREE

VENGEANCE WAITS AT THE DOOR

BLACK
HOOD
PRESS

Published by Black Hood Press
An imprint of Lightning Bug Press
5535 Robinhood Village Drive, #103
Winston-Salem, NC 27106

www.blackhoodpress.com

First Print Edition: April 2019
ISBN-10: 1-949352-02-1
ISBN-13: 978-1-949352-02-3

Printed in the United States of America

10 9 8 7 6 5 4 3 2 1

PROLOGUE

Silverton, 1919.

EDWARD MORRIS stood dutifully by with cloche in hand as Chef Arturo masterfully prepared the most lavish plate of food to ever leave the kitchen at the Wyman Hotel. The proud culinary artist began by plating their most expensive cut of steak, served only to guests in the presidential suite. He topped it with a béarnaise sauce and added a hearty serving of Lyonnaise potatoes and grilled artichoke. Also included was a bottle of their very best wine and a loaf of their famous onion bread, straight out of the oven.

This, of course, was nothing terribly unusual. As the premiere restaurant west of Terminal City, Morris had served many a fine meal to their most illustrious guests. But what *was* unusual on this occasion was *where* he was to serve. Outside the kitchen door a bellman waited in the hotel car with the engine running.

Just as soon as Arturo finished and gave the dish his blessing, Edward covered the plate and the two men carried the wine and tray out the back door. Within seconds they were speeding the two blocks out to the rail yard where their guests awaited.

NATE GREGOR sat down next to his beautiful wife of 33 years and peered over her shoulder. Neither the passing decades nor the toll of tuberculosis could erase the girlish beauty that had so smitten him in her father's general store all those years ago.

With his fine suits and bushy, grey beard, Nate was even more of a distant shadow of the brash young man who'd repeatedly attempted to sweep his beloved "Kitty" off her feet. And had, at long last, succeeded.

Katherine Gregor sat up in her hospital bed reading, with every effort seen to her comfort. The parlor of their private rail car had been converted into a mobile infirmary, complete with an ample supply of pharmaceuticals, medical devices, and a young, live-in nurse at her side.

The Smithson & Gregor coach represented the height of luxury in rail travel. At the fore end was the galley, in which Mr. Coleman prepared their meals. Next was the dining room where eight could sup in luxury and comfort. The narrow hallway led to the collection of sleeping quarters, each with its own private bath. First was the master bedroom, followed by two smaller rooms for guests or servants. Finally, there was the lounge, a spacious room at the end of the car with six comfortable chairs, a sofa, and large picture windows to watch the passing scenery.

"Might I ask what you're reading, Lass?" Nate asked.

"Nathaniel Gregor, you know very well," Katherine chastised him playfully, her voice soft and raspy. "You just gave it to me this morning." He'd given her so many books over the years, she'd hardly had time to read them all.

Even in her debilitated state, she never failed to bring light and joy into his life. He couldn't bear the thought of losing her and had spared no effort in finding a cure. The prevailing wisdom of medical science was outdoor air, exercise, and a healthy diet. For that reason, they'd spent the entire Spring in the mountains of North Carolina. And while she'd gotten better, it hadn't been the remedy for which either had hoped.

Katherine dropped her book in her lap and quickly reached for a linen to cough. Nurse Olive instantly helped her get it to her mouth. Fortunately, there was no blood. This time.

The Gregor matriarch laid back down on her bed and put a hand to her chest. Nate held her other hand firmly as she struggled to catch her breath.

"Just take your time, Mrs. Katherine," Nurse Olive instructed. "Just got to let it pass." After a few minutes, she was finally able to relax once again.

Nate got up cheerfully as he heard the car pull up outside. "I expect that'd be our dinner."

Katherine put aside her book as Nurse Olivia wheeled the table over. Nate opened the rear door of the car to let in Arturo carrying a bottle of wine, followed closely by Edward Morris, who held the cloche-covered tray high above his head with the experienced skill of a master.

Nate recognized them both immediately. As head waiter at the Wyman, Edward Morris had served them many times and always provided nothing less than excellence. And just as on this night, Arturo had routinely outdone himself in the kitchen.

"Mrs. Gregor, Mr. Gregor," Edward greeted them as he set the tray down on the rolling table. "Dinner is served."

It mattered not that they were in a train car that looked more like a hospital. He and Arturo would spare no flourish.

Arturo introduced the meal as Morris took a corkscrew from his jacket and poured a sip in one of the two wine glasses on the tray. "Tonight I have prepared for you a most succulent and delicious meal." He then described each dish in mouth-watering detail.

Morris pulled away the cloche in the most dramatic fashion. A cloud of steam billowed out and filled the air with the most enticing of scents.

"And for your dining pleasure," Arturo concluded, "I have paired it with our finest bottle of French wine. Please enjoy."

Morris offered Nate the glass. The aging tycoon sniffed it carefully, swirled it around in the glass and finally gave it a taste, along with his approval. "Excellent."

Katherine watched the whole production with deep appreciation. The smile in her eyes said more than her words ever could. "Thank you both so much," she told them. "This is all just so wonderful."

The two men both bowed in appreciation. "Our pleasure, Ma'am," Morris replied. "Always a distinct joy to see you again. We pray for your speedy recovery."

Arturo rushed back to his kitchen while Morris stayed on hand to assist. "If there's anything else you need, Mrs. Gregor, Mr. Gregor, please don't hesitate to ask."

"A bigger appetite for one," Katherine chuckled. Even though it was only one steak, it was large enough to easily serve three.

"Now now, I won't be hearing that," Nate reminded her. "Got to keep your strength up. Remember, after dinner we're going dancing at the Handlebars Saloon."

"I think that old place closed twenty years ago," she reminded him.

"Oh, you don't say, now do you?" Nate remarked. "Well then, I suppose we'll just have to make do right here."

SADLY, it was only a matter of days before his beloved Kitty took a turn for the worse. Nate called for Dr. Graves and had him rush out to the Gregor Mansion. Sarah Gregor and Nurse Olivia sat dutifully by her bedside as Nate accompanied the respected physician upstairs.

After more than an hour, Nate led the doctor out and joined Thomas in the study. Thomas Gregor stood up as his father closed the door and sat down in one of the high-backed leather chairs. The deep look of concern on the old patriarch's face told the young D.A. that the news was not good.

"What did the doctor say?" Thomas asked, almost afraid to hear the answer.

His father let out a deep sigh. It was difficult to summon the strength to even speak the words. "Just as we feared. With rest and plenty of fresh air there's a chance she might improve. But she's not long for this world, I'm afraid. A few months. Six or eight at best."

Thomas sat back down in thoughtful resignation. "What if you take her back to North Carolina?"

Nate was just about to answer when little Brent, all of eight years old, ran into the room. In the safety of the estate, he could be quite the rambunctious little boy. Always finding his way where he didn't belong. Somehow, closed doors seemed to never keep him out.

The two men quickly bottled their emotions. No need to share their pain with Brent. Especially at his young age. There would be difficult conversations in days ahead, to be sure. But neither men were in any rush to have them.

"Come here, you!" Nate scooped up his grandson in his strong arms. The young boy instinctively let out a giggle and reached for the old man's bushy beard. Such a welcome distraction from the ever-intruding realities of life.

"I've got something for you, Boy," Nate informed his growing heir.

"You do?" Brent immediately quit squirming and looked up at Grandpa Nate with excitement. He loved to get presents, no matter how big or small.

Thomas looked on with equal surprise. He quickly assumed his father had picked up some trinket in Silverton. The old man always managed to pluck some small and unique object from his pocket. Thomas could have filled a museum with all of the interesting items his father had given him growing up.

As always, Grandpa Nate reached into his suit jacket. Little Brent watched with wonder as Nate produced an old, scuffed pocket watch in his bony fingers and opened it with one hand.

"Do you know what this is?" his grandfather asked.

"A watch," Brent answered. He looked up with a puzzled expression. He knew this watch. He'd seen Grandpa Nate pull it from his pocket many times. He'd marveled when the old man had popped it open and shown him the two dials. He even remembered that the larger one told the time. And that the smaller one at the bottom counted the seconds.

"Not just any watch," Grandpa Nate told him. "It's a very special watch. You see, when I was young, younger than your father even, Uncle Dick and I used to work on the railroad."

Nate pressed the latch and again revealed its contents. "One day I got hold of a whole box of these watches. From your Great Grandpa Dawson, as a matter of fact. Anyway, I got this idea in my head. I thought if I could sell them, I could maybe start a business of my own. Only problem was, I didn't have any money."

"Oh," Little Brent sighed. Though he'd never wanted for anything in his young life.

"Well, the good news was," Grandpa Nate continued, "I knew someone who did. Your Uncle Dick. It took some cajoling, mind you, but that's how we become partners. And that's how we started Smithson & Gregor. Just from this *one* watch."

"Wow!" Brent gasped with excitement.

Grandpa Nate handed him the timepiece. Brent fingered it carefully.

"I want *you* to have it," Grandpa Nate told him. "Keep it safe. And keep it as a reminder. You can do whatever it is you set your mind to."

"When he's older, Pop," Thomas smiled. He graciously took the watch from Brent's small hands and carried it to the large oak desk.

"You be sure to give it to him then," Nate instructed.

"I will," Thomas assured them both. He picked up a narrow manila envelope from his desk and dropped it inside. "When you're older, Son."

CHAPTER ONE

Seventeen Years Later.

WILLIE "POTATOES" BINAGGIO bolted into the Emergency Room at Terminal City General. With his arm still in a sling, he looked more like a patient than a visitor.

Willie took a quick look around. He knew the place well. The waiting area was long and narrow. The furniture comfortable. The magazines out of date. He'd scoped out the place in hopes of getting to Nails McCarthy. But the cops had it too well guarded.

Of all the hospitals in the city, this was the largest. And the least likely to have what he wanted. So he wasn't about to waste any time finding out.

His young backup waited by the door. They didn't expect any trouble. But they wouldn't discount the possibility, either.

Willie immediately locked eyes on the Amazon that ran the joint. He remembered her, too. Reminded him of Sister Gertrude.

Nurse Muriel Plunther peered up from the charge desk. A tall, no-nonsense woman, she looked like a spinster with her pinched face, hair pulled into a tight bun, and cat-eye glasses with a chain around her long neck. It was clear that nothing much phased her. During her many years there, she'd seen it all. From kids with broken bones to gangsters full of lead.

"What's the nature of your injury? Are you feeling any

pain?" she asked.

"Looking for a guy," Willie replied. "Dressed all in black. Shot up like Swiss cheese. We was concerned. Just wanted to see if he was okay, you know."

She just glowered down at him with a disapproving sneer. The fancy clothes didn't fool her. She'd seen his kind enough to recognize him on the spot.

"We don't have anyone like that here," she informed him. She took off her glasses and let them drop on the chain. "Now, if you two gentlemen don't have any other business here, I'd appreciate it if you'd move along."

Willie didn't care for her disdainful attitude. Nor did he have time for it. He wasn't above slapping around a dame. Including one that had him by a good foot.

"Why don't you take a look real quick?" he asked. "'Cause we been combing all the hospitals and we gotta be sure."

She stepped around the desk with her arms crossed and glowered at him further. She'd long ago learned to use her height to intimidate even the strongest of men. "I'm most certain," she affirmed. "Now you two run along like I said before I call the law."

Willie grabbed her by the glasses chain and slapped her hard across the face. The blow was so stinging she dropped to one knee. Even with his bad arm he was lightning fast. And strong.

She looked back at him in stunned disbelief.

He tightened his grip and slapped her again. Just to make his point. She fell to both knees that time.

"Let's try this again, Gertrude," Willie informed her. "And this time how's about you don't give me any more lip?"

"He's not here!" she sobbed as he kicked her to the floor. She threw up her large hands and cowered into a ball. "I swear! Look anywhere you want! I promise!"

Willie glowered back at her angrily. Had half a mind to plug her right there, just for good measure. But he'd wasted enough time already. He rubbed his sore arm and put it back in the sling.

"That's more like it," Willie barked. "Maybe next time you'll show some manners."

TOMMY "CLAMS" AUFERIO rapped on the glass one last time before kicking in the office door. Just as he'd expected, all the lights were out and, at first glance, it sure looked like nobody was there. That was a relief.

He'd worked a few guys over, but never had to take a guy out before. And after what he'd just heard about this Ghost Man trying to plug Big Jack, *on his own turf no less*, he wasn't exactly sure he wanted to face the guy alone. Even all shot up.

He'd kill a man if he had to. He just hoped he didn't have to.

Tommy was tempted just to scram and mark this one off. But this being one of the few times he was out on his own and not backing up Willie, he needed to check the place over and be sure.

It was a small doctor's office of just a few rooms. The waiting area had old furniture and dark wood paneling. Just a one-man operation. And an old man at that. With the lights out it was difficult to see. He almost tripped over the coffee table heading into the back.

He'd never been there before, but he knew the practice. Dr. Harlan Murphy was a family physician with just one nurse. His wife. Wasn't the best doc in town, but a good one to see if you didn't have much money and really just wanted some pills to fix you up.

He checked the examination room, the Doc's own office, and even the storage closet. Not a soul there. And no sign of blood or anything. The place was totally clean.

Was tempted to raid the drug cabinet, but that's not what he was there for. Willie had told them not to get distracted. They had one job and one job only. Find the Ghost Man. Nothing else mattered.

Even so, Tommy still managed to grab a handful of lollipops on the way out the door.

FRANKIE "EGGS" MILANO barreled into the front entrance at the Our Lady of Mercy Infirmary. The young Soldato that rode with him stood guard by the door.

Eggs didn't have far to look. The place was small and cozy. Just plain white walls and tile floors. And, with all the crucifixes and Nuns, looked more like a church than a hospital. So much that he instinctively crossed himself and said a quick *Hail Mary* as soon as he entered.

The hospital was quiet as usual, and this was friendly territory. But he had to be sure before he marked it off and moved on. These old Penguins would help anybody. No questions asked.

He'd been there a couple of times already to visit Cherry Nose. Big Jack's trusted driver was still camped out on the third floor, where they were taking real good care of him. As much as Eggs wanted to stop by for another visit, he wasn't there for a social call. He had a job to do and it was much too late for one anyway.

Still, if the Ghost Man had gone there, he was sure they'd have known about it already. They had the place well guarded. But the order was to check every hospital and doctor's office, so that's what he was going to do.

Seeing the Penguin on duty always gave him the shivers. But she was a nice enough old broad, and he knew she'd cooperate. No need to get rough. Lucky for her, she'd never whacked him with a paddle. That would've been a different story.

Eggs marched up to the desk and tapped on the wooden surface. Sister Helena put down her book and peered at him over her reading glasses. Her wizened little face actually lit up when she recognized him.

"Mr. Milano, what can I do for you?" she asked. "I'd tell your young friend that he's welcome to come inside, but I'm afraid visiting hours are long over. Though I do say that Mr. Caifano always enjoys your visits."

Such a nice old broad, Eggs thought. *Why couldn't he have had her instead of Sister Gertrude?*

"Actually, Sister, we're looking for a guy," Eggs informed her. "He got injured pretty bad just about half hour ago. But I'm afraid we don't know where he went. Just want to make sure he's okay, is all."

He didn't exactly like lying to a Penguin. He could still feel all the wraps across the knuckles he'd gotten from Sister Gertrude. But it was more like *stretching it*. And it was for her own good.

Sister Helena stepped out from behind the desk. She was a tiny woman made even smaller by the stoop in her posture. "Well, my goodness. I'm afraid there's nobody here. We don't usually get emergency patients, you know."

She meandered through the front hall as if to demonstrate by the addition of her mere presence that the place was, in fact, empty. What's more, she was just her usual kind self, not at all flustered, and with nothing to hide.

"Well, thank you for your time, Sister. I suppose I'd better look elsewhere," Eggs told her. "You go back to enjoying that book of yours."

She actually blushed in appreciation. He hadn't been able to catch the title, but it clearly wasn't the Good Book. "Good luck on finding your friend. I do hope he's quite all right."

"Thank you, Sister," Eggs replied on his way out the door. "And please tell Cherry Nose we says hello."

"You drive carefully now, Mr. Milano," she called out to him. "It's getting terrible dark out. You don't know what kind of people come out at this hour."

THE BLACK SEDAN hurled to a stop in the middle of the intersection at State Street and Temple Avenue. Willie Potatoes jumped out of the passenger's seat as two more black sedans screeched to a halt right after him. Tommy Clams and Eggs Milano hopped out and joined him for an impromptu meeting in the middle of the road.

"Okay, I just done Terminal City General. No sign of him there," Willie informed the group. "How 'bout you guys? Anything?"

"Checked Our Lady of Mercy," Eggs replied. "Nothing there. But they been taking real good care of Cherry Nose."

Tommy shook his head in agreement. "All clear at that old doctor's joint over on Prospect. Won't nobody there, neither."

"Where's Fingers?" Willie asked.

"State Street Receiving," Eggs told him.

Willie was just about to hand out further orders when a car pulled up to the intersection and honked for them to move. The middle-aged driver stuck his head out of the window and shouted, "Out of the way! I'm trying to get through, here!"

Willie and Fingers both whipped out their pistols and charged towards the vehicle. The driver had just laid on the horn again when he saw them coming.

"Holy Hell!" the Driver shouted as he threw it in reverse. Willie and Fingers both rushed in his direction as the stunned motorist sped backwards. He nearly ran into a shoe store trying to escape.

"Dumb bastard," Willie grumbled and shoved his gun back inside his jacket. "Who's he think he is?"

Fingers laughed as the driver swerved back and forth until he finally made it to the next intersection and turned around.

"Okay, listen up," Willie barked, "I don't want none of us going home till we find this guy, got it? There's no way he coulda went that far. We gotta check every pharmacy, doctor's office, you name it. Any place that even looks like it's got needle and thread."

Tommy Clams and Eggs affirmed their agreement. They both knew that this would be a long night. There was no way this guy was going to get away. If he was lucky, he'd bleed out before they discovered him.

"Eggs, you take that pharmacy over on 8th," Willie commanded. "I'll check the Vet over on State Street. Tommy, you check out that funeral home down on LaMonte."

Tommy wasn't exactly thrilled about his assignment. "Let me do the Vet," he suggested.

"Don't be such a Nancy boy," Willie chided him.

"Then you do the funeral home," Tommy protested. "Those places give me the creeps."

"Yeah, yeah. Okay," Willie consented. "Such a Momma's Boy."

Tommy was relieved and had almost gotten back into his car when Eggs had a thought. "Hey Willie, didn't you say there was a Chink doctor over in Chinatown?"

"Yeah, right," Willie suddenly realized. "It's a little far, but he maybe coulda gone there. Good thinking. Tommy, you go do the funeral home."

Tommy threw up his hands in disgust. Eggs just laughed

as the fellow gangster went back to his car.

"Somebody tell Fingers to check out the vet," Willie concluded. "I'm heading over to Chinatown."

DOMINICK "FINGERS" SCARRONE marched into the State Street Receiving Hospital. It was an old facility and looked it, with a gothic exterior, uneven tile floors, and cracks in the white walls which had somehow acquired a yellowish hue over the years. It had been hastily built in the 1850s after a smallpox outbreak and was later used to quarantine typhoid patients at the turn of the century.

Its present use was for immediate trauma care, such as burns, severe injury, and severed limbs. This was where most guys went when they took a bullet. Of all the medical facilities in Terminal City, it was also the most likely place they'd find the Ghost Man. And the perfect place for him to hide.

Fingers knew this place well and knew they did good work. They'd pulled two slugs out of his own chest three years earlier. Just missed his heart by a fraction. Even so, he was back there for a reason and was willing to search the whole place himself if he had to.

With his young backup covering the door, Fingers marched right past Nurse Schneider, the stocky, middle-aged woman that ran the emergency room. Fingers knew that she wouldn't easily be intimidated. Which was why Willie had sent him in the first place.

"You can't come in here," Nurse Schneider called out in a stern, German-accented voice. "This area is for patients only."

The gangster just ignored her and made a beeline for the young doctor who was busy attending the injured. Fingers needed to make it known right away that he meant business.

He whipped out his pistol and shot the doctor in the leg. The pained groans that had filled the room were quickly replaced with screams of terror. The attending nurses all dove for the floor, leaving their patients unprotected on their beds. Not that they could have done anything to protect them anyway.

"Hope you got more doctors," Fingers shouted, "'cause you're gonna need 'em if I don't get some answers!'"

Nurse Schneider immediately rushed over and put herself between Fingers and the bleeding physician. "Just tell us what you want! I only ask of you, please don't take any of our medication."

Fingers glowered back at her and offered an amused smile. "I'll take whatever I want. Or you're gonna need some body bags to clean this place up. And don't think I won't plug you just because you're a broad."

He shoved her aside and announced to all, "I'm looking for a guy. Just got shot up real bad. Last twenty minutes."

Fingers shoved his way past her, went to each bed, and pulled back every curtain. A weaker man would have likely vomited at the sight of protruding bones, blood-soaked sheets, and burnt flesh that met his eyes. Tommy especially. But Fingers had seen a lot worse and was more often than not the cause of it.

There was no sign of the Ghost Man.

Scarrone turned back to Nurse Schneider as she attended to the wounded doctor. "You got anybody else here? Or should I turn this place into a morgue?"

"No, please!" she begged through tear-filled eyes. "Look anywhere you like. But I swear to you, there's nobody like that here!"

Fingers just laughed. "Why'd we have to make this so hard, huh?"

EGGS MILANO kicked in the door of Mobley Pharmacy on Temple Street and forced his way inside. It was an old, brick building with the entrance on the corner and a large neon sign overhead. The many rows of shelves were well stocked with medicines, bandages, vitamins, and assorted remedies.

On the left was the service counter where they used to operate a soda fountain. But Eggs couldn't remember a time when they ever did. Old Man Mobley had been in a wheelchair for years and just couldn't manage it anymore.

Behind the counter and in the connecting back room were more rows of shelves. These were where the pharmacist kept all of the prescription medication. If he'd known what to look for, Eggs would have been very tempted to grab a few for himself. He was sure they'd fetch a good price on the street.

He made his way in the dark between the racks. It wasn't the easiest to see, but luckily there was a light on in the back. He just aimed for that and felt his way along.

The employee door was locked, so he set his pistol on the counter and hopped over. Just as soon as he retrieved his firearm he heard something in the next room. It wasn't much of a sound, but enough to tell him that he wasn't alone.

The Ghost Man had to be there. He was sure of it.

He rounded the corner and found himself face-to-face with the business end of a shotgun.

But that wasn't what surprised him. It was held by a young girl with a dimpled chin and a very determined look on her cute little face. Couldn't have been more than seventeen. Looked like a tomboy with no warpaint and light brown hair cut off at the shoulders. She wasn't the prettiest thing he'd ever seen, but she filled out her overalls nicely.

Eggs immediately put his hands up. "Whoa! Careful where you point that thing, Sweetheart."

"Why don't you back right up and get the hell out of my store?" she demanded. "I promise you, I'll call the morgue before I call the police."

He'd heard Old Man Mobley had a daughter. He'd no idea she was such a spitfire. He soon realized she meant business.

"Come on, I ain't looking for trouble," Eggs smiled. "What's your name, Sweetheart?"

"None of your damn business," she told him.

Old Man Mobley called out from the next room. "Keechie, you okay in there?"

"Don't you worry none, Pop," she shouted back, never taking her eyes off Eggs. "Call the police. Tell 'em we got ourselves a first class thief in here."

Eggs was surprised to see Old Man Mobley round the corner in a wheelchair. He was a wiry fellow with a bow tie and round glasses. What few hairs remained on his bald head had long since turned grey.

Eggs was getting impatient. Every minute he spent yapping with them was another minute wasted. He could've easily taken them both out. But that wasn't his style. Especially a young dish sweet as this one.

"Look here," Eggs offered and took a step back. "I ain't here to steal nothing, promise. I'm just looking for a guy is all. Real bad fella, too. We're trying to find him before he hurts anybody else. Be all over the morning papers, honest."

Eggs took another cautious step back.

"Don't take your eye off him, Keechie," her father instructed as he wheeled himself over to the phone.

"Hold on, just a minute," Eggs countered with a charming smile. "I told you, I ain't looking for trouble. Swear on my mother's grave. Look, I'm just gonna put my gun away. No funny business."

Keechie raised her shotgun as Eggs carefully opened his suit jacket and slowly re-holstered his pistol. Then he raised both hands again. She relaxed her grip just a bit.

"Trust me, you don't want to shoot nobody. Especially not a pretty little thing like you." Eggs gave her a wink.

She smiled back.

TOMMY CLAMS barged into the foyer of the Mroczek & Son Funeral Parlor. He was immediately met by Jakub Mroczek Sr., a soft-spoken man in a finely tailored black suit. The elderly gentleman's white hair was combed neatly back and his small moustache perfectly trimmed.

Mroczek & Son was a family-run business that had served the grieving households of Terminal City since their founding in 1904. It was a small establishment with one visitation room, a tiny chapel, and a pair of empty caskets on display in the foyer.

Judging by the young man's harried expression, Mroczek Sr. quickly surmised that Tommy was exceedingly late for the Jefferson wake, which was nearly over. That is until Tommy whipped out his firearm and waved it in the old man's face.

Mroczek Sr. quickly threw his hands up in stunned confusion. He'd never heard of anyone robbing a funeral home before and shuddered at the thought of what this young man could possibly want.

"Sir, we are hosting a wake!" Mroczek Sr. protested.

"Yeah, well you're gonna be hosting another if you don't keep your yap shut," Tommy snapped. The place already bugged him out enough as it was. Last thing he wanted was any lip from a mortician.

Mroczek Sr. could readily tell from the shakiness in Tommy's voice that he was not a young man with whom to be trifled. That and the gun, of course.

"Where do you patch up the stiffs?" Tommy asked.

This was exactly what Mroczek Sr. feared. He looked back at Tommy Clams with pleading eyes.

"Please, have some respect for the dead, I beg you," Mroczek Sr. implored.

"Lookit, I don't want to be here any more than want me to," Tommy explained. "I'm just looking for a guy, is all. He ain't here, I promise I'll be out of here fast as you can say *and how.*"

Mroczek Sr. looked back at Tommy with a puzzled expression. "Is the gentleman in question deceased?"

"Just show me where..." Tommy had to swallow hard as his voice trailed off. "Just show me where you fix 'em up."

Mroczek Sr. opened a nearby door and led Tommy downstairs. With each step into the basement, he could tell that the young man was becoming even more unnerved. On the one hand, he thought that the young hoodlum might bolt in repulsion. But, on the other hand, he feared that a worse reaction was also possible.

Mroczek Sr. led Tommy into the preparation room and turned on the overhead lights. It was cold, with white-tiled walls, cabinets of embalming fluid and tools, and a big metal table in the center of the room. On one wall were six large drawers where they kept the *guests of honor*. The place stunk of formaldehyde.

Tommy immediately ran to the sink and threw up.

FINGERS banged fiercely on the door of the Fifth City Animal Hospital, but there was no answer. He was about to kick the door in, even shoot through it if needed, before he changed his mind. If the Ghost Man was there, he'd probably be around back anyway. So he opted to do the same and cut through the narrow pathway between the low, brick buildings.

Fingers reached the back alley where he found a small dirt parking lot with an old, red pickup truck. Beside it was Enzo, a young Italian kid having a smoke. He was dressed in rubber boots and overalls and looked about Tommy's age. Maybe younger. Mostly he looked fresh off the boat.

"Hey, kid!" Fingers shouted as he stepped towards the open back door.

Enzo dropped his cigarette when he looked up to see Fingers with a gun pointed straight at him.

"I'm looking for a guy," Fingers commanded as he waved Enzo towards the open door. "He didn't come here for help, did he?"

Enzo just stared back at him with his hands in the air. Fingers didn't know if the kid was deaf or just soft in the head. But either way, the boy didn't answer.

"You hear me?" Fingers shouted. "You ain't stupid, are you?"

Enzo finally shouted back. "Non capisco. Non parlo inglese."

Poor kid, Fingers quickly realized, he really was fresh off the boat. Straight from the old country. Just like his own parents and older sister. Fingers had never been there himself. He and his two younger brothers had both been born in America.

"È il dottore qui?" Fingers conversed in Italian. "I'm looking for a guy. He might have come here looking for help."

"No," Enzo assured him, relieved to be understood. "There's no one else here. It's just me and the animals."

The kid seemed sincere. But Fingers knew better than to trust anyone. He'd already had to leave his mark at the hospital when they didn't listen. He wasn't about to walk away from this place without checking every inch.

Fingers waved Enzo towards the door again and followed him inside. "Come on. I need to look around and make sure."

The back room was cramped and smelled of excrement. It was chock full of metal cages of every size. Large ones on the bottom and small ones on the top. Inside were dogs, cats, and even a monkey. You couldn't hear a thing for all the barking and screeching. Right by the door was a shovel and a bucket. Poor Enzo's tools of the trade.

"Where does the doctor operate on the animals?" Fingers inquired.

Enzo waved for him to follow. The young man led him into the next room and switched on the lights. It was a small operating room with a light overhead, big bottles of ether on the shelves, and surgical tools neatly arranged on the tile counter. The table in the middle had leather straps. Just like the first room, there was a drain in the cement floor.

Looked more like the House of Pain than an operating room. Dr. Moreau would be right at home.

Fingers quickly checked it over. The table was clean and dry. No sign of blood. Same with the counter and floor. Everything sure looked like it hadn't been touched. The only thing he saw was animal hair. If the Ghost Man had been there, there was no way they could have cleaned the place up so fast.

He looked up just in time to see the shovel come flying at his head.

Fingers ducked as Enzo hit the cabinet and smashed open two giant bottles of ether. He fired two quick shots and the young boy collapsed on the floor.

The gangster grabbed the corner of his jacket and covered his mouth. He stepped over the young man's body and coughed his way back through the cages.

The Vet would sure have a surprise in the morning.

Poor kid, Fingers thought. *He'd come a long way just to shovel shit and die on the floor of an animal hospital.* But Fingers hadn't survived that long without always staying on his toes.

When it came time to pull the trigger, he was always ready.

WILLIE POTATOES jumped out of the car outside Chinese City Hall. He'd barely made it into the front entrance of the immense Oriental building before he ran headlong into the man he needed to see. Yo Hing, right hand of Sam Yuen.

Willie bowed and offered his respects. "We're looking for a guy. Got shot up real bad. Thought he might've come see the doc here."

"Dr. Tung?" Yo Hing queried.

"Uh, yeah," Willie nodded in hesitant affirmation. He couldn't remember the name. Wasn't sure he'd even heard it when they'd met on the stairs just a few weeks earlier. *But how many Chink doctors could there be in Chinese City Hall?*

"Just want to ask him a few questions is all," Willie explained.

Yo Hing didn't know all the answers. But he knew enough. He knew that the Doctor had been called to the Parish. That he, himself, had been asked to dispose of a car that had been shot full of bullet holes.

But Dr. Tung and the Parish were both under Sam Yuen's protection. And no matter what kind of arrangement they had with the Italians, he wasn't about to tell. Especially not to Willie.

The Chinese were very good at keeping secrets.

"Doctor Tung left at his usual time," Yo Hing stated. "No patients came here. This is not a hospital."

Under normal circumstances, Willie would have checked the doctor's office. Every room and closet. Just to be sure. But Willie knew better than to ask. This was as far as he would get. Sam Yuen had already let them search for Whitey. There was no reason to expect he wouldn't help them find the Ghost Man.

He'd just have to take Yo Hing's word for it.

"Well, all we know is, this guy didn't just disappear into thin air," Willie exhaled in frustration. "If he did, he *really* must be a ghost."

CHAPTER TWO

DAILY CRUSADER reporter Vicky Rose dropped her shoes on the stairs and rushed for the hallway phone in Mrs. Hershey's Boarding House for Women. Though it was late at night, she'd just gotten another urgent message from her sister. But the one that really got her attention was from *Standard* news hound Charlie Hecht. If Charlie was working this late, she reasoned, something must have happened. Something big.

She grabbed the phone and immediately dialed Charlie back.

Her landlady, Mrs. Hershey, was not at all happy about Vicky's blatant disregard for the rules. "Miss Rose!" the older woman complained. "I must protest the usage of the telephone at this late hour!"

Vicky just waved at her to shush. Hecht picked up on the first ring. "Charlie, what's this all about?" she asked him excitedly.

"Hiya, Doll!" Hecht answered with surprise. "Can't believe you called me back! Heard you been out hobnobbing with the hoi-poloi."

"Cut the crap, Charlie," Vicky retorted. "What gives? Something happen at the Four Diamonds to-night?"

Mrs. Hershey couldn't believe her ears. "Miss Rose! We do not tolerate that kind of language! Especially from a young lady!"

Vicky shooed her off again.

"Well, I never!" Mrs. Hershey exclaimed, fanning herself. She quickly turned on her heel and went back into her apartment.

"Lookit, Doll Face, I know you been grounded," Hecht began. "That's the only reason I'm calling you. Heard a little something to-night and you, of all people, might know the answer."

"What happened at the Four Diamonds?" she demanded.

"Well, it's like this," he told her. "Somebody tried to drop a dime on Big Jack."

I knew it! Vicky was beside herself. Something big had happened all right, just like she said it would. And she'd missed it!

"Who was it? she asked. "Whitey? Squint Mulligan? Dapper Sheridan?"

"That's just it," he replied. "They don't know. But *a little bird told me...*" Way to rub it in, Charlie.

"Now, I didn't see it myself, but I managed to overhear some conversation. Said he was dressed all in black. Wore a mask with a skull on it. And that Vito Spats had seen him before," Charlie continued. "Said it was *the same guy from the Asylum.*"

Vicky practically dropped the phone.

"You wouldn't happen to know anything about that, would you, Doll?" Charlie asked.

She just stood there shaking. Silent.

"Hey Doll, you still there? Hello?"

Mrs. Hershey stuck her head out again. "Miss Rose! It's far too late an hour — "

"Can it, Mrs. Hershey!" Vicky barked. That told Charlie loud and clear that she was still on the line.

"Before you say what you're thinking," he told her, "let me remind you again that you're grounded."

Not the best tactic, Charlie, she thought. But she wouldn't have expected anything less.

"No, I don't know a damn thing," she told him and slammed the phone down.

Mrs. Hershey had to clutch her pearls. She was about to exclaim yet another "Well, I never!" But Vicky stopped her before the older woman could make a sound.

"I don't want to hear it!" Vicky snapped. Then she turned and charged back up the stairs.

So, the Man in Black was real after all. Vito Spats had seen him, too. That was all the confirmation she needed.

This was her story, she fumed. And Charlie Hecht, of all people, had beaten her to it!

And it was becoming clear that she'd need to find a new apartment. With her own telephone. But she didn't have time to think about any of that just then. She had bigger things to worry about.

She felt her headache coming back.

With a vengeance.

DR. EUGENE TUNG emerged from the kitchen-turned-operating room in the Chinatown Parish and joined Worthington, Father Pacelli, and Sister Amelia in the tiny prayer room. Worthington looked up with hope in his eyes as the good doctor wiped his forehead with a towel.

Dr. Tung had been gone for what seemed like an eternity. In truth, it had been several hours, well past midnight and closer to dawn. The only comfort Worthington had been able to find, aside from his prayers and the company of Father Pacelli and Sister Amelia, was that each passing hour was another in which they hadn't been found.

Worthington had prayed most of the night and found himself in tears. He'd already lived through this tragedy once in his life. The last thing he wanted was to see it to its logical, tragic end.

"Is he alive, Doctor?" Worthington barely managed to ask. "Will he survive?"

Dr. Tung stretched his tired back and sat down with Worthington. His expression showed a combination of amazement and bewilderment.

"I'm afraid I couldn't say at this point," the middle-aged doctor explained. "One of the bullets has passed clear through his internal organs. From the loss of blood and the location of the puncture, he should be dead already. And yet he still lives."

Worthington let out an exhausted sigh of relief. It wasn't

the definitive answer of good news for which he'd hoped, but it was enough. He'd already witnessed one miracle these last few weeks and was certainly open to the possibility of another.

"With God, all things are possible," Father Pacelli happily confirmed as he clutched Worthington by the shoulder.

"We can only wait and see," Dr. Tung concluded. "And continue to pray. Considering the resources, I did the best I could. But I'm afraid I can make no promises."

Worthington had heard those words before. And under the very best of circumstances. This time, he prayed that the outcome would be different. But at least he had hope.

"Clearly, the hand of God is at work here," Father Pacelli observed, shaking his head. "When the time is more appropriate, you'll have to tell me by what miracle he's able to walk. And how you came to be here to-night."

Worthington struggled to hold back the tears that suddenly overwhelmed him.

"It could very well be a miracle," Dr. Tung added. "This is certainly the place for such things."

"There are greater forces at work here, Doctor," Worthington commented. "That much, I truly believe."

CHAPTER THREE

Three Years Prior.

BRENT GREGOR stared out at the mountains through the large picture windows at the Heiße Quellen Clinic high in the Austrian Alps. He and Worthington had arrived by train the night before, so this was their first opportunity to take in the majestic beauty of the area. They were surrounded by snow-peaked vistas, endless green forests, and bright blue skies.

Equally intriguing was the bevy of beautiful blonde-haired, blue-eyed young women exercising on the large veranda outside. Each wore an identical white leotard as she performed calisthenics, meditation, or gymnastics.

Brent was particularly impressed by the young woman who worked the parallel bars. He marveled as she swung her lithe form in between and over the bars with the honed skill of an Olympic athlete.

"Wilkommen, Herr Gregor!"

Brent reacted with a start. He looked up as Dr. Wilhelm Gaebeler clicked his heels and greeted them both with a firm and enthusiastic handshake.

Gaebeler was a tall man with a balding head and bushy, white moustache. Educated in both Vienna and London, he'd made numerous advancements in the field of neurosurgery and was respected the world over. He'd founded the clinic five years earlier, after practicing for many more in Munich. Its stated mission was to constantly push the boundaries of what was possible in medical science. The building was formerly a three-story mountain chalet. The retreat had been built seventeen years earlier on the site of a natural hot spring, for which it was named.

Brent was certain that when he left this place, he would forever leave his wheelchair behind.

"Here at the clinic," Dr. Gaebeler explained, "our approach is somewhat unique. We aim to repair both the mind *and* spirit. Before your surgery, you shall spend the next couple of weeks in preparation."

Following his operation, it would be at least a month before he was ready to travel. All told, he would be there for at least a good two months.

Brent had one order of business that weighed upon his mind. "I've left the clinic as my forwarding address. I'm expecting a very important telegram in the next several weeks. I would greatly appreciate it if you could see to its prompt delivery."

"Yes, of course," Dr. Gaebeler confirmed. "You shall have it the moment it arrives."

How Worthington felt about any of this, he made no comment. Brent assumed the older man had few objections to the surgery (other than, perhaps, it being experimental and the long journey to get there). The *healing of the mind and spirit* was likely a different story. Brent knew his beliefs in that area were far more traditional. But in a surprising turn, he kept those thoughts to himself.

Dr. Gaebeler signaled outside. The girl from the parallel bars had just finished and dried off. She threw the towel around her neck and came inside. "Herr Gregor, may I introduce you to Ilsa. She will be your personal caretaker during your time with us at Heiße Quellen. She shall assist with every step of your journey here."

She took Brent's hand and, in a soft accent that sounded more British than German, said, "So pleased to finally meet you, Herr Gregor. Please forgive my appearance. I was just doing my morning exercises."

Brent couldn't help but notice the tiny drops of perspiration as they cascaded down her smooth skin. He didn't have to wonder what Worthington's thoughts were then. The older gentleman's raised eyebrow spoke volumes.

"Please excuse me while I go make myself more presentable," she added. "I so look forward to our many sessions together." Brent couldn't help but follow her with his eyes as she left the room.

Worthington cleared his throat and finally spoke up. "What are his chances, Doctor, if I may?"

Dr. Gaebeler took a step back and gazed thoughtfully at Brent. "After careful examination of the X-rays and study of his records, I feel very optimistic. However, we can't know for certain until I operate. I can make no promises, but I shall endeavor to do the very best that I can."

ILSA rejoined Brent on the veranda after lunch. Treatment was scheduled to begin bright and early the next morning. So, she suggested, this was an opportunity for them to converse and get better acquainted. This time she was dressed in her crisp, white nurse's uniformed and looked much more the part of a professional caretaker.

Worthington had already taken a car back to the nearby village. He was scheduled to leave on the afternoon train back to London for an extended visit with his family. Dr. Gaebeler had assured him that Master Gregor was in very capable hands.

Worthington could only imagine.

Brent offered a brief family history. How his grandfather came from Scotland, worked on the railroad, and co-founded Smithson & Gregor. Much to his surprise, she was unfamiliar with the company. He told her about his parents, how his father was once the District Attorney, and that they had passed away years earlier. Finally, he talked about attending Emerson University, from which he had recently graduated.

Ilsa immediately stated that her own story was far less interesting (though Brent would quickly disagree). She grew up in Vienna, where her parents were both musicians. She'd spent most of her life there, except for many summers spent in England (*That explained the accent*, Brent thought). Ever since she was a small girl, she'd practiced gymnastics. She eventually went to Munich and trained for three years to compete in the Olympics.

"But one day I fell and suffered a terrible knee injury," she explained. "There was much doubt as to whether or not I'd ever be able to walk again without a cane."

Brent could certainly understand. She clutched him excitedly by the hand. "That was where I met Dr. Gaebeler. He repaired my knee just a year ago and now look at me. This is how I came to work here. I want to help others the same as he helped me."

Brent couldn't help but wonder just how complete her recovery had been. "Are you able to compete?"

"That remains to be seen," she told him. "There is another Olympics in a few years. Perhaps."

She got up and admired the beautiful vista below. Brent watched as she took in a deep breath of the fresh mountain air and turned back to him. "I hope that as we get to know each other, you will want to be more honest with me."

Brent was taken aback, though he shouldn't have been. "Whatever do you mean?"

"You haven't said a single word about the tragedy that befell your parents, why you're in this chair, or about the woman who broke your heart."

Brent instinctively backed away. Avoiding himself as much as her.

She turned back to face him. "Just know that if you want this treatment to be successful, there can be no secrets."

ILSA wheeled Brent down to the gymnasium first thing in the morning. He'd attempted to follow his usual routine of breakfast and the morning paper. When he'd requested to have his meal brought to his room, the clinic had readily complied.

The headline of the *London Times* had troubled him. The National Socialists of Germany had just passed the Law Against the Establishment of Parties, which outlawed all political opposition. Very troubling indeed.

But before he'd been able to read further, Ilsa showed up in her white nurse's uniform. She took away his newspaper and announced that it was time to get started. Brent looked at his watch in disbelief. "Already? But what about your morning practice?"

"I've already done my exercises," she announced. "Now its your turn."

The gymnasium was a large room that Brent surmised had previously been used for social functions. The furniture had all been removed and replaced with cushioned treatment tables, tumbling mats, weights of every size, medicine balls, and rowing machines. It was all very impressive.

She pushed his chair up next to one of the tables and locked the wheels. "Are you able to get up on your own?"

"Of course," Brent told her. Despite his inability to walk, he'd never considered himself fully dependent on others. As he pulled himself up onto the table, Ilsa unbuttoned her uniform. Underneath she wore the same white leotard from her gymnastics performance.

"Lie down on your stomach," she instructed him.

He complied and much to his surprise, she got up on the table with him. She reached into his lower back and began to massage where he still had feeling. She dug her nimble fingers deep into his muscles. He was more than surprised at the level of pain she was able to elicit.

"You'd be very effective at interrogation," he winced.

IT WAS another two days before she again broached the topics which he'd kept to himself. She told him that she was very pleased with his progress in physical therapy. She'd given him a series of exercises that he could perform both in his bed and in his chair. All of which he'd done religiously.

As a reward, she took him down to the actual hot springs where they could soak and relax. It was a welcome respite from the physical contortions he'd been forced to endure.

This time they needed the aid of a pair of male Orderlies. Brent had seen them around the few days he'd been there. Like the nurses, they were also dressed in white. They maintained the gym and performed any tasks requiring heavy lifting. In this case, that meant putting Brent on a stretcher and carrying him down a mountain path to the nearby springs.

As soon as Brent and Ilsa arrived, they were welcomed by the shimmering, crystal water and rising steam. The springs themselves were a series of shallow pools situated under several natural alcoves. This gave each one a feeling of seclusion. They were accessed by wooden walkways and stairs that easily pre-dated the clinic.

"Why don't you tell me about Abigail?" Ilsa asked after they'd gotten settled and had time to relax.

Brent was even more guarded than before. During their first conversation, he'd at least had the pretense of being forthcoming. "Obviously, you already know quite a bit," he replied.

She wasn't the only one collecting information. The fact that Ilsa referred to her as "Abigail" and not "Abbie" told him quite a bit.

She readily admitted as much. "I know the general details, of course. But what I really want to know is how these events have affected *you*."

That she said "I" (as opposed to "we") told him something else, too. Of course she was sharing everything she learned with Dr. Gaebeler. But her tactic was to make it truly personal. For him to feel like he was speaking only to her. That would make him more willing to divulge.

In theory, at least.

IT WAS another week before she once again attempted to pry into his past. Physical therapy was going extremely well. Brent had gotten more used to her contortions and was thoroughly committed to his exercises.

She only wished that she could say the same for his spiritual journey. There she found long-twisted knots that seemed impossible to unravel.

Brent knew it was coming. They'd spent the late afternoon at the springs again during which she hadn't asked a single question about Abbie, his parents, or what had happened to them.

Then she arranged for the two of them to have a private, candlelit dinner together on the veranda. Instead of her usual nurse's uniform, this time she wore a short floral dress. Her entire appearance much more suitable for a romantic evening.

And when she did finally say something, it was after

dinner. And so much more gingerly than before. This time she was more caring and empathetic, as if she could feel every ounce of the same pain that he did.

"I was wondering," she asked, "if you wouldn't mind telling me about that night."

Brent instinctively pushed himself back in his wheelchair. He stared off into the darkness of the mountains. "You know what happened," he responded. And said nothing else.

She leaned across the table and did her best to look into his eyes. "You were just a little boy," she pleaded. "I can't even imagine what that must have been like for you."

Brent exhaled deeply, his eyes still firmly locked on the darkness beyond. He sat there for the longest moment. Then finally turned back to her. The agony so deep and evident in his eyes.

"I tried to save them," he admitted. "But I should have just stayed upstairs. It's my fault I'm stuck in this damn chair."

He closed his eyes and took a deep breath. "And it's my fault that they're both dead."

THE NEXT DAY Brent didn't wait for Ilsa before going to the gymnasium. By the time she arrived, he'd already spent an hour on the rowing machine and lifting weights.

"So there you are," she exclaimed. "I've been looking all over for you." Brent didn't answer. He only continued his repetitions.

Finally, he climbed back into his chair and wheeled himself over to the treatment table. He was just about to hoist himself up when he stopped and looked up at her sternly.

"Tell Dr. Gaebeler that I'm ready for my surgery," he announced.

She wasn't surprised. She took a moment to think as she removed her uniform. "Does this have anything to do with the telegram you received last night?"

Of course she knew about that. He wondered just how much she knew. And if she'd known about it over dinner the previous night.

Even before he did.

"Yes, as a matter of fact," he responded sharply. "I've business at home to which I must attend." He climbed up on the table and lay face down.

"Of course, I'm sure you're already aware," he added, "it's from a man named Sam Donohue. He's the private detective I hired to look into my parents' murders."

She climbed up on the table with him and massaged his lower back.

"You realize that after the surgery," she explained, "it will be at least another month before you're able to travel."

She dug her hands in deeper, but it made no difference to him. She still marveled at the fact that she'd learned the exact point at which he had any feeling.

"Which is why I want it done now," he told her.

"You understand that Dr. Gaebeler has other patients," she inquired. "He is in very high demand. With a rather busy schedule."

"Tell him I'll pay whatever he requires."

BRENT AWAKENED in his room, still under the haze of anesthesia. He looked about groggily, unsure of where he was. The last thing he remembered was being given ether in preparation for surgery. He could just make out a figure dressed in white standing by the foot of his bed. He struggled to focus.

"Ilsa?" he mumbled.

"Ah, good morning, Herr Gregor," Dr. Gaebeler replied, an unmistakable tone of concern in his voice.

Even more unmistakable, especially as Brent began to come around, was the worried look on Gaebeler's face as he studied the charts. Brent quickly surmised that the surgery had not gone as planned.

"I do suggest that you eat something," Dr. Gaebeler suggested. "We must rebuild your strength."

Brent looked to his left and found a tray with a simple breakfast of oatmeal, orange juice, and toast. The doctor was right. He was starving. He reached for the bread.

"Was the surgery a success?" Brent asked hopefully.

Dr. Gaebeler let out a deep breath and chose his words

carefully. "I'm afraid the situation was more dire than we anticipated. However — "

Brent was quick to interrupt. "Will I be able to walk?"

"You must understand," Dr. Gaebeler continued, "the nerves were completely severed."

Brent grew more impatient. "Can I *walk?*"

"No, I'm afraid not," Dr. Gaebeler admitted with defeat. "The damage was too severe. However, I feel that with the right combination of physical and mental therapy..."

"Get out!" Brent demanded and threw his breakfast tray across the room.

BRENT waited only a few days before he cabled Worthington and instructed him to make arrangements for their long voyage home. He was still on a great deal of pain medication and had only just begun sitting up again in his wheelchair.

As soon as Ilsa realized his intentions, she strongly advised against it. The prescribed recovery time was four weeks before he could travel, and even then only a short distance.

When he wouldn't listen to her, she appealed to Dr. Gaebeler. The respected surgeon went straight to Brent's room to confront him.

"Herr Gregor, I simply can't allow you to leave!" Dr. Gaebeler countered. "As your physician, I must inform you that it is far too soon to travel."

Brent just looked back at him with heavy disdain. He'd placed so many hopes in this man. He'd paid thousands of dollars. All for nothing.

"I'm already unable to walk," Brent grumbled. "What more damage can be done?"

CHAPTER FOUR

VICKY, her head pounding, stormed into Frank's office first thing in the morning. She threw a copy the morning *Standard* on his desk. The headline screamed "MYSTERY ASSASSIN ATTEMPTS BIG JACK MURDER."

"What the hell, Frank?" she shouted. "I told you something would go down at the Four Diamonds! I told you!"

Everyone in the newsroom scrambled for cover. Perry Phillips had made his escape as soon as he heard her coming down the hall.

"This was my story!" she shouted. "I *told you* he was real! And Charlie Hecht *of all people* beat me to it!"

She planted both fists firmly on his desk and glowered over him. Hell hath no fury.

"You have to put me back on this story!" she demanded. "I know what I saw at the Asylum! This can't be a coincidence. Either someone out there is standing up to these people, or someone is trying to take over!"

Frank just eyed her calmly. Once he knew she was finished, he responded firmly. "I'd rather lose a scoop than lose a reporter any day. Now, unless you want me to ground you completely, I don't want to see you in this office until the Doc says it's okay."

Vicky wasn't used to Frank standing up to her. And for him to do it in such a calm, authoritative manner, either. Well, that just completely threw her for a loop. Especially since he was doing it for her own good.

She fumed a second longer, but he just stared back at her and held his ground. It was clear he wasn't going to budge.

Her tantrums usually did the trick. But not this time.

She turned on her heel and stormed back out.

DETECTIVE SHAYNE covered his face with a handkerchief as he made his way into the back rooms of the Fifth City Animal Hospital. Even with all of the doors and windows open, the smell of ether still hung in the air so bad it stung the eyes. He'd only be able to examine the crime scene for a few minutes before he'd have to go back out for some fresh air.

The quiet was the first sign of trouble when the Veterinarian came in early that morning. The animals closest to the fumes were all dead and the rest still out cold. That's what they told Shayne when he'd arrived.

Slumped in the doorway between the operating room and the kennel was the body of the victim. Young kid named Enzo d'Antonguella. According to the Vet, he was from Castellaneta and had only been in America a short time. Someone from the Terminal City Italian League had been by a few months earlier to secure him a job. Didn't speak a word of English. But that wasn't a necessary job requirement for cleaning cages.

At first glance, it just looked like a dumb accident. Broken pair of ether bottles. Dropped shovel. Poor kid had likely succumbed to the vapors before he could get out.

But closer inspection revealed a different story. It usually did. First the blood on the floor. Then the two slugs in his chest.

Didn't look like anything had been stolen. Not even the medication. Could have been a thief. Could have been young Enzo got the drop on him, broke the bottles in a skirmish, and took two slugs for his troubles. That would have explained why the fellow had hightailed it out of there empty-handed.

Could have happened that way.

But Shayne's gut told him otherwise. Especially after what happened last night.

The hospital visits. The surgeon who took one in the leg. The break-ins at the doctor's office. The pharmacy. And the raid at the funeral home.

Shayne was dead certain that they'd come there, too.

But the only witnesses were a bunch of animals in cages. And a good third of them dead. Even the monkey.

Shayne would talk to the neighbors, see if any of them saw anything. But he already knew the answer. No one would sing.

No way to prove it. No way to bring these people to justice.

Just another dead end.

DR. TUNG returned to the Parish first thing in the morning to check on his patient. He well knew that in all likelihood, Mr. Gregor hadn't made it through the night. And if that were the case, he didn't want to even think about the consequences.

For that reason, he was more than surprised when he entered the back room. Mr. Gregor was not only alive, but awake. Though heavily sedated.

Worthington, who'd stayed by Brent's bedside all night, looked both exhausted and relieved. Even so, he still jumped to his feet and happily made the introductions. "Master Gregor, this is Doctor Tung. He's the skilled surgeon who came to our rescue."

"Very pleased to make your acquaintance, Mr. Gregor," Dr. Tung greeted him warmly. "Now, let's see how we're doing this morning."

Brent looked up at him weakly. "Your English is very good."

Dr. Tung smiled back and replied, "On me dit que mon français n'est pas trop mauvais non plus." *I'm told my French isn't too bad, either.*

To which Brent replied, "Mes excuses, Monsieur. Je ne voulais pas vous insulter." *My apologies, Sir. I did not mean to insult you.*

"Not to worry, young man," Dr. Tung reacted with a smile. "You're not the first to make that assumption."

Dr. Tung looked Brent over carefully and checked his wounds. His patient was clearly weakened and devoid of strength. His skin was ashen and it pained him to move. But considering what he'd survived, Dr. Tung couldn't help but shake his head in astonishment.

"Again, I have to say," Dr. Tung commented in disbelief, "it's an absolute miracle that you're still alive. God has truly intervened."

Worthington shook his hand vigorously. "Thank you so much, Doctor! We shall forever remain in your debt."

Dr. Tung added with a smile. "I would be remiss in telling you that my wife simply adores your catalog. You've managed to furnish our home with a great many things."

Abbie had taught him years ago to stop explaining that he had little to do with the company and that it was actually run by the Smithsons. "Thank you," he replied simply. "Tell your lovely wife that she's welcome to anything we offer. It's the least I can do."

"Now if I were to do that," Dr. Tung replied, "we'd hardly be able to keep this arrangement a secret, would we? Perhaps you should just promise to rethink whatever it is you're up to. I won't say any more than that."

Brent replied simply, "Understood."

"Is it safe to take him home, Doctor?" Worthington asked. "Or at least to the apartment in town?"

"He really should be in a hospital," Dr. Tung replied. "But I understand your reasons for not doing so."

"I just feel," Worthington explained, "he'd be far more comfortable at home. And that I can better attend to him there."

Dr. Tung thought it over carefully then finally relented. "As long as you're careful. I'll send some medication for the pain. If he begins to run a fever, call me immediately."

DENNY returned from lunch to find drawer after drawer pulled open. Random files were turned sideways to be easily spotted and yet not lose their place. He didn't have to look far to find the shapely figure responsible. "Can I help you find something?" he asked quietly so as not to startle her.

"Denny!" Vicky exclaimed as she quickly turned around. "Did you see *The Standard's* morning edition?"

"You mean about the Mob hit at the Four Diamonds?"

He'd easily guessed what had motivated her to ransack his basement domain.

"Yeah, and it wasn't a Mob hit," she informed him. "It was a man, and he was dressed all in black. Sound familiar?"

"This isn't about your mysterious phantom again, is it?" he queried. It was obvious from his response he hadn't seen it.

"Vito Spats saw him again at the Four Diamonds," she informed him.

"And you know this how?"

"A little bird told me," she replied, grabbing her copy of *The Standard* and throwing it to him. Which he barely managed to catch.

"Last night he tried to kill Big Jack," she continued. "Dressed all in black, just like I told you. And he was *real*."

Then she jammed her fingernail into his chest. "Told you so!" Denny did his best not to wince.

She stood there, hands on her hips, and stared him down. He knew exactly for what she was waiting. He looked back at her like a scolded puppy.

"Okay, I'm sorry," he admitted. "I shouldn't have doubted you. It's just that I was all over that building and I never saw him. And after what they did to you, well, I just assumed... Anyway, I'm just really, really sorry."

Denny glanced back at her with a look of defeat. He seemed to have tripped over his own two feet a lot lately. And he was justifiably worried that he would lose her when they'd only just begun their courtship.

"Anyway," he stammered, "I am certain that there's nothing here. Nothing like that's been in the paper. Sounds like the only people who've seen him are you and Vito Spats."

She slammed a file drawer shut in frustration. She leaned against the filing cabinet and wrestled with it in her mind. There had to be something else she could do. Some other lead that she could follow. And that's when it finally hit her.

"You're right!" she exclaimed happily. "Thanks, Denny! You're a genius!"

She gave him a big kiss on the cheek and charged out the door. Denny just stood there, dumbfounded. One second she was fuming. And the next she was joyous.

"What did I say?" he called out to her.

And that's when he had his own epiphany. "Oh no, what did I say?"

CHAPTER FIVE

VICKY stopped and took a deep breath as she approached the Belmont Hotel. This was a crazy notion indeed. She was determined to get answers but was, unfortunately, short on options.

She could've gone back to the Asylum and tried talking to the Orderlies, though she seriously doubted that they would say anything to her. Besides, that was the last place she wanted to go.

No, as much as she disliked this idea as well, the two people with whom she needed to talk were "Three-Finger" Ned Vogel and Vito Spats. Of course, she had no idea where Ned was, obviously. But everyone knew where to find Vito Spats.

The middle-aged Doorman happily greeted her in his resplendent red uniform. "Afternoon Miss! Welcome to the Belmont!"

He pulled open the large glass and iron door and bid her to enter. She assumed he was a replacement for the usual Doorman who'd caught a bullet in the leg during the recent shootout. In fact, they'd only recently repaired the many dozens of bullet holes on the outside of the hotel.

She walked determinedly into the ornate lobby with its dozen crystal chandeliers. The light that they cast across the light brown marble floors, walls, and columns gave the vast room a golden hue. She could have easily lost herself exploring every detail and corner, but she was there for a purpose. And despite the lush surroundings, her heart pulsed a mile a minute.

She still couldn't believe what she was about to do. She'd just entered the lion's den and was about to demand an audience with the king of the jungle himself. Or rather, his second in command.

Before she could lose her nerve and stop herself, she marched straight up to the front desk. The lovely Desk Clerk, a pert blonde in a starched white blouse, greeted her warmly. She looked the same age as Vicky, if not a year or two older. "Good afternoon, Miss. How can I help you?" the girl asked in a soft, French-Canadian accent. "Checking in?"

Vicky put both hands on the hotel desk and announced herself with friendly assertion. "Yeah, hi. I'm Vicky Rose with the *Daily Crusader*. I need to see Vito Spats."

The young Desk Clerk offered a brief apology. "I'm sorry, but I'm unaware of a guest by that name…"

"No, my fault," Vicky offered, realizing that, of course, he wouldn't be registered under his usual moniker. If he were even registered at all. "Vittorio Gennaro."

Again, the Clerk shook her head. "No, Miss. I'm sorry."

"Okay, how about 'Henry Green' then?" she asked, citing his primary alias. She had imagined this process going much smoother.

"No, Miss, I'm afraid not," the Desk Clerk replied. This time she didn't even bother to look at the register.

By this time, Vicky had lost her patience. "Cut the crap, you know who I'm talking about. *Vito Spats Gennaro*. Everybody in town knows who he is. Half the country, for that matter. He's got the whole damn 7th floor, for crying out loud."

The Clerk just smiled and recited her usual response. "I'm sorry I'm unable to help you, Miss. But it appears the person for whom you're searching just isn't here."

"Fine," Vicky retorted with a huff of frustration. "Thank you for your time."

She marched across the grand lobby to a side hallway where she found the elevators. She sharply punched the

Up button three or four times, then waited impatiently. She felt another headache coming on.

As she watched the dial overhead slowly count down the floors until the elevator's arrival, a large, muscular man in a dark, pinstripe suit walked up beside her. "Excuse me, Miss Rose. But is there anything I help you with?" he asked in a tone that was both kind and threatening.

Vicky gazed up at him. He was a good two-feet taller than she was, and easily twice as large. She'd seen him before. Both at Michael Memoli's funeral and... well, she couldn't remember where else.

What she didn't forget was his name: "Big Joey" Frogameni. Also known as "Joey Frogs." Since he already knew who she was, that put them on equal footing. In at least one aspect, anyway.

She should have been very intimidated. But she wasn't. Maybe it was her determination to get answers. Or her impatience. Or just the headache.

"I need to talk to Vito Spats," she asserted, as if that would have any effect on him.

"And what is the nature of your inquiry?" He over-emphasized his words in an attempt to sound polished.

"It's about the Man in Black," she told him, happy to finally have someone acknowledge that she was in the right place. "You know, the Ghost Man that attacked the Four Diamonds last night? I just want to ask him a few questions. I'm not here to talk about anything else."

Big Joey offered a quick shrug. "Well, I'm afraid Mr. Gennaro is not available at the present time."

"Will you give him that message then?" she asked.

"I would be happy to do so," he responded politely.

She fished in her purse for a pen and her card, quickly jotted down the apartment phone number, and handed it to him. "Tell him to call me anytime. Day or night."

This took her disbelief to another level. She was already bothered that Spats knew where she lived. She could only imagine Mrs. Hershey's reaction if he were to phone her there.

"I will tell him you called," Big Joey offered. "And may I say you're looking quite lovely this afternoon, Miss Rose. You have a good day, now."

BEN SANDERS grabbed a seat at the counter in Turtle's Bar & Grill in Bronzeville. It was a small, welcoming establishment that felt like home. Nothing fancy. Just dark wood, plaster walls, dim lighting, and tiled floors. A place for working men. He'd known the establishment for years and had known the bartender and co-owner, Fred, even longer.

As Editor, Chief Reporter, and everything else at *The Evening Hubbub*, Ben knew *everyone* in Bronzeville. Even the businesses that didn't advertise with his tiny paper. If something entertaining was happening in the neighborhood, he wanted to know. And what was more, he wanted his readers to know.

"Thought you might want to try a quarter page after the Fourth," Ben suggested.

Fred just shook his head and laughed. Sanders had been trying to get him to advertise for years. But he'd never had any problem filling his barstools, especially around a holiday. "You kidding? This place is going to be packed solid. Why would I need to advertise?"

"The holiday don't last forever," Ben countered with a friendly smile. "Got to think about what happens afterwards."

Ben was just about to get up when he heard the bell ring on the front door. He looked up to see two men walk in and stop. It took a minute for his eyes to adjust to the afternoon light that had spilled in. And even when they did, he wasn't sure they weren't playing tricks.

The sudden hush of silence that gripped the establishment told him they weren't. Just like in a movie Western. Even for a small-time entertainment reporter, Ben knew enough to know who they were. Even if he hadn't, he'd have known they were trouble. He also knew that this was real news. Even if it wasn't the kind he usually covered.

Willie Potatoes took a seat near the door. Vito Spats made his way to the bar and looked around. Even with their black hair and olive complexions, they stuck out like sore thumbs.

Spats grabbed a stool two chairs over from Ben. He tipped his bowler. He could tell Sanders was nervous. Along with everyone else in the bar.

He liked it that way. "Don't mind us," Spats reassured him. "We're just here for a social call."

"What can I do for you, Sir?" Fred asked. He was understandably nervous, but didn't let that stop him from extending every courtesy.

The door opened again and Spats quickly turned to look. Willie just let the newcomer go by, clearly not concerned.

Spats saw that it was just a young negro boy. Couldn't have been more than ten. He just skipped right past them and ran straight to the back. *Mother must work in the kitchen*, he thought.

"We're looking for an Irishman," Spats turned back to Fred with a sly grin. "You'd know him if you saw him."

Fred attempted to smile back. "Yessir, I'd have to say you're right." He wasn't sure if he should laugh or not. Spats just smiled back.

"But I promise you," Fred added. "Ain't seen nobody like that around here."

Spats sat quietly and rubbed his pinky ring with this thumb. Everyone watched anxiously as he reached into his jacket.

"If you do, you just be sure to let me know." He pulled out a roll of bills, peeled off a few, and put them on the counter. "Happy Independence Day."

"Yessir, I sure will," Fred told him with a quiet sigh of relief. Then he added, perhaps a bit too enthusiastically, "You have a happy Fourth, too, Sir!"

Spats gave him a nod of approval. He glanced around the establishment once more then made his way back to the door. Willie opened it for him as they went to leave.

The young boy rushed right past them on his way back out.

THE JOURNEY back to Gregor Mansion was not without difficulty. Worthington had to enlist the help of another trusted young man, Lee Jun-fan, to retrieve another car from the downtown apartment. He felt reasonably certain that the staff wouldn't notice one missing from the fleet.

Once he had gotten Master Gregor home, Worthington

took him straight up to his bedroom with the aid of Mr. Donaldson. He instructed Mrs. Poole that Master Gregor had taken ill and was not to be disturbed. The medication Dr. Tung had prescribed had put Brent right to sleep. And his wheelchair made concealing his injuries that much easier.

The greater question was how they'd continue the ruse. With Master Gregor's history of poor health, Worthington hoped that the questions would be minimal. But that was a concern for another day.

He had just gotten Brent settled in his bed and was on his way out when Elyse stopped at the door. The look of total concern on her face told him exactly why she was there. "Will you be needing anything, Sir?" she asked.

"No, my dear," he answered, doing his best to sound unconcerned. "Run along now. I'm sure there's work to be done."

She curtsied obediently and took only a few steps before she stopped again. "Will he be okay, Sir?"

"Not to worry, my dear," he reassured her. "Master Gregor just needs to rest. I'm sure he'll pull through just fine."

Not wanting to invite more conversation, Worthington pulled the door closed. When he looked back at Master Gregor, he saw that blood had seeped through his shirt.

He only hoped that she hadn't noticed.

VICKY returned to her new desk by Leonore's office. It was the last place she wanted to be, but considering her conversation with Frank, she thought it best if she made a show of it while she considered her next move.

She'd just noticed the latest stack of messages waiting when Leonore approached and loomed over her. "And where on earth have you been? As if I didn't know."

Vicky really hoped she didn't *actually* know the whole truth of it.

"What do you care?" Vicky shot back. "I went to your party, I rubbed elbows, and dropped off my story just like I said I would."

"Yeah, well," Leonore retorted, not to be outdone, before

heading back into her office. "I'll have you know I held up my end of the bargain, too. Don't be surprised if her father sends you a giant wreath or something."

Vicky grabbed a copy of the morning edition. She'd been so incensed over the *Standard*'s cover story, she hadn't even bothered to look at the *Crusader*'s. She went straight to the Society page. It was at the bottom, but it was there. It had been trimmed a bit, but otherwise her attempt at capturing Leonore's style was all there, word for word. Complete with every "a little bird told me" and "dot dot dot." At least something good came of it.

Finally, she turned to her stack of messages. They were all in Perry's handwriting. He'd obviously dropped them off earlier. The first was from Louisa, of course. She'd telephoned to say how proud father was to see her listed on the Society page. And that he wanted to send her a small thank you gift. Vicky just hoped it wasn't a giant wreath.

Just as she suspected, the rest were from that Spider character again. He was certainly tenacious, if nothing else.

But at the bottom of the stack was a familiar yellow envelope. From Western Union. She had to wonder. *Who in the devil would send me a telegram?* It was dated yesterday. Her curiosity thoroughly piqued, she tore the envelope.

It was from her sister, Lizzie.

ELYSE went down to the laundry and quickly pulled Mollie aside. She looked around to make sure no one else was listening. It was very unlike her to spread gossip, but she just had to tell someone. "Where's Mrs. Poole?" she asked.

"She's in the kitchen taking her lunch," Mollie answered, then huddled close. "Bridget's upstairs changing the linens."

Elyse took a deep breath then whispered, "Master Gregor's fallen ill again. When I was upstairs, Mr. Worthington was careful not to let me look into his room."

Mollie took Elyse by the hands and clutched them tightly. "What did you see?"

The fear in Elyse's eyes said everything.

"Blood."

FRANK was hunkered down at his desk reviewing the latest stories when Vicky walked in and sat down. The fact that she hadn't stormed in and immediately started shouting should have told him clearly that something was wrong.

That and the fact that she'd recently been crying. He'd been married to Betty long enough to know that look. She'd obviously waited before coming in there. She wouldn't have wanted the men in the newsroom to see it.

Still, he was too focused on layouts to realize what was going on. "I, uh..." she began, then let her voice just trail off. "Need to take a few days off."

"About time, Red," he replied, happy to finally hear it.

"No, it's not that," she sniffled. "It's...." She took another moment. She had to fight back the tears that welled up inside.

That was when he finally realized that something was *terribly wrong*.

"My mother died."

CHAPTER SIX

VICKY ROSE stood on the platform at Union Station early the next morning with her ticket in hand and the same suitcase that had brought her there five years earlier. She'd only had a few hours to pack and get things in order. She got the distinct impression that despite the circumstances of her departure, Mrs. Hershey was probably relieved to see her go. Even if it were just for a brief time.

"Help you, Miss?" the young porter, Raymond Rawlins, asked as the Conductor called again for everyone to board.

"Yes, please," she replied. "It's just this one." She gave him a small gratuity as he picked it up.

"Thank you kindly, Ma'am," he replied with a tip of his hat. "Much obliged."

She was just about to board when Denny, of all people, ran up and shouted. "Vicky! Vicky!"

"Denny, what're you doing here?" she asked with surprise. "You didn't have to see me off."

The fact that he carried a small overnight bag should have clued her in to the contrary. But her mind was duly occupied with things of far greater importance.

"Vicky, I'm so sorry to hear about your mother," he told her. "I hope I'm not over-stepping my bounds here..."

"Denny, please," she implored as the train whistle blew.

He quickly got the message and cut to the chase. "Anyway, I just couldn't let you make the trip alone. As your... boyfriend, I just really wanted to be here for you."

"Oh, that's so... sweet," she told him, taken aback by his surprise show of gallantry. "But you don't have to do that. I can manage just fine on my own."

As much as she appreciated the gesture, she was not entirely thrilled about the idea of him coming along. The reunion with her family would be awkward enough as it was.

"Nothing doing, Vick," he insisted. "You need an arm to lean on. Whatever it is. I'm here for you. Day or night."

"But, where will you stay?" she asked.

"Oh, I can just get a hotel room in town," he offered. "They do have hotel rooms in... where are we going?"

"All aboard!" the Conductor shouted again as the engines made ready.

She still wasn't crazy about him coming, but it was hard to say no. As much as she'd pushed him away and chastised him previously, she realized that this time, she might actually need his companionship.

"Well, okay then!" she finally agreed. "Gibsonville. We're going to Gibsonville, Missouri."

WORTHINGTON peered down the third floor hallway and, certain that no one was watching, opened the door and quietly made his way up to the attic. With Master Gregor asleep and improving somewhat, he at last had a few moments to further address his own mystery.

He carefully checked each and every article of clothing. Both the full inventory of shoes and hats were accounted for. However, one of the dresses was most definitely missing. As was a brooch from the jewelry.

He strongly suspected that someone was stealing Mrs. Gregor's belongings. Or at the very least had *borrowed* them without permission. It hardly seemed the time to worry about such a thing, but it was his job to protect the Gregors. Even in death.

He took a moment to ponder the possible culprit. Most likely one of the maids. He would need to watch them more closely. But short of searching them every day when they left, how to find out which one?

Master Gregor was much more suited to this sort of mystery. But Worthington couldn't very well involve him at this time.

DETECTIVE SHAYNE sat down in the confessional at the Cathedral of the Holy Name. He was pleased to see Father Sean Ryan when the small window opened from the other side. As a former military man himself, Father Ryan understood him well.

"Bless me father, for I have sinned," he confessed. "It's been almost two weeks since my last confession. I didn't come last week — well, that's the whole reason I'm here. I, uh... I witnessed something wrong."

Shayne hesitated as he searched for the words. It was difficult to speak it out loud. Even in this holy setting. "Go on, my son," Father Ryan coaxed him.

"Yes, Father. You see, this other fella and I, we both got a promotion," Shayne continued. "But it's all a lie. We don't deserve it. Him especially. If anyone knew what really happened, we'd both be locked up."

"I see," Father Ryan replied. There was a long silence.

The good Priest easily ascertained that he was speaking about the Nails McCarthy incident. He had to contain his own shock and surprise. As much as he wanted to pry for more details, he had to put curiosity aside. He was there to provide absolution and guidance.

"What does your heart tell you to do?" Father Ryan asked.

"It's telling me to say something," Shayne quickly replied. "To make it right."

"So, why don't you?" the Priest asked.

Shayne hung his head low. "'Cause I'm afraid, that's why. There's a lot of people involved. People in charge. It could cost me everything."

"My son, the Holy Book tells us to follow the Lord's example," Father Ryan comforted him. "Remember the money lenders. They were powerful people as well. But he stood up anyway. Overturned their tables. And chased them out."

"But he's my boss," Shayne quickly shot back.

Father Ryan thought for a moment. He knew it was hard

to be the one righteous man in a corrupt world. But still, he could only advise the struggling detective to follow the example provided by the Lord himself and so many others.

"Then go," Father Ryan advised, "confront him."

Again Shayne hung his head in defeat. "Yeah, I tried that already."

"And?" Father Ryan asked.

"Didn't go very well."

BRENT rang his handbell over and over, to the point where his arm grew tired and he simply gave up with exhaustion. As he slumped back against the pillows in frustration, he accidentally dropped it on the floor. He finally resorted to shouting for help, but in his drugged and weakened condition, that proved to be even less effective. "Worthington!"

Hurried footsteps that sounded very much unlike Worthington resulted in a welcoming face at the door. It was one of the maids. The dark-haired, shy one who usually cleaned his room. She apologized and tried to catch her breath. "I'm sorry, Master Gregor. I ran up just as quick as I could."

"Where's Worthington?" Brent complained. He winced as he struggled to sit up. "I rang so many times I dropped my bell."

"I'm afraid I don't know at the moment," Elyse told him and walked around the bed, careful not to look directly at him. This time, at least, there was no blood.

She spotted the bell on the floor. She quickly picked it up and returned it to the night stand. "I'm glad to get whatever you need, Sir."

Brent just exhaled in frustration, then moved painfully to the edge of the bed. "I'm *tired* of being in this room. I wish to repose in the solarium. Where in the hell is Worthington?"

This was more than she had expected. She stood silently for a moment, unsure of just what to do. How she wished Mr. Worthington were there. "Are you sure about that, Master Gregor?" she asked.

"Of course, I'm sure!" he commanded. "Bring my wheelchair!"

Again she hoped that Mr. Worthington would soon arrive. She reluctantly moved the wheelchair next to the bed and locked the wheels.

He held out his hands. "Pull me up, will you?"

She instinctively took a step back. "Perhaps if I call for Mr. Worthington myself?"

"Don't worry," he reassured her, "I just need a little boost."

She reached out hesitantly and he clutched her tightly. His hands were strong, yet soft. So soft. She could only imagine what it felt like to be caressed by them. "Okay, now pull," he instructed.

She took another step back and, bracing her small feet against the floor, did as he instructed. In one smooth, swift move, Master Gregor popped off the bed and pivoted into the chair.

Brent looked back at her appreciatively as Worthington rushed into the room. "That will be all, Miss Thompkins, thank you."

She gave a quick, relieved curtsy as she rushed past him and out the door. "Thank goodness you're here, Sir! I didn't know what else to do."

Worthington just as quickly put himself between Brent and the path to the door. He stared at the young, obstinate man and spoke in a calm, firm voice. It was a voice that Brent had heard many times before in his younger years. "Master Gregor. What on earth do you think you're doing?"

Brent stared back at him, just as determined. It was a look Worthington had *seen* many times as well. "I'm tired of being in this room, Worthington," Brent stated emphatically. "I want to repose in the solarium. I'm certain that the sunlight will do me good."

"Are you sure that's advisable, Sir?" Worthington felt compelled to ask. "Dr. Tung insisted that you remain in bed for several more days at the least."

Brent snapped back. "I'm tired of staying in this room! I want to go down to the solarium!"

At once he again sounded like the petulant child who would slam his fists and throw books across the room. Worthington could tell it was the medication doing most of the talking on this occasion, however.

Dr. Tung hadn't warned him about that. But Worthington should have expected it.

The older man stood silently and considered it for a moment. He was inclined to make Master Gregor lie right back down. If for no other reason than his distasteful behavior.

But it was a miracle that he was still alive. And as petulant and spoiled as he may have been, getting him out of that room and into the sunlight could actually be of a benefit.

"Of course, Sir," Worthington answered. He stepped aside and unlocked the wheels on the chair.

"I called for you repeatedly and you didn't answer," Brent scolded. "I was beginning to wonder if anyone heard me ringing until that maid, Elsie, finally came. Thought I'd have to get *her* to take me downstairs."

"Elyse," Worthington corrected as he placed a blanket across his lap.

"What?" Brent asked, confused.

"The Maid in question, Master Gregor," Worthington explained as he wheeled Brent to the door. "Her name is Elyse. Elyse Thompkins."

"Well," Brent sniffed, "at least she's around when I need someone."

"Yes, I've noticed, Sir," Worthington replied.

"It's more than I can say for you," Brent reprimanded. "What could you have been doing that was so important?"

"I can't imagine, Sir."

CHERRIES HOGAN stepped cautiously out of his girlfriend's apartment building and made a beeline for the alley where he'd parked his car. He'd been extra careful to watch his back, and even had her on lookout to make sure it was safe. But what he hadn't counted on was her using the phone before he even got there. At least she got one last kiss good-bye.

As soon as he rounded the corner into the alley, he found Spats and Willie there waiting for him. He was just about to bolt right back out when Fingers stepped up behind him with a gun in his back.

"How's it going, Cherries?" Willie asked politely. "Nice visit with your gal?"

Spats stepped up closer and gave a whiff. "From the smell of her perfume, I'd say that you did."

Cherries was bewildered. He thought he'd done everything to cover his tracks. This wasn't even her building. He quickly got his answer. "She's going to look real beautiful in that new mink coat," Willie smiled. "A real doll, that one."

Cherries' expression quickly turned to disgust. *What a dame*, he thought. *Sold me out for a fur coat.*

"Why don't you get in the car, Cherries?" Spats told him. "Time we had a little talk. Just want to ask you a few questions."

"Like you did with Kid Yellow?" Cherries shot back. Then he spritzed one directly on Vito's pristine white spats.

Spats took out a handkerchief and wiped them off. "That ain't gonna make it any better," Willie told him as he opened the door. "Trust me."

"You're just wasting your time," Cherries said as he climbed in. "I don't know nothing 'bout where Whitey is. But I do know you ain't never gonna find him."

"Good thing that's not all we want to talk about," Willie replied as he closed the car door.

VICKY just stared out the window from her seat in coach and watched the endless cornfields roll by. It was a six-hour train ride to Gibsonville. A good hour past St. Louis. So many times she'd dreaded the day she'd have to make this train ride home. But always for her father. She never dreamed it would be for her mother.

The reality had finally begun to set in. Most especially that she hadn't gotten a chance to say goodbye. She'd always assumed her mother would be there long afterwards. So much so that she'd ignored the repeated messages from her sister, Lizzie.

All in an effort to keep her job on the crime beat. That had been her only focus. Her health and her family be damned. And now she'd lost so much more. With no possibility of getting it back.

She barely even had time to cry. Having just gotten the news the day prior. She had to immediately pack and leave first thing that morning. And with so much emotion bottled up inside, her head throbbed even worse. Even after taking her medication. She just needed to let it all out. But not on the train. And certainly not in front of Denny.

He was sweet, though. As annoying as he could be at times, he'd been just the shoulder she needed to lean on. He'd graciously seen to her every need. And for once he'd actually just been quiet when she needed that the most.

Try as she might, she couldn't just sit by the window for the entire trip. She finally felt the need to get up on her own. Ever the chivalrous gentleman, Denny immediately leapt into action. "What do you need? I'll be glad to get it."

She stood up anyway. "Denny, I do appreciate the effort. But there's just some things a girl must do on her own."

"Oh?" he answered, not understanding. Luckily, he caught on before she had to explain.

"Oh!" He turned beet red with embarrassment.

VITO SPATS sat down at the tiny kitchen table and took off his bowler hat. Across from him sat Alvin Bruckman, one of the five Orderlies who'd encountered the Ghost Man that night at the Asylum. Still sporting a broken arm and black eye from the encounter.

Three-Finger Ned had fought with the Ghost Man the most. But Spats couldn't talk to Ned again just yet.

Willie stood by the door. Even with his arm in a sling, the message was clear. Spats wanted answers. And after the attack at the Four Diamonds, he needed better ones. Spats could only shake his head in disgust. And anger. "Five large men. Each of them used to working with mental patients. And yet here we are. Just look at you."

Bruckman searched his memory for any detail he might have missed before. Fearful he had forgotten something important, he was rightfully worried about the repercussions.

"It was just like we told you before, Spats," Bruckman stuttered. "He was strong. And fast. I never seen anybody that could fight like that."

"Ned didn't seem to have any problem," Spats admonished. "I saw Ned throw the guy right through that door like he was a little rag doll."

But what Spats couldn't explain was everything that had happened afterwards. And he wasn't about to, either.

"Yeah, but I mean," Bruckman continued anxiously, "it was like he'd appear right out of thin air. Catch you by surprise, you know?"

"Like a ghost?" Spats sneered cynically. He was beginning to think he might need to break a few bones himself to get the answers he wanted.

"Yeah, you could say that," Bruckman replied, not knowing how else to explain it.

Spats tapped his fingers on the brim of his hat and shifted it on the table. Clearly, he wasn't satisfied.

"But he was weak, too," Bruckman added.

"Oh?" Spats asked sharply, his anger starting to get the best of him. "I thought you just said he was strong."

"He was, real strong, and really fast, just like we said," Bruckman attempted to clarify. "But what I meant to say was, he had a weakness. He had trouble walking."

"You mean a limp?" Spats queried, thinking he might actually be getting somewhere.

"No, no," Bruckman explained. "Like he'd been hurt or something."

"Clearly, he's had time to heal," Spats grumbled angrily. *Well, this was definitely more information*, Spats thought. But he doubted how useful it would be. Especially since this Ghost Man had no trouble walking at the Four Diamonds.

Of course, considering the number of times they shot him, walking was probably the least of his troubles at this point. If he was even still alive.

As Spats picked up his hat to leave, a thought occurred to him. *What was the Ghost Man doing there that night, anyway? If he's working for the North Side, why go to the Asylum?*

The answer was obvious, even if it didn't make any sense. Same reason the pencil neck was there. To rescue that dame reporter.

Who just so happened to come knocking at his very door yesterday.

CHAPTER SEVEN

DENNY watched excitedly out the window as the train pulled into Vicky's hometown. It was 2:30 in the afternoon. Right on schedule. It was a reasonably sized community, bigger than he'd expected. Though not nearly as big as Terminal City or even St. Louis.

The railroad tracks went right through the center of town, right alongside Main Street. Among the many shops and businesses, he immediately spotted the Rose & Harwood Savings and Trust. He felt pretty certain that this was her father's bank. But she didn't say a word, so he didn't mention it, either.

"So this is where you grew up, huh?" he remarked, as if he'd just been let in on a big, personal secret. Vicky didn't answer.

"Gibsonville!" the Conductor shouted and strode down the center aisle. "All off for Gibsonville!"

The depot was the equivalent of a railroad wharf: a long collections of shops, warehouses, and a diner, all connected to the station. There was even a Smithson & Gregor store where people could pick up their larger shipments, straight off the delivery train.

The sight of it brought a smile to Denny's face. Not just because it was a little taste of home, but because he owed a slight debt of gratitude to Brent Gregor for directing him to the Asylum the night he'd tried to find Vicky.

Just as soon as they'd disembarked, they were met by her

younger brother, Henry. He was about the same height, a little pudgy, and had a tinge of his sister's auburn hair. With him was his short, chirpy and equally pudgy wife, Bitsy. She squealed with tempered delight at the sight of them.

"Oh, my goodness! Look at you! So sophisticated!"

Denny took a careful step back as Vicky quickly hugged them both. "So happy to see you, Sis," Henry said through a forced smile. "Just wish it was under better circumstances."

It was clear that both of them had been crying.

Henry and Bitsy stood there awkwardly for a moment. No one was sure of how to address the tall, lanky man standing behind Vicky. Finally, she spoke up.

"Oh, I'm so sorry. Henry, this is my... boyfriend, Denny."

"Boyfriend?" Bitsy exclaimed. "Won't everyone be surprised! We could sure use any little ray of happiness."

Denny stepped forward and shook Henry's hand heartily. He was determined to make a good impression on her entire family. "Pleased to meet you, Henry. I'm so very sorry for your loss."

Bitsy forwent the handshake and gave Denny a big hug. She barely came up to his chest.

Vicky happily noticed that Denny was less awkward than usual. Then she looked around. "Where's Patsy?"

"Oh, she's back at the house with Lizzie," Bitsy chirped. "She's gotten so big, you won't recognize her."

That was an understatement, Vicky thought. It had been nearly five years since she'd seen any of her family. The last time she'd seen her niece, the youngster was still in diapers.

"Didn't know you were bringing a *gentleman friend*," Henry stated.

"Actually," Vicky explained, "that makes two of us. Denny surprised me at the station this morning. Didn't want me to have to make the trip alone. Isn't that thoughtful?"

Bitsy happily agreed. "Oh yes, it most certainly is!"

Henry helped Denny collect their bags from one of the Porters. "Before I forget," Denny asked, "would you mind pointing me towards a good hotel?"

"Sure, sure," Henry replied. "But we can worry about that later. Come on to the house first. Everyone will want to see you right away."

"Everyone?" Denny asked anxiously.

MOLLIE peered into the solarium to check on Master Gregor. A good hour or more had passed since Elyse very nearly had to push him downstairs on her own. He hadn't looked well then and she'd wondered about the wisdom of it. But they all had to answer to Master Gregor's whims, whether they were detrimental or not. Mr. Worthington included.

She thought it wouldn't hurt to check in on him, just to make sure he was all right. And if perchance he needed something, all the better. She glanced through the doorway and her heart nearly stopped.

There was Master Gregor, slumped over in his chair. She immediately rushed to his aid. His skin was ghostly white and cold to the touch. His breathing was hard and labored.

And there was blood. A lot of blood. It had soaked through the front of his pajamas in several places. "Mr. Worthington!" she cried out. "Mr. Worthington!"

Though only the barest of moments had passed, it seemed like forever before the heavyset Valet appeared in the hallway and rushed to her aid.

"Oh, my Heavens," was all he managed to get out.

There was young Master Gregor, now looking so much like his father, before him once again bleeding from a gunshot wound. He was again taken back to that Halloween night fifteen years earlier when an intruder had entered the house.

Elyse was close behind him. Though she was silent, her reaction said the same.

And once again, as he had done before, Worthington had to put his own feelings aside and take charge. He quickly knelt down and lifted the young man's head. Brent looked back at him weakly. He was still alive, thank God.

Worthington just knelt there silently for the longest moment, desperately trying to decide what to do. His concern, though, was that anything at all would be too late. He feared the worst. "Shall I telephone Dr. Graves?" Elyse asked anxiously.

"No!" Worthington stood up quickly.

She took a step back, stunned by his reaction.

He required another moment to collect himself. "No," he told her again, this time much more calmly. "Help me get him on the couch first. We must elevate his feet."

The three of them worked quickly, yet gently, and carefully moved Brent to the floral sofa. Mollie grabbed all of the pillows from the room and placed them under his legs.

"Mollie," Worthington asked in a kind, but firm tone, "would you be so kind as to go to the kitchen and bring back some orange juice."

"Yes, Mr. Worthington," she answered tearfully before racing off as instructed.

Worthington stood up tall and straightened his vest. There would be time for tears later. "Elyse, I need you to watch over him whilst I make the call."

"Yes, Sir," she answered dutifully.

HENRY ROSE drove Vicky, Bitsy, and Denny to the house in his two-door convertible. It was quite fortunate that it had been a sunny day and the top was down. Between the four of them and their luggage, the car was rather crowded.

Equally fortunate, Denny observed, was that the house was less than four blocks away. As Vicky had mentioned, they could very easily have walked it. Even with their bags in tow. Something Vicky had done herself more than once.

"Well," Vicky shrugged, an air of surrender in her voice, "this is where I grew up."

The house was a fine, dark red, two-story cottage with a big front porch that wrapped around two sides and a white picket fence. Just the kind of house in which Denny had always dreamed of living.

In the back yard, Denny spotted an extremely large, muscular man throw a football back and forth to his three young sons. They all had their suit jackets and ties off. The oldest son looked to be twelve, with each brother a year younger. Denny got the instant feeling that even the youngest was more masculine than he was.

"That's my brother-in-law, Will Harper. My sister's husband," Vicky informed him. "And their boys, Will Jr., Frankie, and Chris. They really love the outdoors, as you can probably tell. I'll have to introduce you later." Denny just nodded in agreement. *If that's the kind of man who'd won her sister's hand,* he thought, *he didn't stand a chance.*

Vicky couldn't help but feel the first tinges of guilt creeping in. The last time she'd seen her nephews, the oldest had just started kindergarten.

"Don't mind the luggage," Henry instructed them as they got out. "I'll bring it in."

Denny was about to ask about a hotel again, but then changed his mind. Better to do it later when things had settled down.

Bitsy hurried them along and ushered Vicky and Denny into the house. "Come along, come along. Everyone is so anxious to see you."

Before they had made it two steps, a five-year-old girl in a lovely dark dress bolted from the front door and into Bitsy's arms. She had round, rosy cheeks just like her mother.

"Mommy!" she exclaimed.

"Have you been good for Aunt Lizzie?" Bitsy asked. With her eyes locked on the two newcomers in the driveway, the little girl nodded and clutched her mother tightly.

Vicky ignored her deepening guilt and greeted her niece with a warm smile. "Hi, Patsy! How are you?"

"This is your Aunt Vicky," Bitsy told her reassuringly. "She's your Daddy's sister."

Denny took a shy step back towards the car. He thought one introduction was enough for the little girl.

"My heavens, look how much you've grown!" Vicky exclaimed with child-like excitement. "The last time I saw you, you were just a baby!"

Little Patsy stared at Aunt Vicky for another long moment. A puzzled expression crossed her tiny face. "You look like Aunt Lizzie."

"That's right!" Bitsy chirped. "She's Aunt Lizzie's sister, too!"

ELYSE stood nervously and watched over Master Gregor as he lay on the couch. Mollie paced the room anxiously, almost afraid to look in his direction. He coughed and then winced from the intense pain. The orange juice they'd given him had brought some of the color back to his skin. But the blood stain on his pajama shirt had grown larger.

"Can I get you anything more, Master Gregor?" Elyse asked anxiously.

Brent struggled to speak. "Where's... Worthington?"

"He's off calling the doctor, Sir," she anxiously informed him.

"Tell him... hurry," Brent struggled.

Mollie waved for Elyse to join her across the room. She stepped away and towards the other girl, but kept her gaze firmly on their patient.

"Why in the world did he not want to call Dr. Graves? Especially with that blood!" Mollie whispered. "There's plenty he's not telling us."

VICKY clutched Denny by the hand, as much for her own sake as for his, and led him into the living room. Naturally, it was filled with people, most of whom she knew and just a handful whom she didn't. It was immediately obvious from the size of the wake that her mother had been loved by one and all. Many her former students.

The house was just as she remembered it. The small, white-walled foyer with a coat rack and umbrella stand. The doorway into the dark wood-paneled living room. Couches and chairs with big floral patterns and crocheted doilies on the head rests.

Vicky pulled Denny through the crowd of mourners. Many of whom were surprised to see her. "Vicky, my dear! So glad you could make it!"

At last the crowd parted to reveal a lovely young woman dressed all in black. Even with her face covered by a veil, Denny immediately noticed the striking resemblance. Though her hair was a shade darker, there was no mistaking her. This was Vicky's older sister.

The two women burst into tears upon seeing each other and immediately embraced. Denny just stood back and waited awkwardly, yet patiently. After they had cried for several minutes, Vicky finally introduced him. "Lizzie, this is Denny Morris, my... boyfriend."

"Oh my!" Lizzie stood there in stunned silence for a moment, then wiped away her tears with a handkerchief.

"What an unexpected surprise!"

"So nice to finally meet you," he replied politely. He awkwardly reached out for a handshake, but then shyly drew back when she didn't reciprocate. "I'm so sorry for your loss."

Finally, she reached out and gave him a warm and welcoming hug. "Please forgive me, it's been such a difficult day. So nice to meet you! Thank you so much for coming."

"Vicky has told me much about you," Denny added warmly, even though he and Vicky both knew that not to be entirely true.

"Denny works with me at the paper," Vicky told her. And before Lizzie could ask if he was a reporter, she added, "He works in the archives."

"Sort of like a librarian," Denny explained, then added with a smile. "Except, I never have to shush anyone."

"I'm just so glad you were able to make it," Lizzie welcomed him. "I'd introduce you to my husband and our boys, but I think they're outside keeping busy."

"How's everyone holding up?" Vicky asked.

"Well as can be expected," Lizzie replied. She started to say something else, but didn't.

There was a long, awkward pause.

Denny could tell that there was a lot left unsaid between the sisters. And a lot more that needed to be said. He was tempted to leave them alone, but Vicky grabbed his hand. It became readily apparent that she didn't want to be alone with her family any more than he did.

But somebody had to say something. Which was a job that had never once fallen on his narrow shoulders.

"So, Lizzie," he spoke up nervously. "Is that short for Elizabeth?"

"Why yes," Lizzie replied. "It certainly is." It wasn't much of a conversation starter. But it was enough.

"Such a lovely name," Denny commented, still doing his best to both bail out Vicky and make a good impression. "Lovely home, too."

Vicky watched his face and waited for the lightbulb to come on. She was sure it would only take a minute.

And then Bingo! There it was.

WORTHINGTON stood watch by the closed French doors of the solarium as Dr. Tung administered the final of two injections to Master Gregor. The first had been to help him sleep and the second was to combat the infection that had suddenly plagued him.

Outside the glass-walled room, Elyse and Mollie watched with dread and concern. If only this had happened upstairs, Worthington thought. There he could have shielded them better. But downstairs in a room that was transparent from every side, it was impossible to hide the truth.

They'd seen the blood. And now they'd seen Dr. Tung. There would be many more questions. For which he didn't yet have plausible answers.

He'd have to deal with that later, however. One problem at a time.

"How has our patient fared?" Dr. Tung asked.

"Much better, up until to-day," Worthington answered stoically. "He seemed to be well on his way to recovery."

Dr. Tung shook his head in disbelief. "I'm still amazed that he's alive at all, to be honest. God's hand is truly at work here."

"Will he survive, Doctor?" Worthington asked, his stoicism finally showing signs of weakness.

"Yes, I believe he will," Dr. Tung replied optimistically. "You've done an excellent job changing his bandages. Better than some of my nurses, in fact."

"I've had many years of practice caring for Master Gregor," Worthington explained with just a tinge of pride.

"The bullets left traces of bacteria that caused the infection," Dr. Tung explained. "I've given him a shot of penicillin. You should see a marked improvement by to-morrow. I'll call to check on him then."

"Shouldn't we take him to a hospital?" Worthington asked, prepared to face the inevitable.

Dr. Tung thought carefully for a moment. "As a physician, I'm inclined to say yes. But considering the circumstances and the repercussions that are sure to follow, for each of us, I believe that we can handle this on our own."

CHAPTER EIGHT

VICKY spotted her father in the back of the room, looking very stern and stoic. For a man who'd been in poor health for most of his adult life, he knew how to look strong when the moment arose. And this had certainly been one of those moments.

The only thing worse than the complete and utter sadness that had engulfed her had been the feeling of dread on top of it all. She hadn't at all looked forward to seeing him again. They hadn't exactly parted on the best of terms.

But at least she had Denny there to shield her. Surely, she thought, between the funeral and having Denny at her side, her father would leave things unspoken.

She was just about to succumb and make the necessary introductions when Denny quickly pulled her aside and whispered. "So, your name is Victoria, your brother's name is Henry, and — "

"Yes, my sister's name is Elizabeth," she confirmed. It had been just the diversion she'd needed. A way to delay the inevitable, even if only for a few more minutes. "My mother was quite the Anglophile. Just so glad she finally got to go after we left home. Twice in fact. Father took her to London for their 25th anniversary."

"How wonderful," he commented.

"I can usually tell how smart someone is by how quickly they figure it out," she added. "Record time I'd say, Mr.

Morris. Bravo."

"Thank you," he replied. He was about to say something else, but couldn't think of anything appropriate.

"I could really use a drink." She took a deep breath and grabbed him by the hand. "Come on, let's get this over with. If we're lucky, he'll throw us both out."

ELYSE checked outside the laundry room and carefully shut the door. It was the one room of the house that Mr. Worthington rarely frequented, but she still wanted to make completely certain that he could not overhear.

She and Mollie had both just helped Mr. Worthington move Master Gregor back up to his bedroom. After all that they had just witnessed, they had expected some form of explanation. But there was none.

Just a simple "thank you" and an instruction to "go on about your business."

"Just who is this Chinaman doctor?" Mollie pondered incredulously. "And why in the world ain't he in a hospital?"

Elyse, who'd worked there a good two years longer, replied, "I've seen all sorts of quacks come and go at this house. But never one in place of Dr. Graves."

"And you see all that blood?" Mollie retorted. "No telling what all that's about. I lay you ten to one he's dying, I do. And that's the least they're not telling us."

"Well, one thing's for sure," Elyse reasoned. "We'll be out on the street, looking for a new job before you know it."

COCKEYE DUNNE sat on the front stoop of Terry Milliken's brownstone on Elm Street. Milliken owed him two sawbucks and it was time to collect. He'd been waiting there for a good half hour and suspected that Milliken was wise to him. It wasn't a total waste of time, however. If Milliken didn't show up soon, Cockeye knew Terry's sister would keep better company.

The Irish tough wondered how Milliken managed to live in such a decent neighborhood. A butcher shop across the street, young mothers walking with their children, and a tavern right on the corner. Milliken should have loaned money to *him*.

Cockeye was just about to head inside when a black sedan pulled up to the curb. After what happened to Kid Yellow and Cherries, instinct told him to get the hell out of there. Too bad instinct wasn't fast enough. Willie Potatoes and Fingers Scarrone were already getting out of the car before he could make it down the stoop.

Cockeye only had a second to make a choice. He could get in the car and do as they said. On the other hand, he could try to shoot it out right there. Or he could just follow his first instinct and run like hell. He went with with the latter.

He'd barely made it past the next brownstone before the South Side gangsters opened fire. Screams filled the street as Cockeye went down in a splash of crimson. Bullets ricocheted off the stone wall and struck a woman passing by. Willie hoped she was only injured.

"Let's get the hell out of here!" Willie commanded. The two men jumped back into the car and quickly sped off.

VICKY sheepishly tugged Denny through the crowd towards a thin, stoic man in a black suit, with a white goatee and wire-rimmed glasses. He could feel her usual bravado and self-confidence melt away with every step. She was practically clutching his arm for strength when they finally stood before the Rose family patriarch.

"Father," she greeted him politely.

"Victoria," he greeted her in return.

"Denny, this is my father, Mr. Edward Rose," Vicky said demurely, much quieter than he'd ever heard her before. "Father, this is my... boyfriend. Mr. Denny Morris."

Apparently, Mr. Rose had already been informed of Denny's presence, judging by his lack of surprise.

Since Vicky had described her father as a frail man, which had certainly been supported by his gaunt appearance, Denny was unprepared for the firmness of the older gentleman's handshake. He immediately felt that Mr. Rose was sizing him up. And he was sure that he had failed on every level.

"I'm so sorry for your loss," Denny offered.

"So, what do you do, Mr. Morris?" Vicky's father asked bluntly.

"Actually, I work in the morgue," Denny replied hesitantly.

Mr. Rose leaned back slightly with eyes widened. He wasn't sure if Denny's response was meant as a joke in extremely poor taste, or just a most unfortunate coincidence.

"How interesting," was his only response.

Vicky immediately jumped in to the rescue. And not for the first time, of course. "Actually, Father, Denny works in the archives at the paper. He doesn't really work in a morgue. That's just what we call it. He's sort of a librarian."

"Oh, is that so?" Mr. Rose replied, clearly relieved.

"Yes, that's how we met actually," Denny added, trying again. "Vicky, Victoria… came down to the, uh… archives, looking for research on a story. We searched all night until we found it."

"All night you say?" Mr. Rose asked, eyes widened once more.

Denny immediately realized he'd done it again. He was about to clarify, but thought the better of it. Vicky was back to the rescue.

"Not actually *all night*, Father," Vicky explained. "Just very late. Denny wanted to make sure I got home safely."

Mr. Rose eyed him carefully, then said, "Well, I do appreciate you bringing my daughter back to me, Mr. Morris. For that, I will be forever grateful."

Denny started to respond, but opted instead to just smile and nod.

WILLIE POTATOES and Tommy Clams opened the front door of Mrs. Hershey's Boarding House for Women. They glanced around the entrance hallway and looked for mailboxes or some other indication of who lived in which apartment. "I don't see nothing," Willie snorted. "Come on, we'll ask one of the neighbors."

They'd just made it to the stairs when Mrs. Hershey quickly opened her apartment door and poked out her little, round head. A disapproving frown crossed her already well-lined face.

Just as she'd suspected. Two gentlemen callers in dark, pinstripe suits and wide-brimmed fedoras had begun to make their way upstairs. They looked like a couple of toughs, even with one in a sling. *But they had another thing coming*, she thought. *Not in her building*. None had ever gotten past her watchful eye. And they weren't about to anytime soon.

"Excuse me," she snipped in her usual disapproving tone. "May I help you gentleman?"

The two men turned around when they saw her. Willie gave Tommy a friendly jab and smiled back at the old woman. *This old busybody would have all the answers*, he thought. And it would be a bit of fun, to boot.

"Yeah, we're looking for Vicky Rose," Willie answered. "She's a red-headed gal, hot little number. If you could just tell us which room she's in, you can go back to your knitting."

Mrs. Hershey just crossed her arms and glowered. She didn't know who these greasy-looking hoodlums were, but she wasn't about to let them just roam around in her building. She ran a respectable boarding house. And, as such, it would stay.

"I'm sorry," she retorted firmly, "but gentlemen callers are not allowed above the first floor. And Miss Rose is not at home. Perhaps you should arrange to meet her elsewhere."

She opened the front door for them to leave.

The smile momentarily disappeared from Willie's face. He had a job to do. And old broad or not, he was beginning to tire of her attitude. "You hear that, Willie?" Tommy chuckled. "Looks like we ain't wanted around this place. Maybe we ain't respectable enough for Grandma Moses here."

"What's your name, Lady?" Willie asked as they slowly walked back down towards her.

"It's Mrs. Elmira Hershey," she informed them.

Willie nudged Tommy in the ribs. "Hey, just like the chocolate bar!"

"And this is *my* boarding house," Mrs. Hershey continued. "Which means that when you come through that door, you abide by *my* rules."

She soon found herself directly addressing the two men, face-to-face. They pressed themselves even closer, just to make sure she knew that they meant business, too. "Maybe you could just tell us where she is and we'll be out of your way?" Willie suggested.

Tommy didn't like leaning on a broad, much less an old one. But he wasn't about to disobey direct orders.

Mrs. Hershey finally realized that she wasn't dealing with the usual sort of ruffians. She just hoped it hadn't been too late. *That Victoria Rose*, she thought. *Knew that girl was trouble the moment she'd laid eyes on her.*

"She's, uh — " Mrs. Hershey stammered. "She's not here, I'm afraid. She had to go out of town suddenly."

"Can you believe this old broad, Tommy?" Willie asked. "Miss Rose had *to go out of town all of a sudden*. Well, ain't that just convenient."

"A little *too* convenient if you ask me," Tommy sneered.

Willie pressed even closer to make his point known. She practically had to look straight up to see his face.

"Listen here, you old hag," he glowered, "apparently we ain't made ourselves clear. Now why don't you tell us where we can find Miss Rose before we have to make things uncomfortable? Capisce?"

Willie opened his jacket to reveal his shoulder holster tucked inside.

"Oh, on the contrary," she stammered with a nervous smile. "I understand perfectly well! I swear, I'm telling you the God's honest truth. Her mother passed away and she had to go back home."

She smiled again, awaiting their approval. She'd readily told them all she knew. She'd just hoped it was enough to save her from any harm.

Willie took a step back. "You don't say? And where is home?"

"Gibsonville," she offered quickly. "Gibsonville, Missouri. She left on the train just this morning."

Willie finally smiled again and tipped his hat to her. "Thank you, Ma'am. It's been a real pleasure. Now you go and enjoy your evening."

They brushed past her and made for the door. They'd just gotten it open and were halfway out when she'd gotten her salts back about her again.

She called out to them. "And when you see her, you can give her a message for me. Tell her that she needs to find a new place to live. I'll have her things boxed up and waiting!"

AGNES SHAYNE stirred from an uncomfortable sleep. Something wasn't right. She could just sense it. And the feeling had awakened her. She reached over to touch her husband. But he was wasn't there. He still hadn't yet come to bed. She missed having his strong body there next to her.

"Poppa?" she called out. There was no answer.

She turned on the lamp and shielded her eyes from the light. She fumbled for the alarm clock. It was after two a.m. She reached for her robe.

Moments later, Agnes found her husband in the living room. Sitting in his easy chair, alone in the dark, nursing a glass of whiskey. They'd never had alcohol in the house before.

"Aren't you coming to bed, Poppa?" she asked.

"Can't sleep," he mumbled then took another drink.

She just didn't know what to make of it. With all the honors he'd received, he should have been elated. Something was clearly eating him up inside. He wasn't even like this after he got shot. Even Bobby Junior had noticed he wasn't the same.

They had found happiness together. He had given her light when she'd run away from darkness and tragedy. He'd given her marriage and a son. He'd given her comfort and safety. Yet somehow the darkness had followed her. And now it was taking him away. She couldn't help but wonder if she deserved it.

"Can't we talk about it, Poppa?" she asked. "Why won't you tell me what's wrong?"

He just sat there silently. She kneeled down at his feet and implored him. "That's what wives are for. Better or worse, remember?"

"You go on back to bed," he grumbled. "I'll be there in a little while."

She got back up and stared down at him. "All right then. You just know I'll be waiting. As long as it takes."

She did as he instructed and went back to bed. She lied there for close to an hour before she finally, fitfully, fell back asleep. Waiting for him to return to her side.

He never did.

And when she awoke the next morning, he was already gone.

CHAPTER NINE

SATURDAY MORNING brought a day of sunshine, birds chirping, and children playing outside. And while the rest of the country gathered together to honor their nation's independence, the Rose family faced a gathering of a different kind. One that didn't involve fireworks, waving flags, or any sort of celebrations.

The cemetery, like the train depot and pretty much everything else in Gibsonville, was also just a few short blocks from the Rose home. And though a few people actually opted to walk, the majority followed the hearse in their automobiles. In was not the parade in which they'd wanted to participate.

Despite Lizzie's insistence that he was welcome to join the family, Denny didn't want to impose. He already felt that he'd encroached enough when they suggested he stay over with the family instead of going to a hotel.

Vicky had even agreed. She certainly could have used his shoulder on which to cry. But he just didn't feel it was his place. Unlike Will and Bitsy, he was just the... boyfriend. And barely one at that. So, he opted to walk as well and hang in the back with the other family acquaintances.

The casket was a beautiful mahogany with brass trim and surrounded by dozens of lovely floral arrangements. Vicky and Lizzie looked over all the flowers that had been sent by friends and other mourners. The majority were from people they knew, but there were a few arrangements from names that the family didn't recognize.

"This one's from Jerome Cooper of Terminal City," Lizzie noted. "Friend of yours, I take it?"

She had to think for a second before she realized who that was. "Oh, that's Jerry," she explained. "He runs an ice cream shop near the office. Sweetest guy you'll ever meet."

She most especially did not mention how Jerry'd taken her to the hospital when she'd blacked out in front of the Carousel.

Another was from Elmira Hershey, which appeared to be a bit on the *frugal* side. "That's my landlady."

Vicky reasoned (correctly) that Mrs. Hershey must have sent it out of a sense of decorum, rather than any actual caring on her part. She'd later find out just how right she'd been with that assessment.

Finally, there was one very large, very impressive floral arrangement. It was a good three times bigger than any of the others. The assembled mourners had never seen anything like it. But Vicky recognized it immediately.

She'd seen plenty of arrangements just like it in Terminal City. At the funeral of Michael Memoli. And Dion O'Boyle. Vicky was about to look at the tag when Lizzie whispered quietly. "Was just about to ask you about this one. From someone else in Terminal City, a Henry Green. Friend of yours as well?"

Vicky sighed nervously. "You could say that."

"Must be someone pretty important," Lizzie added.

"Yeah, you could say that, too," Vicky replied as the family minister announced that they were ready to begin.

To everyone else, it was just a huge, gaudy arrangement that was terribly out of place. To Vicky, however, it meant something else entirely.

Vito Spats had gotten her message.

ELYSE, Mollie, and Bridget followed Mrs. Poole into the back room of the kitchen. They sat down at the servant's table with the cook, Mr. Coleman. They were followed by the groundskeeper, Mr. Olstead, and Mr. Donaldson, the chief of security for the estate.

Mr. Coleman was one of the few servants who'd been with the Gregor family since Thomas was a young man himself. He could well remember the days when the staff was so large that it would have taken several kitchens to hold them all.

Over the years, however, Mr. Worthington had continually cut back. It wasn't due to lack of monies (a fate which had, sadly, befallen some families). Brent's Grandfather, Nate Gregor, had seen to that. With just Master Gregor there by himself, a large staff simply wasn't needed. The Wentworths had done the same after their move to Europe. They'd kept on a minimal staff to maintain the house for whenever Billy or Abbie chose to visit.

Mr. Coleman was the only one who wasn't worried. He'd seen staff come and go for over thirty years. "If there's one thing I'm sure of," he always said, "people gotta eat."

"What's this about? Does anyone know?" Olstead asked, as puzzled as the rest of them.

"Hope he's going to tell us what's been going on around here," Mrs. Poole stated.

"Is Master Gregor dying?" Mollie asked.

"Oh, I certainly hope not," Elyse added. "But he doesn't look well, I'm afraid. He doesn't look well at all."

"Most of us are probably going to be sacked, I'm sure of it," Mrs. Poole surmised, defeatedly. "Seen this happen plenty of times before. But you younger ones'll still have a job for a time. You and Mr. Coleman, here."

"People gotta eat," Mr. Coleman commented.

DESK SERGEANT COFFEY leaned back and cocked an eyebrow. He and the other Buttons watched with puzzled interest as Dapper Sheridan, Mossy Egan, and Spike Kinney all marched into the Southside Precinct. They went straight up to the desk and proudly presented themselves.

Coffey peered down at them with suspicion. "What's this all about, boys?"

Dapper offered up his wrists. "We're here to surrender. Turning ourselves in."

"Surrender for what?" Coffey couldn't believe his ears.

"Parole violation," Dapper explained. "The three of us

just drove down from Wisconsin this morning, and we can prove it."

He handed Coffey a traffic violation. The sergeant took the paper, put on his glasses, and gave it a read. It was legit, all right. From the Milwaukee Sheriff's Department. Even had all three of their signatures.

"Which, I believe, is a clear violation of parole," Dapper offered proudly. "So, in the interest of the taxpaying public, we hereby surrender ourselves to the bosom of the law."

Coffey just stood there in disbelief. These three were clearly working some kind of angle. But for the life of him, he couldn't yet figure out what it was. *Better to err on the side of the law*, he thought.

"Okay, take 'em on back, boys," Coffey instructed. "We'll get this all sorted out upstairs."

Dapper, Mossy, and Spike all readily surrendered to the uniformed Buttons, happily cooperating as they were cuffed one after the other.

Coffey just scratched his head as he watched. Then signaled to a nearby Rookie. "Better go get Detective Flynn," he instructed.

He called the Rookie back as the gang obediently followed the boys upstairs. "Better get LaSalle, too."

FATHER PACELLI sat down across from Brent Gregor as Worthington checked the younger man's temperature. As Dr. Tung had predicted, his fever had come down and his color was returning to normal. He still looked very weak, however, so Worthington opted to get him some more juice. "Do you mind, Father?"

"No, of course not," Father Pacelli answered. "I'll do my best to keep him company in your absence."

"Thank you," Worthington replied and went to the door. He pulled it shut as he left. "I'm afraid the walls sometimes have ears."

"We've all been praying for your recovery," Father Pacelli said anxiously. "Just wanted to check and see how you're faring."

Brent easily sensed that was not the only reason. "And?" he asked.

"And we wish to return the rather sizable donation. As much as we appreciate the generosity, I didn't want you to think it was necessary."

Brent was taken aback at the suggestion, however true it might have been. "Fine, just give it back then. But, seeing the state of your parish, I thought it was the least I could do."

"Not quite the answer I was seeking, but it does erase my concern," Father Pacelli told him.

"And what was that?" Brent asked.

"That the gift was an attempt to purchase our silence," the Father explained. "May I ask by what miracle are you able to walk again?"

"I'm afraid it's somewhat temporary," Brent told him. "I only have the ability to walk when I use it to help others."

"Is that how you managed to get injured?" the Priest asked.

"Does not the Holy Book talk about the *root of all evil*?" Brent asked. "Big Jack is just that for Terminal City. He's taken so much from so many. I thought if I could..."

Brent hesitated for a moment. He didn't want to fully admit what he'd been there to do. But they both knew full well his objective. And he couldn't lie to a Priest. To whom better to confess his sin?

"I thought that if I were to kill him," Brent admitted, "it would save many other lives in return."

Brent paused as the pain got the better of him once again. Finally, he implored, "Please, don't let the folly of my actions outweigh the good you can accomplish with the donation."

"Very well then," Father Pacelli agreed. "We shall gladly accept your gift. Though I do hope that you will visit the parish again under better circumstances. Faith will get you through this, my son," Father Pacelli assured him.

Faith, Brent considered. He'd had faith once before, or so he'd thought.

CHAPTER TEN

Two Years Prior.

TRUMPETS sounded the arrival of Sister Audrey in her enormous, 5000-seat auditorium. The entire audience, some forced to stand in the back, focused their attention on the rear doors. The giant Kimball pipe organ (one of only three that size in the entire world) filled the cavernous hall with music. Both the Choir and the Amen Chorus, dressed in their immaculate white robes and positioned on opposite sides of the stage, sang "Hallelujah!" The orchestra was positioned below.

At last the doors opened. The crowd burst into thunderous applause.

Sister Audrey entered in her glistening white robe adorned with a red cross. A dark blue cape flowed behind her. She beamed with a triumphant smile. In one arm was an enormous bouquet of red roses. She waved to the crowd with the other as she made her long ascent to the stage.

The crowd stood up and continued their accolades.

Finally seeing her in person took both Brent and Worthington by surprise. In the news reels they had watched, Sister Audrey was a dowdy, plumpish woman with dark brown hair piled up on top of her head. Now, however, she was thin, her hair dyed blonde, and cut into a fashionable bob. All very fitting for someone firmly rooted in the heart of Los Angeles.

Worthington marveled in appalled curiosity at the

unrivaled spectacle. He and Master Brent were seated on the front row. Waiting for their appointed time to take the stage.

The auditorium was one of the largest that either had ever seen. With an enormous seating area and two elevated balconies, the Seraphim Temple was nearly as large as Radio City. Were it not for the stained-glass windows built high into the walls on each side and the giant cross over the dais, it could have easily been mistaken for a concert hall. Outside, the Temple building looked like a Roman coliseum with a large dome on top and a light-up cross that could be seen for miles away.

The path that had brought them there had been a challenging one indeed.

Following his unsuccessful surgery in Austria, they had rushed home upon receiving word from private detective Sam Donohue regarding the long ago attack on the Gregor family. Still in recovery, Brent had arranged for Worthington to retrieve a package from the gumshoe at Union Station.

Donahue never showed. The next day, his body was found. Afterwards, Brent received the file in the mail but was unable to make much use of its contents.

Fresh from yet another setback, Brent began his search for another surgeon. Every hospital and clinic, no matter which country, all demurred and offered the same recommendation. Dr. Wilhelm Gaebeler at the Heiße Quellen Clinic in Austria.

His options in the field of medical science exhausted, Brent embarked in the opposite direction. The healing power of faith. Worthington assumed this would lead him to Father Ryan at the Cathedral of the Holy Name. Better still, a path of prayer and redemption. Instead, it brought them to Los Angeles.

Worthington was understandably skeptical. He had no doubts regarding the healing power of faith. Or the existence of miracles. What he doubted was Master Gregor's commitment to faith. And whether or not this woman was a worthy vessel. She struck him as far more P.T. Barnum than Apostle Paul.

"How is this any different from the pomp and circumstance of the Catholic Church?" Brent asked. Worthington was about to illustrate that the Catholic service was far more reverential when he suddenly realized Brent's greater point. It was all a creation of Man.

In addition to the grand spectacles she performed each week (Sunday night services resembled Broadway reviews, complete with costumes and dance numbers), she also published her own magazine, *The Shepherd's Call*. And had her own radio station which broadcast her sermons, radio dramas, and music. It was all a masterful mix of religion and entertainment.

As much as he didn't care for her theatricality and self-built cathedral, there was no denying the good works that she performed for her community. A very large part of her organization was dedicated to charity. When men got out of prison they were given jobs. Needy mothers were given baby clothes, diapers, food, and assistance.

When the city was unable to provide for the ever-increasing numbers of people in need, Sister Audrey opened up her own commissary. It provided food, blankets, clothing, and medical care. It was staffed 24 hours a day, seven days a week. And all of it was free of charge. No questions asked.

She'd recently garnered an enormous amount of publicity after a faith healing service in Santa Barbara. While her usual home was the Temple, she still liked to travel the country as she had done in her years as an itinerant evangelist on the Sawdust Trail. Before the trail had led her to the West Coast and a permanent home.

She'd performed numerous faith healing services before, but this one had been for the largest crowd ever. She was understandably nervous and had already experienced a few failures. But never in front of that many people. Or surrounded by so many members of the press. All ready to snap their pictures.

A young girl who'd spent most of her life in a wheelchair was brought up to the stage. Sister Audrey was tempted to turn the child away, but like Moses before Pharaoh, asked the Lord for strength. Undeterred, she laid hands on the young girl and prayed.

She then called for the child to get up. Moments later, the child did just that and took her first few uneasy steps. The girl and her family were quick to heap endless praise and gratitude upon Sister Audrey. But as she had always done, she took no credit for herself. "This was the work of the Lord," she told them. "It was He and He alone."

Some people believed that she was a living apostle. Others that she was a charlatan. Her reputation as a holy woman wasn't helped by a pair of scandals involving a possible illicit romance and misuse of church funds.

Following the service in Santa Barbara, a pair of enterprising reporters, looking to make a name for themselves, sought to prove without a doubt that she was, in fact, a fraud. They left no stone unturned. They dug up every bit of information they could find on the supposedly healed girl, her family, the doctor who'd treated her, every eyewitness they could find, and even the manufacturer of her wheelchair. And, of course, the scandals as well.

But despite all of their efforts, they were unable to *disprove* that the girl had been healed. When asked for comment, Sister Audrey replied as she always did. "Those who came to scoff stayed to pray."

In a time when many people struggled just to survive and desperately wanted to believe in even the *possibility* of miracles, the story received more than the usual attention.

All the way to Terminal City.

BRENT and Worthington had arrived by private rail car the day before. They had attempted to arrange a discreet meeting with Sister Audrey. Accompanied by a sizable donation to her organization, of course. The donation was happily accepted, but not the private service.

The denial came with a message. "There are no rich nor poor here, no white or black, no class nor nationality. All are equal in the eyes of the Lord."

Brent was dismayed, though Worthington could hardly disagree with that sentiment. Faced with attending a regular service as his only option, Brent quickly warmed to the idea.

If he was going to attend with the masses, he reasoned, they should certainly blend in. He had Worthington purchase plain, brown suits for the two of them. Brent let his stubble grow and arranged for the use of another wheelchair that was decidedly less expensive.

The Sunday morning of the service, they happily joined the thousands of other attendees outside. The line stretched for blocks on end. When the doors opened, the crowd poured inside.

On their way to the auditorium, they passed a museum room dedicated to Sister Audrey's healing services. The walls were adorned with discarded canes, leg braces, artificial limbs, and even a few wheelchairs.

The sight had its intended affect. It gave Brent more hope than he had already.

The auditorium filled quickly. They were not alone in wanting to be healed. With them were numerous others. Each week a fleet of ambulances parked in front of the Temple. They delivered the sick and frail from miles away. Had Brent not been in a wheelchair, they would have easily ended up in the topmost balcony. But the ushers, and even a few men and women of the congregation, saw to it that Brent and Worthington be given prime seating near the front.

There they listened to her message with wrapt attention. Brent purely focused on what was to come afterwards. Worthington on what she spoke then.

Aside from the expected dramatic flourishes, her theology was reasonably sound. She spoke with the Good Book in her hand. She jumped from lesson to lesson, each one illustrating the unwavering faith of those who were healed by the Lord. The blind man who put mud on his eyes. The lame man who was lowered through the roof. The bleeding woman who merely touched His cloak. The lepers outside the village.

In true evangelistic style, she spoke in a measured cadence, rolled her Rs and over-emphasized the final syllable of many words. But unlike the usual fire and brimstone preachers that had also risen up from the Sawdust Trail, her message was one of love and redemption.

At last she spoke of miracles.

The Ushers called forth an elderly Mexican man who walked with a cane. She moistened her hands with spiced oil, then touched and prayed over him. Then she called out to him, "Cast away that walking stick! The Lord will support you now!"

The Older Man hesitantly dropped his cane. With his eyes firmly locked on Sister Audrey, he made his first tenuous step across the stage.

Sister Audrey stood there with her arms open wide, ready to embrace him. But after each step, she backed away, urging him to go further. By the time he finally reached her, he'd walked over half the stage. The choir burst into song of praise.

Brent was enthralled by what he'd just witnessed. Ushers dutifully picked up the discarded cane, surely to be added to the museum. They took the gentleman by the hand. He thanked Sister Audrey profusely. She graciously refused all credit. "This was the work of the Lord. It was He and He alone."

He did a shaky little quickstep as they led him offstage.

Brent watched patiently as Sister Audrey went back to her message. She told the story of a father who merely asked that his son be healed. Of the paralytic who picked up his bed and walked home. Of Lazarus who was risen from the dead.

"That's the kind of faith I'm talking about to-day!" she sang out. The crowd shouted their Amens in response.

At last, it was Brent's turn. Sister Audrey called out to him. The choir sang out as the Ushers took the chair from Worthington and steered Brent up onto the stage. Sister Audrey beamed and greeted him with open arms.

"Welcome, Brother!" she acknowledged. "The Lord tells me you've come a long way to be here this morning."

Brent nodded in affirmation. The Choir continued to sing and the Amen Chorus chimed in.

She raised a hand high in the air. "Please tell me your name, my brother."

He answered simply, "Brent." He hadn't realized that one of the Ushers behind him had held up a microphone. He reacted with a start as the sound of his own voice echoed across the great hall.

"Tell me, Brother Brent, you've suffered great pain, haven't you?"

Brent nodded again. He wasn't sure whether or not she was actually reading his soul, or was just making reasonable suppositions. Worthington firmly believed it was the latter.

"Tell me, Brother, how long have you been in that wheelchair?"

Brent hesitated before leaning into the microphone, this time aware of its presence. "More than ten years," he replied.

"Tell me, Brother Brent, do you have faith? Do you have faith that the Lord will give you the strength to walk once again? Do you have faith that, with the Lord at your side, you can stand up out of that chair? Do you have faith that, like Peter stepping from the boat, you can once again have the strength to walk across this stage?"

"Amen!" Brent shouted. Yes, he truly believed. Yes, he *wanted* to believe.

Worthington held his breath and watched. Hoping for an actual miracle.

Just as she'd done with the Older Man, she moistened her hands and touched his head. Brent thought it smelled like olive oil with some kind of spices mixed in.

Brent clutched the armrests of his chair. Be it real or just the excitement of the moment, he felt the strength within. He felt the power of faith give him the courage to stand.

"Dear Lord," she prayed, "let this young man know the power of your wisdom, your love, and your mercy. Give him the strength to rise up out of that chair and walk across this stage!"

He actually rose up out of his chair. The Ushers held him by the arms to keep him from falling. She backed away quickly and called out to him.

"The Lord commands you! In His name! Rise up and walk! Follow in his footsteps!"

Brent felt something come over him. But as soon as the Ushers relaxed their support, he sank right back into the chair.

He hadn't been healed.

He was just the same as always. Nothing had changed. Nothing at all.

Sister Audrey immediately rushed to his side. This didn't look good for her, either.

"I sense a heaviness in your heart, Brother Brent," she told him. "I feel a great pain that clouds your soul. It's a deep and residing agony that's been there a very long time. There's more than just a weak and broken body keeping you in that chair."

Brent nodded hesitantly. This he hadn't expected.

Any of it.

He just shook his head in frustration. He'd come there to be healed. Not to have his motivations questioned.

She hadn't done that with anyone else. She hadn't *failed* with anyone else.

Brent and Worthington left for home that very evening.

CHAPTER ELEVEN

VICKY, still in her black dress from the funeral (though her veil had been ditched the moment they'd walked in the door) searched determinedly through the kitchen cabinets and pantry, all to no avail. Flustered, she leaned against the counter and let out a deep sigh.

As usual, Denny was right on her heels and ready to offer support. Normally, this irritated her to no end. But lately she'd come to depend on it. "Need a hand in here?" he asked, ever wanting to be chivalrous.

"I really need a drink," she stated flatly. "Alcohol or chocolate, it doesn't matter. But Prohibition had nothing on this house, and apparently that still hasn't changed. Couldn't even find a bottle of cooking wine."

Denny could easily tell something more was going on. "Something wrong, Vick?" he asked, then realized how stupid that sounded. "I mean, something else happen?"

The exasperated, determined look on her face made him wonder if he'd regret having asked. She fumed a moment longer, then blurted out: "Father just informed me that he wishes to have a talk. Barely been home forty-five minutes."

"Did he say what he wanted to talk about?" Denny asked, doing his best to be helpful.

"Didn't have to," she retorted. "It's the same thing we always talk about. Same lecture every time. How disappointed he is. Everything I'm doing wrong with my life."

She put both index fingers to her temples and exhaled again.

"Least he waited until after the burial. And this time he wants to lecture me in Mother's garden. That was a surprise! Usually he lectures me in his study."

She immediately burrowed through her purse for her medication. Then grabbed a glass from the cupboard.

Denny was tempted to ask if her headaches were coming back. But that was patently obvious.

"Might as well get it over with," she determined, then tossed back her pills and chased them with a swig of water.

She snapped back towards Denny. "Just going to have to tell him off once and for all. I'm not a little girl anymore! I make my own choices."

She threw the pill bottle back into her purse. "Yeah, I've made my share of mistakes," she resounded (the headaches were a sure reminder of that). "But they're... *my mistakes!*"

She jabbed her index finger into his chest to emphasize the last two words. He did his best not to wince too much.

She tossed the glass into the sink. "Maybe we can make the four o clock train back home."

BY THAT AFTERNOON, Brent had shown even more progress in his recovery. Unfortunately, however, his mental state had worsened considerably.

"I must say, Master Gregor," Worthington intoned with unconvincing cheerfulness, "you've made a marked improvement this morning."

Brent refused to answer.

"I'm afraid you gave us all quite a scare these few days prior," Worthington continued with feigned optimism. "But judging from the look of you this morning, I'd say we've clearly turned a corner."

Confined once more to his bed, his every movement brought only pain and discomfort. Unable even to move about the house in his wheelchair, Brent felt more trapped than ever before.

He'd tried to read the paper, but that just brought more pain. Not physical pain. Pain of a different kind. The kind that seemed to torment him at every turn.

Right on the front page was a story about Abbie. She'd just secured a contract for her "to appear in up to three motion pictures for MGM Studios." All thanks to the *brilliant skills of her manager and new husband*, George Parkhurst.

This, of course, was on top of her recent win in the Bendix race. Try as he might, he just couldn't put her out of his thoughts.

VICKY barreled out into her mother's garden, her head still pounding. She stopped and took a moment to compose herself. If she didn't, she thought, there was no telling what she might do or say.

Her father sat on a cement bench surrounded by her mother's gardenias. If she hadn't known what was about to transpire, she'd have thought he actually looked peaceful. Sad. Broken.

But as weak as his body was from years of sickness, he'd always been strong of mind. And that's with which she'd always had to contend the most. Ever since she left teaching, never an agreement as to where she went or what she was to do with her life.

Until it had all just exploded and she'd left for good. And it had cost her the chance to say goodbye to her mother. More than anything, that was what saddened her the most.

She rubbed her forehead once more. The pills couldn't begin working fast enough. She took a deep breath, gathered herself again, then stormed over to where he sat.

"Father, I — "

"Victoria, please, sit down with me here," he said gently. "Don't your mother's gardenias just look so beautiful?"

"Yes..." she said, taken aback.

"I used to never come out here," he continued weakly. "Never took the time. But now it's the first thing I do every morning. And the last thing I do at night. She lives on in this garden."

Vicky didn't know what to say. She didn't know what to think, either.

Finally, she just sat down next to him.

He took her gently by the hand. "I so wish I'd had the

chance to bring you out here, to speak with you *before* the service. With your mother's passing, I've come to realize that there are a great many things I haven't said. That I should have said. And now that you're here, for however long, I just wanted to make sure that not another day passed before I did so."

Vicky was flummoxed. She'd expected a battle. But this was anything but. She didn't know at all what to say.

"I'm just so very sorry for everything," he continued. "For all that I said. For all that I did. I just wanted to tell you that I was wrong. Wrong to insist that you had to follow the course I'd set for you. Wrong to expect you to not have goals of your own. So wrong that I drove you away. And for that I'm so *terribly* sorry."

"Father, I..." was all that she could manage to get out.

"And I'm just sorry that I didn't tell you until now. It's my fault that you didn't get to see her again before she passed. She used to tell me every day to reach out to you. But I was just too stubborn and pigheaded. And now it's too late."

With the words finally out, he could hold back the tears no longer. He clutched her hand tighter. "Could you ever find it in your heart to forgive me?"

Vicky just sat there in stunned silence.

Then all at once, she felt like a little girl again. In her short, pink dress. With ribbons in her finger-curled hair. Her loving father by her side.

She collapsed into his arms and cried. It was a cry that she'd needed for a very long time.

THE COLD, DEAD fireplace called to Brent. Just an empty pit of blackness that was situated in the corner of the room. It's coals and ash long dormant for months.

Abbie's name screamed at him from the newspaper he held in his hand. The smiling faces of her and Parkhurst dug their way into his memory.

Perhaps he could just burn them away.

With some pain and difficulty, he reached over and retrieved a small matchbook from the nightstand. Then slipped it into the pocket of his robe. With even more pain and difficulty, he reached for his chair. He carefully slid himself across the bed and into it, landing with a painful, sudden stop.

He took the newspaper and wheeled over to the hearth. He struck a match, lit the pages, and watched it burn for a moment.

Watched as her face and name disappeared into ash.

Once the flames licked near his fingers, he tossed it into the fireplace.

In his weakened condition, however, he was unable to throw it quite far enough.

Bits of burning paper fell onto the corner of his lap blanket. Within seconds, it had managed to catch fire.

Brent wheeled back in a panic.

He tried to grab his bell from the nightstand, but only managed to knock it over. Frantic, he tried to push the blanket off, but it only bundled up around his feet.

He bent over to push it further, but toppled out of his chair. He hit the floor with a loud, ungainly thud. The burning wool still around his ankles.

He tried to drag himself across the floor. But still couldn't pull himself away from the flames.

He could feel the heat against his skin.

At any moment, his robe and pajamas would catch fire.

He screamed out in fear.

CHAPTER TWELVE

One Year Prior.

AMRISH SINGH sped through the crowded, dusty streets of Chandrapur in his sleek, convertible Roadster. He swerved left and right, narrowly avoiding carts of fruits and vegetables, pedestrians, and the various animals that wandered about freely. The town was a cacophony of clapboard buildings, exotic sounds, and bright colours.

Amrish was a young Indian with an ever-present smile and a ready eye for opportunity. He'd discovered his greatest fortuity in a Hindu Shaman who lived in the hills and had done many wondrous things. Amrish had already made a small fortune arranging travel for the scores of wealthy Europeans and Americans seeking a cure for their many ailments. Usually these cures involved afflictions such as gout, lumbago, rheumatism, and general nervousness.

In the back seat, Worthington clutched both his hat and his stomach. Brent Gregor held onto both the door and his older companion.

"Mr. Singh," Worthington intimated, "I do say, we're really in no hurry."

It had been a long voyage to get there. They'd first taken a train to New York, then traveled by ship to London. Then another ship to Mumbai, followed by a two-day train ride across India to Chandrapur.

Amrish turned around and smiled back at them, with no concern for the road. "Not to worry, Mr. Gregor! I take care of everything!"

Worthington's expression quickly went from nervous to abject fear. His eyes grew big as saucers as he stuttered and pointed excitedly at the road ahead.

Amrish turned back around just in time to see a large cow directly in front of them. Brent and Worthington were tossed back and forth as he swerved wildly around it.

"Please take care to look at the road, if you don't mind," Brent requested.

Twenty minutes later, the two men were finally able to breathe a deep sigh of relief when Amrish skidded to a halt at their destination. They both said a quick prayer that they had arrived unscathed.

The Hotel Mirabar was a white, two-story Georgian manor that sat in the shadow of the Siwalik Hills. It had a wide porch on the front which wrapped around to an even larger veranda on the side overlooking the Ganges River. The Union Jack flew proudly in the wind.

Amrish jumped out of the automobile and rushed around to open the door for Worthington. He pointed proudly at the entrance ramp which had already been installed. "See! I take care of everything! I will get you all checked in. Not to worry."

No sooner had he dashed inside than the Bellman, a young Indian named Hadid, quickly arrived with a wheelchair. This was just a temporary measure until Brent's arrived from the train station with the remainder of their luggage.

"Welcome to the Hotel Mirabar," Hadid greeted them as Brent climbed into the chair. "Anything you require, just ask and I will get it for you."

"A very cold drink would do nicely," Worthington suggested. He took a kerchief and wiped the unending perspiration from his neck.

"Halloo!" a voice called out as they reached the porch.

They were welcomed by Colonel Nigel Hewlett, resplendent in his white suit, bushy white moustache, and tan pith helmet. He stood up from his rocker and twirled his cane. Hewlett, they would soon learn, was both the owner of the hotel and the local magistrate.

"You must be Brent Gregor!" Hewlett called out.

"Welcome to Chandrapur. What on earth brings you to this corner of the Empire?"

"A local Hindu shaman," Brent replied as they shook hands.

"Yes, of course," Hewlett replied. "Should have known. He's done miraculous things, I hear."

How Hewlett could manage in that heat, Worthington had no idea. He fanned himself continuously. Even the overhead fans provided little comfort. Both he and Brent were already covered in perspiration.

"I actually knew your grandfather back in the day," Hewlett informed Brent. "How is Old Nate doing these days? Still living in Paris with that new wife of his? Or so I hear."

"Still the same as ever. Still enjoying Paris," Brent answered with a manufactured smile.

Brent was at a loss on what else to say when Worthington felt the sudden need to sit down. He grabbed a nearby rocker and fell into it. Brent was worried that he might faint. He wasn't the only one who was concerned.

"Worthington, are you all right?"

"Just need to sit down a moment, Sir," Worthington replied. "Not to worry."

Hewlett called on Hadid to bring him some wet towels and cold water to drink. Within a few minutes, Worthington was looking more like his old self again.

"The Crown has done much to tame India," Hewlett commented, "save for the oppressive heat. You should try the ice baths. Fix you right up."

Worthington's ears immediately perked up. "Ice baths, you say?"

"Yes, of course," Hewlett confirmed. "Most wonderful things, I tell you. Mix of salt water and chips of ice. Bring the stuff down from the Himalayas, or so they say. Don't know how they do it without it melting the whole way, of course."

That sounded very appealing indeed.

BEFORE he could head back into town, Worthington saw to his required duties and got Brent situated in his room. Brent told him there was no rush, but of course, Worthington wouldn't hear of it. Then the trunks arrived from the train station and there was no getting rid of him.

"Sir," Worthington commented as he hung up the last of Brent's clothes. "I think it best that we should take a few days to settle. Rest up a bit before the remainder of the journey."

Brent knew this was coming. He'd expected no less. And was well prepared to stand his ground.

"No," he replied emphatically. "I want to get going right away. I've waited long enough."

That was just what Worthington had expected as well. Only his response wasn't thought out. It was just one of duty and emotion. "Then please, let me go with you," Worthington implored. Though he very well knew that he was in no physical condition to do so.

"No," Brent replied, just as emphatic. "This is something I have to do on my own."

"But, Sir..." Worthington protested.

Young Master Gregor wouldn't hear of it. "I've told Amrish I want to leave first thing in the morning."

WHILE Worthington explored the healing power of ice baths, Brent stayed behind at the hotel. Once he'd finished getting the last details in place for his journey the next morning, Hadid helped him out on the veranda for an early dinner by himself. Just the way he preferred it.

Most of the meal was perfectly quiet until a small group of fellow guests took a nearby table. Brent tried not to pay them any mind, but with all of their laughter, it was hard not to do so. He was nearly done when the ringleader of the group took notice.

"Oh my heavens, is that Brent Gregor?" the jovial man shouted with surprise. "I dare say it is!"

Brent looked up to see Archie Leach. Brent didn't so much know him as *knew of him*. Everyone in polite society did. He was round-faced, impeccably dressed, and a bit of a fop. He'd had enough good taste to marry into wealth. For his arrival in India, he'd traded in his usual bowler for a straw hat.

With him was his beautiful and elegant wife, Grace. And another couple, Clive and Mary, two of the most uninteresting people Brent had ever met.

But the person who most got his attention was Abbie.

It had been three years since that night at Vicedomini's. Three years since he'd seen her last. She wasn't the same Abbie he remembered. Her hair was shorter and she looked more grown up. More refined.

Though he'd never met the handsome, dark-haired gentleman who's arm she clutched tightly, no introduction was necessary. He was George Parkhurst, newspaper publisher and Abbie's current suitor. And a good ten years older than her.

Archie, true to form, was keen to make introductions, despite the objections of nearly everyone there. "Abigail, you simply must introduce him to George!"

"Please, perhaps some other time," Abbie protested.

Archie grabbed her by the arm and drug both her and Parkhurst to Brent's table. Mary gave Clive a disapproving look over Archie's behavior. But, of course, did nothing to discourage him.

"Abbie, what a pleasant surprise," Brent remarked.

"Yes it is, isn't it?" she remarked, unable to let go of Parkhurst. It could not have been a more uncomfortable situation.

"Go ahead, Abigail," Archie urged with a prod of his elbow. "Don't be rude."

Brent noticed that she now went by her full name.

"This is my... well, he's my manager," Abbie offered. "Mr. George Parkhurst."

Thanks to Leonore's Society column, Brent knew exactly who he was. And the true nature of their relationship.

Brent offered Parkhurst a handshake. "Forgive me if I don't get up."

Parkhurst smiled nervously, unsure if he should laugh or not. Abbie would explain to him later that it wasn't actually a joke. Just Brent's subtle way of getting back at them both.

"So, Brent Old Boy," Archie asked, "what brings you all the way out here to India?"

"Healing of the mind and spirit," Brent replied and signaled for Hadid.

"Well then," Archie exclaimed, "you simply must join us for the polo match to-morrow!"

That was the last thing he wanted. And behind Abbie's feigned smile, it was obvious she felt the same way.

"I appreciate the invitation, Archie," Brent replied, "but I'm afraid I've already made other arrangements. Some other time, perhaps."

"Hats off to you then, Old Boy!" Archie laughed and patted him on the shoulder.

Hadid showed up just in time to take him away. As he left, Brent overheard Archie comment to Abbie, "He doesn't seem at all as unpleasant as you described him."

EARLY the next morning, Amrish arrived at the hotel as promised with two elephants and a half dozen porters. Worthington watched nervously as the men used ropes, a pulley, and a great deal of effort to hoist Brent up onto one of the towering pachyderms.

"Once I reach the temple," Brent instructed, "I want Amrish to lead the entire group right back. Just leave me a handful of provisions. Enough to last a few days."

"Sir," Worthington protested, "they can't just abandon you."

"They won't!" Brent exclaimed. "Once I am finally cured, I intend to *walk* down this mountain on my own. And she'll be right here waiting when I do. This has worked out far better than I had hoped!"

Though Worthington outwardly agreed with Master Gregor's optimism, inwardly he worried that Brent was headed towards yet another heartbreak. Or worse.

But he wasn't about to have Brent left unattended up in the hills. Duty dictated that he should go with him. But he knew that he'd only be a liability himself. He quickly pulled Amrish aside.

"Mr. Singh," Worthington instructed, "after you drop off Master Gregor, I should very much like for you to camp a safe distance away and keep an eye on him. I'm rather concerned for his safety."

"Master Gregor will be just fine," Amrish reassured him. "No worry. I take care of everything."

Worthington opened his billfold and quickly produced a large handful of British pounds. "Do this for me, please won't you?"

Amrish happily agreed. "Yes, sir! Of course, Sir."

THE JOURNEY up the jungle-covered hillside took the better part of two days. Amrish rode at the front on the first elephant. Brent rode second on his, followed by the porters and their load of supplies. The overhead canopy was filled with the chattering of monkeys. Their shadows danced across the jungle floor below. They seemed to follow the group for the entire journey.

Despite the intense heat, bugs, and the discomfort of riding by elephant, Brent was determined to soldier on. Knowing that Abbie would still be there when he returned from the jungle gave him the strength that he needed.

The sun was just beginning to dip in the evening sky when they reached the ruins of an ancient Hindu temple. It was nearly hidden by the jungle. A swarm of monkeys stood guard over the entrance. Amrish quickly climbed down from his elephant and shouted excitedly, "We are here! We are here!"

Getting Brent down from the elephant was still a chore, though a much easier one than getting him saddled. Amrish instructed the porters as they tossed ropes over the animal's back and carefully lowered him down onto a stretcher.

The other Porters opened a crate full of fresh fruit. They tossed mangoes, bananas, and melons to the monkeys. Once the simians were well occupied, they picked up Brent and carried him to the ruins.

Inside the temple was pitch dark. Amrish lit a torch and led the way. They passed through a long, overgrown corridor towards a light beyond.

Brent shielded his eyes as they reached the heart of the ruins. It was a stone courtyard whose only roof was the trees above. There was a square pool in the center.

The Shaman sat at the edge with his spindly legs dangling

in the clear, blue water. He was nearly naked save for a loincloth, with scraggly hair and red and yellow paint on his face and beard.

The Shaman offered a silent welcome as the Porters set Brent down beside the pool. He put a shell necklace around the young man's neck, then painted red and yellow marks on his face.

Amrish translated. "Welcome to this sacred place. The journey you are about to take will be difficult. But if your heart is true and your soul determined, at the end of this journey you shall reach your goal."

The Shaman pointed a scrawny finger at Brent's chest and asked, "Are you ready?"

"Haan!" Brent affirmed in Hindi. *Yes!*

THE NEXT several days were one long, hallucinogenic dream for Brent, dotted with visions that may or may not have been real. They included vague images of smoking a pipe full of mystical herbs, endless chanting, high fevers, and being soaked in perspiration.

The days and nights ran together as he endured treatments of hot stones placed all over his bare skin. He vaguely remembered trying to scream but was unable to make a sound.

Ghostly voices echoed inside his head.

"You could have saved us," his mother accused.

Brent tried to escape but found only darkness.

The voice of his father echoed over and over.

"I expected more from you, Son."

THE SUN had just gone down as Worthington returned to the hotel suite from his latest ice bath. Their cooling properties had not been overstated by Colonel Hewlett. In fact, they'd gone a long way in helping him adjust to the sweltering climate. Worthington dabbed his forehead with the towel around his neck. He was tempted to lie down under the fan, but knew full well that he'd never make it down for dinner.

He couldn't help but once again think of Master Brent. Up in the hills with who-knew-what-kind of witch doctor.

Unable to walk and unable to contact anyone for help, should he need it. And try as he might, Worthington couldn't imagine a situation where he wouldn't.

He had to place his trust in Amrish. He'd paid the man handsomely to keep check on Master Gregor. And with no word from their Indian host, he could only assume that all was well.

At least that was what he hoped.

He was just about to get ready for dinner when he heard a soft knock outside. He assumed it to be Hadid.

"Miss Abigail! What a pleasant surprise," Worthington exclaimed as he opened the door. "Please, do come in."

Worthington offered her a seat and told her, in true gentlemanly fashion, how wonderful it was to see her again and how much she'd grown these last few years. He was tempted to say more, such as how much he'd missed her laughter around the house, but thought the better of it.

Judging by her own uneasiness, it was the right decision. "You can't imagine how surprised I was to see Brent at dinner the other night," she told him, searching for just the right words.

"Yes, I'm sure I can't," Worthington agreed. "I trust that he was a gentleman, however?"

"Yes, of course," she affirmed, much to the older gentleman's relief.

He smiled at her with fatherly eyes. "To what do I owe the honor, my dear?"

She struggled for the right words. "I was wondering, if you don't mind my asking, what brings you to India?"

AMRISH sat by the campfire, stirred his morning tea, and glimpsed up at the sun as it peered down through the jungle canopy. It had been nearly a week, and he had seen no sign whatsoever of Mr. Gregor's return from the Shaman.

Each dawn, he'd instructed a scout to head back to the temple and check on the situation. And each morning, the scout had returned to report his findings.

He was tired of camping up on that mountain, despite being very well paid to do so. If Mr. Gregor wasn't walking by now, it was surely time to carry him back down.

He soon got his answer. It was only moments later before the scout ran anxiously back into the camp and shouted, "Come! Come! I think he may be dead!"

They rushed up the hillside and combed through the jungle until they finally reached the nearly lifeless body of Brent Gregor. He was stripped down to his undergarments, unshaven, and his back bore many burn marks from the hot stones. His hair was disheveled and his face streaked with red and yellow paint. Worse, he was malnourished and still under the effects of heavy narcotics.

Perhaps believing he could walk, he'd apparently attempted to drag himself down the mountain on his own.

The men huddled around Brent and sat him up. Amrish grabbed the water flask from around his shoulder and threw it to them. They did their best to get him to drink.

"Quick!" Amrish commanded. "We must carry him back up to the temple!"

Amrish and the porters hoisted Brent across their shoulders and made the difficult climb back up to the top of the mountain. They marveled at how he was able to drag himself down that far on his own.

At last, they finally reached the ruins. The place was deathly quiet. To the man, they were all frightened of what they would find.

Amrish quickly lit a torch and led the men inside. They gently carried Brent into the pool. There they worked to clean him up and gave him more to drink.

There was no sign of the Shaman. As much as he was afraid to do so, Amrish picked up the torch and ventured deeper into the temple. There would be many questions when they returned. He would have to find answers.

He reached a juncture with three corridors, each leading off into a different direction. The left and right tunnels were softly lit by beams of sunlight that forced their way down through cracks in the roof. The remaining tunnel was black as pitch.

He stopped to listen.

At last he heard a soft moan. It was barely perceptible over the flickering of the torch. But then he heard it again.

It came from straight ahead.

Amrish steeled his courage, readied his pistol, and cautiously ventured forth. There was no telling what he might encounter. A snarling panther perhaps, or even a rabid baboon.

Step by step he continued forward, moving his torch back and forth, quickly studying every patch of wall and ground that the light struck.

Finally, he reached the end.

There, huddled up against the far wall, he found the quivering figure of the Shaman.

"What are you doing here?" Amrish asked in Hindi. "What has happened?"

"Please, it is too great!" the Shaman cried out. "Please! You must take him away. It is too great!"

"What is too great?" Amrish asked. "His ailment?"

"No!" the Shaman cried out with fright. "The dark spirits within!"

WITH the sun setting over the Ganges, Brent had a late dinner by himself on the veranda. Despite a full day's rest, a hot bath and a shave, he still appeared quite worse for the wear. Following his lost days in the temple, he'd returned shockingly gaunt, with scratches on his face and dark circles under his eyes. His temperament was even worse.

He tried to eat, based on Worthington's instructions, but found it increasingly difficult to muster an appetite. No matter where he went or how much he spent, the result was always the same.

He'd be stuck in that chair forever, he realized.

Surely the universe had conspired against him. If it weren't bad enough that he was still crippled, he'd come back to find that Abbie and her obnoxious friends hadn't yet left the hotel.

The irony was too rich for words. He'd expected to walk down the hillside in triumph and win her back. But instead, he once again returned in failure. Only to be mercilessly taunted by seeing her there in the arms of another man.

As if to rub salt in the wounds even further, she was right there as he tried to eat dinner. Just inside the hotel and well within earshot. The group had gathered for a parlor game in the sitting room next door. The French doors wide open. The sounds of drunken laughter carried all the way out onto the grounds. Taunting him further still.

Leach, true to form, lead the group in a game of Guess the Character. Each person wore a headband with a card stuck inside that only the others could read.

As loud as Archie was, the only laughter Brent could hear was Abbie's. It was Parkhurst's turn, and she giggled like an enamored schoolgirl at his every simple utterance.

"Am I man?" Parkhurst asked.

"Yes," Abbie squealed with delight. Brent had never heard her behave so insipidly before.

"Do I have a moustache?"

"Yes," Abbie confirmed.

"Charlie Chaplin," Brent muttered to himself.

"Do I speak with an accent?"

"Possibly," Abbie replied after some thought. "Hard to say, really."

"Am I in motion pictures?"

"Yes," she confirmed again. He could hear the excitement in her voice as he got closer.

Parkhurst became smug with certain accomplishment. "Am I Charlie Chaplin?"

"Yes!" Abbie gushed. "Oh Darling, you're so brilliant!"

Brent pushed his plate away in disgust. He'd clearly had enough. And not just of dinner. He signaled for assistance.

"Hadid," he asked, "would you mind closing the door?"

IN ACCORDANCE with the proper decorum, Worthington took his meals at the servant's table in the hotel kitchen. He was unsure about leaving Master Gregor to dine on his own, but propriety dictated such, particularly in a country where the class system was even more prevalent than their own.

For that reason, one could only imagine his great surprise when Hewlett trotted in carrying his own plate of food. And even more astonished when the Colonel actually sat down with him.

"Mind if I join you, good man?" Hewlett asked.

Worthington immediately leapt to his feet and scrambled

to pick up his plate and silverware. He was sure he could find some spare bit of counter space on which to finish his meal.

Hewlett stared back in confusion. "Where the devil are you going? Sit down, man."

Worthington was confounded by just what to do. Protocol dictated that he not dine with Master Gregor. Yet, here he was taking supper with a man who was both the master of the house and a government official. In the end, he just decided to follow orders and do as instructed.

"Welcome Colonel," Worthington stuttered. "To what, may I ask, do I owe the honor of your good company?"

"Serenity, my good man," Hewlett confessed. "Blessed serenity. I dare confess this is the only quiet room in the whole building."

Worthington was at first surprised by this revelation. "You don't say, Sir?"

Hewlett leaned in close and explained softly, "Forgive my saying so, but the fact of the matter is I simply can't abide that Archibald Leach. There's not a room on the entire first floor where you can't hear his constant braying. And perhaps the second as well."

Worthington had to agree. It was for that reason among many he hadn't wanted to leave Master Gregor to dine alone. And was anxious to dine in the kitchen himself.

"Most distasteful sort of chap," Hewlett complained. "Don't know why on earth the rest of that group even deign to be seen with a ruffian of that sort."

Worthington nodded once more in agreement. He and the Colonel might have been on opposite ends of the societal ladder, but on this they most certainly saw eye to eye.

"Here here," Worthington offered and raised a glass.

"Especially the Wentworth girl," Hewlett continued. "Always thought the better of her family. Comes from good stock."

"Indeed," Worthington couldn't have agreed more.

"Can't say as I know this Parkhurst fellow," Hewlett puzzled and whispered close again. "But if I you ask me, I'd say he smells of new money."

Hewlett pondered over the situation more thoroughly

and offered a raised eyebrow. "Forgive my saying so, but I thought she and your young Gregor were betrothed?"

"Sadly," Worthington replied, "it was not to be."

UNFORTUNATELY, the only route back to his room required Brent to pass in full view of the parlor. Propriety and Worthington both would prefer that he leave Abbie unencumbered by his presence, even if she hadn't shown him the same consideration.

Brent signaled again for Hadid. "I'd like to retire for the night."

Propriety be damned, he wasn't about to *hide out* on the veranda all night. From the sound of things, the group was having too much fun (and was likely too tipsy) to even notice him.

No such luck.

"Oh, there you are, Old Boy!" Archie exclaimed as they passed by the parlor. He'd clearly had plenty to drink. "We've been looking all over for you!"

Abbie could immediately tell that Brent was in no mood for games. She quickly attempted to intervene. "Archie, please. I think he'd much prefer to be alone."

"Rubbish," Archie scoffed. "He could use a good cheering up!"

Archie quickly grabbed Brent's chair from Hadid and wheeled him straight into the parlor. "Come on, Old Boy. Join us for a little fun. We're just playing a round of Secret, Secret."

Hadid stood at a loss, unsure of what to do. Brent raised a hand to signal that it was okay.

Archie handed Gregor a small card. On the underside of which was a criminal activity. He didn't even look at it. Mary glanced at hers and squealed with delight.

"Who wants to go first?" Archie called out.

Grace volunteered excitedly. "Oh, I do!"

"That's the sport, Darling!" Archie cheered.

From the corner of his eye, Brent's focus was solely on Abbie. He watched as Parkhurst reached over and took her by the hand. She hesitated to take it, as if she even cared about his emotions.

Brent seethed angrily as he watched.

"Does it involve breaking the law?" Mary asked, which seemed a rather obvious question. Less obvious, Brent thought, when he considered the source.

"Yes," Grace replied.

This was essentially the exact same game they'd played earlier, Brent thought. Only the guessing is reversed and the subject is different.

"Is it illegal in some countries, but not in others?" Clive asked.

"No," Grace replied with some thought. "All countries, I'd say."

Archie chimed in. "Would you say this is a high crime, or a lesser crime?"

"A lesser crime, I suppose," Grace answered.

"Are you a prostitute?" Archie shot back playfully.

Grace's face turned red as she giggled. "Oh, heavens no!"

Brent stewed with increasing anger. Propriety or no, he'd had enough and signaled for Hadid.

"Brent, Old Boy! Where on earth are you going?" Archie asked with astonishment. "You haven't even offered a single question."

Abbie again did her best to intervene. "Archie, please. Just let him go."

Archie brusquely jostled poor Hadid aside and drunkenly stood his ground. "Not until he's made a proper guess!"

"Fine," Brent huffed in exasperation. "I'll give you one. She's a shoplifter."

"Heavens!" Grace shouted. She held up her card to demonstrate that he was correct. "How on earth did you know?"

Brent tried to back away on his own, but Archie had solidly blocked his escape.

Archie slapped him on the back. "See? I told you! Splendid job, Old Boy!"

That was it. Brent had finally reached his boiling point.

"I don't know why we're all bothering with pretend secrets," Brent complained, "when there are so many real ones that are barely any secret at all."

"Ha!" Archie cheered. "That's the spirit!"

"Brent, please!" Abbie implored. She knew what was about to happen. But it was too late.

"Archie here is a homosexual who's never once pleasured his wife," Brent stated angrily.

The room was struck with a sudden silence. Everyone was stunned.

"I'm sorry, what did you say?" Clive stuttered.

Archie, for once, was at a complete loss for words.

Brent, however, was only just getting started. "Poor Grace, on the other hand, is forced to share a bed with other men. Clive being among the latest."

Mary's eyes widened in absolute shock. She looked sharply at Clive.

Clive's face turned suddenly white.

Abbie glowered at him with increasing anger.

"You'd think Parkhurst here would be the saint of the group," Brent continued. "But he's still married to another woman."

"Stop!" Abbie shouted and jumped to her feet. "Just stop!"

Brent had never seen her so angry before. He stared back at her defiantly. Matched her dagger for dagger.

Abbie did her best to collect herself. It was all she could do to not explode further.

"Brent, I think it would be best if you leave."

That was the moment he realized it. He had gone too far.

Then she added tearfully, "And I never, *ever* wish to see you again."

CHAPTER THIRTEEN

ELYSE bolted into the master bedroom.

Without concern for her own safety, she fell to the floor and grabbed the blanket. The cuffs of his pajamas had already become singed. She stamped out the remaining sparks and threw the burning fabric into the fireplace.

"Mr. Worthington!" she cried out at the top of her lungs. "Mr. Worthington!"

Moments later, Worthington hurried in through the doorway. His senses immediately assaulted by the sight of Brant sprawled out on the floor, the toppled wheelchair, and the smell of burnt wool.

"Oh, my dear!" He exclaimed and quickly rushed to Brent's aid. "Are you injured, Sir?"

The still-panicked Brent answered shakily, "I don't know...."

Worthington quickly checked him over. With Elyse's assistance, they managed to get him upright and back in the chair.

Brent was a bit shaken but otherwise fine. "Thank the Lord."

Worthington then turned to Elyse. "Are you injured in any way, my dear?"

"No, Sir," she replied as he helped her to her feet. "Thank you, Sir."

"I cannot thank you enough, child, for your quick action."

She curtsied in response. "Just doing my duty, Sir."

Worthington's immediate thought was to sharply admonish Master Gregor. But there would be time to assess just what had happened and assign blame later. Of greater importance at that moment was to address the situation at hand.

"Run downstairs and gather the rest of the staff," he instructed Elyse. "I shall be in the kitchen momentarily."

"Yes, of course, Sir," she curtsied again. She knew well enough to close the door behind her.

"You should have just left me alone," Brent complained softly.

Worthington reacted with a start, unsure of what he'd just heard. "I'm sorry, Sir?"

"Up on that mountain," Brent intoned critically. "You should have left me alone."

"Sir, you know that I couldn't have — "

"If you hadn't told them to wait," Brent snapped angrily, "Abbie wouldn't have been there when I got back. It would've been better if you'd just left me up there to die."

Worthington knelt down and whispered firmly, very much like he'd done many times over when Brent was just a boy. "Now, we'll have none of that, Master Gregor! You've survived far worse and come out the stronger for it!"

Worthington grabbed his wheelchair and shoved it towards the bed. "I didn't give up my life just for you to waste yours!"

Brent just stared back at him, sad and defiant.

WORTHINGTON stood silently at the head of the servant's table and searched for just the right words. Each of the staff, save Mr. Coleman, looked to him anxiously and waited. Finally, he straightened his waistcoat and addressed the assembled group.

The solution, he surmised, was to present them with enough truth to satisfy their individual curiosities. But not so much that any of them would know what had actually occurred.

"Considering the events of yesterday and prior," he began, "I'm sure that each of you are both concerned and curious as to the state of Master Gregor's well-being."

Worthington paused for another moment and collected his thoughts. He expected that one or two of them might raise a question, particularly Mollie or Elyse. But neither said a word.

He continued. "I do feel the need to offer a word of explanation. As many of you know, Master Gregor has spent a considerable amount of time and effort in pursuit of a cure for his physical disabilities. Our recent trip to California involved another such attempt."

Worthington hated to be dishonest, but in this instance, it was far better than revealing the truth. Both for Master Gregor's sake and theirs.

"Needless to say, the results have not been as anticipated. But rest assured, we expect a full recovery all in good time. I wish to thank and commend both Elyse and Mollie for your exemplary fulfillment of duty during our crisis yesterday. Your quick and steady action is much appreciated."

A sense of relief filled the room. "So, he's going to live then?" Mrs. Poole asked.

"Yes, quite so," Worthington assured her. "I'm terribly sorry for the fright, but I'm certain that the worst is now behind us. I shall see each of you back bright and early tomorrow. And with any luck, we shall soon return to a state of normalcy."

With the staff dismissed, they each shuffled out to their respective stations. Even Mr. Coleman left the room.

Worthington couldn't help but wonder if his explanation had been sufficient. If perhaps he'd successfully allayed their doubts. Only time would tell.

Worthington had never knowingly lied to the staff. But he'd also never been placed in a situation where it had become so necessary to do so.

VICKY and Lizzie stood at the large kitchen window in the Rose home. The overwhelming sense of sadness that hung like a fog inside the house was at least tempered by the sound of the neighborhood children playing outside.

"This was mom's favorite part of teaching," Lizzie commented. "Just letting the kids get out and run around. Use up all that energy. She used to hate rainy days, even though they were great for her gardenias."

"Oh, I remember," Vicky replied. *"I'd rather have dead flowers than unruly students."*

Vicky swallowed hard and felt the tears well up in her eyes. "How long was she sick?"

"No idea," Lizzie told her. "I'm thinking she was diagnosed a year ago, maybe? But you know Mom, she didn't want anyone to worry. Didn't tell a soul. Not even Dad."

Vicky looked away. She was more like her mother than she cared to admit.

"She did a good job of hiding it," Lizzie continued. "I suspected something was wrong, but she kept telling me it was just old age. And I guess I wanted to believe it."

Lizzie crossed her arms and gave her younger sister that patented school teacher glare. "She's not the only one."

Vicky turned back to her, puzzled. She knew that look. And she should have known that there was no escaping it. Had Vicky been a third-grader, she would have crumbled on the spot. Even as an adult, she didn't hold up much better.

"What're you talking about?"

"You're hiding something," Lizzie observed. "Anything to do with why you haven't had a byline in over a week?"

"You read *The Crusader*?" Vicky reacted with surprise.

"Why wouldn't I?" Lizzie asked. "So does Father, by the way. He pores through every copy. Of course, by the time it gets here, it's usually a day late."

"Do I use the word *puerile* too much?" Vicky asked trying to deflect the conversation.

"Why on earth would you ask that?"

"Someone told me that the other day," Vicky answered.

"Henry Green?" Lizzie asked, bringing it right back around.

"No, no," Vicky quickly replied, anxious not to make this any worse. "No, it was Brent Gregor."

"Is he someone *important*?" Lizzie put a spin on that last word that could be taken multiple ways.

"Important as in *very rich*," Vicky chuckled. "You know, Smithson & Gregor. Had to see him the other week for a story. He actually helped on the O'Donnell case."

It was at that point that Vicky realized she'd said more

than she'd wanted. Brent Gregor's involvement had been left out of the printed story, and hadn't exactly been common knowledge.

Fortunately, that wasn't what had interested Lizzie. But rather that this was someone who's opinion Vicky respected. Greatly.

"You do travel in *interesting* circles," Lizzie commented. "Now that I think about it, I'd have to agree."

"Agree on what?" Vicky asked.

"You do use the word *puerile* too much."

VITO SPATS made himself comfortable at the bar in The Deluxe. As it's name implied, this was the poshest drinking establishment in Bronzeville. Red, white, and blue streamers hung from the chandeliers. It had a huge bar, vast stores of wine, whiskey, and bourbon, decorative palm trees, a large number of tables, and a clientele all dressed in suits and expensive gowns. Save for the color of their skin, this was the type of establishment more to his liking.

The mood there was completely different as well. Spats and Willie sensed it just as soon as they strutted in the door. A quick and jolting reminder that this wasn't their territory.

No one there was afraid of them.

There had been no hush when they entered. That came later. Only then it was more out of reverence than respect. Or even fear.

Teddy Johnson took the stool right next to Spats and set his hat on the counter.

Just like the Italian gangster, he was tall and imposing. And cut a very dashing figure. His suit was every bit as expensive. And with his crisp white shirt, blue bow tie with stars, red cravat, and American flag cuff links, he wore his patriotism well. Very well indeed.

"You look a little lost, Spats," Teddy chuckled. "Shouldn't you be home celebrating with that pretty young wife of yours?"

"Very patriotic," Spats remarked.

"Why shouldn't I be?" Teddy answered with a wry smile.

"I've been very fortunate. And as you can see, I try to do my part to spread that good fortune."

Theodore Johnson hailed from the Louisiana bayou, just outside of New Orleans. Born the son of a sharecropper, he apprenticed as a tailor and part-time bootlegger. Using his earnings from the latter, he moved north to Terminal City. He soon found a job with a Bronzeville tailor. Who also ran a small numbers racket out of the back room. Before long, Teddy found himself doing a lot less sewing and a lot more selling of chances at the lottery.

"Two whiskeys, Ervin," Teddy instructed the Bartender.

"Yessir, Mr. Johnson," Ervin replied and immediately set up the drinks.

"I'm surprised you didn't come talk to me first. Like you did with Sam Yuen," Teddy commented as he tossed his shot back. "You can't show me the same courtesy you show a Chinaman? I'm disappointed."

Spats picked up his glass and was about to do the same when he noticed a boy run past. He only got a glimpse, but he looked a lot like the kid from before.

"My apologies," Spats replied. "No disrespect."

Teddy tapped the bar. Ervin dutifully refilled their glasses. "I'd like to say none taken. So then, perhaps you could tell me why you're cooling your heels here in Bronzeville? I'm sure it's not for the hospitality."

"Looking for an Irishman," Spats indulged him, certain that Teddy already knew.

Johnson gave him a curious look before tossing back his second shot. "Anything else? A Man in Black, perhaps? A Ghost? A Spook?"

Spats just looked back at him defiantly then took his shot.

"You should have come to see me first," Teddy stated as he got up from the barstool and retrieved his hat. "Saved yourself a lot of trouble. Tell Big Jack I said 'Happy Fourth.' Wish him well on his recovery."

Spats had just gotten up when the kid ran out of the back. Spats watched as he went past and right out the front door. This time he was certain.

It was the exact same kid.

"But then we would have missed out on all the wonderful hospitality," Spats replied.

WHILE the rest of Gibsonville watched the fireworks from the town square, the Rose family viewed them from their own front porch. It wasn't the ideal location (the house across the street blocked part of the view), but considering all, it still provided a brief, but welcome respite to sadness of the days' events.

With the loudness of the explosions echoing through the night sky, Lizzie pulled Vicky aside. Gone was the accusatory glare of the school marm. Instead came the concerned and troubled voice of an older sister.

"Tell me honestly, Vick," Lizzie inquired. "Who is this *Henry Green*? You said he's somebody important, but I can't say I've ever read about him in the paper."

"Because it's an alias," Vicky explained. She knew she'd have to fess up sooner or later.

"For?" Lizzie asked, sounding very much like the schoolteacher she was.

Vicky exhaled with exasperation. She really didn't want to have this conversation. But after the giant floral arrangement at the funeral, there was simply no avoiding it. "Vito Spats Gennaro," she confessed.

Then it was Lizzie's turn to stop and take a deep breath. "Are you serious? I'm so glad you didn't tell me that at the funeral."

"Don't worry," Vicky reassured her. "He was just sending me a message."

"This isn't making me feel any better," Lizzie retorted.

"Not *that* kind of message," Vicky explained. "I tried to meet with him before I left."

Lizzie was immediately taken aback. It took her a moment to find the words, and even then she stumbled. "Meet with him? Why on earth would you want to meet with him?"

Again, Vicky tried to reassure her. "Just for a story, that's all."

At least that was partially true. The whole truth was more than she was ready to explain.

CHAPTER FOURTEEN

AS SOON as they had finished lunch, Denny reluctantly packed up his things for the long train ride back home. This time alone. He didn't want to leave. He'd just gone to church with her family and then had lunch afterwards. He was starting to feel a part of them. And what was even better, Vicky seemed to like the idea herself.

Henry had offered to drive them to the depot, but Denny quickly demurred. He only had the one bag and a newspaper, he explained. Though the truth was, he wanted to spend every last second with Vicky that he could.

It was the perfect Sunday afternoon for a stroll. As they walked through the town square, they chanced upon many other couples out together as well. Holding hands, stealing a kiss when the chaperone wasn't looking. But luckily for them, none of them had to say good-bye.

"Really sorry you have to leave," Vicky confessed.

"Honest?" Denny asked. It had been an instinctive reaction, based more on his own insecurities than anything on her part. Especially since he'd surprised her at the train station and not given her much choice.

"Of course!" she reassured him. She felt bad that he would doubt her, but she understood why. Only just a week earlier, she'd been pretty hard on him. Rebuffed his every attempt to get to know her better.

But what a difference a week had made. And what a

trying week at that. And though at first it seemed like he'd wormed his way in, she finally realized just how much she needed him.

"Honestly, I just don't know how I would have made it through this without you," she reassured him.

"Me, too," he happily agreed. "But Frank would only let me go for so long."

"Tell Frank I'll be back soon enough," she stated anxiously. Days earlier she'd risked her life to keep her job. But now she was hesitant.

"You sure?"

"Just a little longer," she assured him. "Promise."

DETECTIVE SHAYNE pushed Dapper Sheridan down into a chair in the cramped interrogation room at the Terminal City Jail. At least the rooms at the precinct had painted walls with wood trim and some sense of comfort. But since these rooms were only used for prisoners, comfort wasn't needed.

"So where you been, Detective?" Dapper snapped. "Your buddies was all in here yesterday." He tilted his head to give Shayne a better look at the brand new shiner he was sporting.

Shayne didn't say a word.

"I'm sure you was home spending Fourth of July with the family," Dapper plucked his hat. "I'd have been doing the same if it weren't for, well, you know."

Shayne plopped down in the chair opposite and glared at him across the table.

Even though he couldn't smell any alcohol on his breath, Dapper could tell that Shayne hadn't been far off from a bottle.

"Why don't you tell me why you're locked up in here?" Shayne grumbled.

Dapper let out a chuckle. "You're the Copper! Don't they tell you these things?"

"Yeah, well when I've got a beef with someone, I don't turn yellow and hide!" Shayne barked.

"Ha!" Dapper bursted with a laugh. "That's rich coming from you!"

Dapper didn't even have time to react before he smashed into the cold, grey wall behind him and watched his tooth skitter across the floor.

DENNY handed his bag to one of the many porters as the conductor called for everyone to board. While he and Vicky attempted to say their good-byes, the platform was a scramble of activity. It was just like in the movies. And he wasn't about to relinquish one more second than necessary.

"Before I go," Denny began, "there's one thing I have to ask you."

Vicky suddenly feared the worst. *This isn't a proposal is it?* she wondered. Had he somehow talked to her father? It would be just like him to do that. And in that moment, she might even have said yes.

She needn't have worried, however. "Your nephews, Lizzie's boys," he began. "Are they named after Shakespeare, Francis Bacon, and Christopher Marlowe?"

"You're a little slower on that one, Mr. Morris," she smiled. "But yes, you're exactly right."

Then she leaned in quietly and whispered, "I'm not even sure their own father's figured that one out."

Denny took her in his long arms and held her tightly. Only after the train whistle blew and the conductor again shouted "All aboard!" did he finally let her go.

He plucked the *Crusader* from his jacket pocket and showed it to Vicky. "You see what's wrong with this paper?" he asked.

The first thing she spotted was a big article about Abigail Wentworth and her movie contract at MGM. It was impossible to miss.

"That Leonore finally got an article on the front page?"

"No, look at the headline," he instructed. She glanced up to read, "IRISH MOBSTERS SURRENDER OVER BAIL VIOLATION." By Chester Lyons, of course.

"That cover story wasn't written by you," he told her. "I can't imagine going back to work to-morrow and you're not there. Won't be the same without you."

Vicky could barely contain the tears of happiness that ran down her face. "You're a good man, Mr. Dennis Morris," she told him. "Even if your full name is hard to say."

He stuttered, then finally said, "I do my best."

And in that moment, she fell into his arms. She didn't just kiss him for the first time. She kissed him deeply, with all of her heart. So deeply he'd still be reeling from it when he arrived in Terminal City six hours later.

"Golly, I sure hate to leave after that," he finally managed to say.

WORTHINGTON strolled into Master Gregor's bedroom and was elated to find him not only sitting up and reading the morning edition, but an empty lunch tray beside him. It was truly a miraculous sight, and one he hadn't expected to see anytime soon. If at all.

"My heavens," Worthington exclaimed, "someone is feeling much the better."

"Yes, much," Brent readily agreed, putting the newspaper aside.

Worthington sat down on the edge of the bed and took a deep breath. He handed Brent an aged, manila envelope sealed with a red tie string. A small, round object was inside. "What's this?" Brent asked.

"Encouragement," Worthington replied.

Brent flipped the envelope over. His name was scrawled on the front. His father's handwriting. "Worthington, is this what I think it is?"

"Yes, Sir," Worthington replied. "Your grandfather wanted you to have it when you were old enough. I'd say that time has come."

Brent carefully unwound the string. It was old and brittle. He thought it might break. He slid open the flap and tipped the envelope up on its end. The contents slid out into his waiting palm.

It was Grandpa Nate's pocket watch.

"Your grandfather built an empire with this small watch" Worthington told him. "In order for you to take down an empire, perhaps you should endeavor to do the same."

Brent looked at him curiously. "I'm not sure I understand."

Worthington thought to himself for a moment. "Before he partnered with Master Smithson, he lived on impulse and whim. He learned, through much difficulty, to exercise patience. That once he'd seized upon a goal, better to examine it, devise a plan. And then follow it through. You would be wise to follow his example."

Worthington got up and looked at him firmly. "There are many answers in your father's office. You won't find them lying in this bed. Or anywhere else, for that matter. The only requirement is that you summon the courage to look."

WHEN VICKY returned to the house, she found Lizzie sitting on the steps, waiting for her. Obviously with more questions on her mind. Once they'd gotten through the pleasantries of Denny making his train, Lizzie jumped right to the heart of the matter.

"So, about your lack of bylines," Lizzie began. "Anything to do with all those pills you're taking?"

"You're just like Mom," Vicky reacted defensively. "Not a detail gets past you."

"I know somebody else just like that," Lizzie retorted. And in that same instance, she was struck by a sudden epiphany. "You were in the hospital were you? That's why you were so hard to reach."

"I'm betting your students hate you," Vicky shot back.

"Of course, they do," Lizzie replied proudly. "A good half of them are convinced I have another set of eyes in the back of my head."

Vicky shrugged in exasperation then sat down next to her. There was no keeping secrets from her sister. And the truth was, it felt good to have someone in which to confide. But perhaps not quite *everything*.

"Okay, there's something I didn't tell you about the Asylum," Vicky admitted. "But promise me, you won't say a word about it to Father. Or Henry."

Lizzie looked at her younger sibling with troubled concern. "What on earth did they do to you?"

THE SKY was getting dark as the evening train pulled into Gibsonville. Only a handful of passengers disembarked. Most had gotten off in St. Louis, while the rest continued on to Tulsa and points beyond.

Among the few were two men in pinstriped suits who clearly didn't belong. One in a bowler and white spats. The other with his arm in a sling.

Vito Spats and and Willie Potatoes.

They strolled down the platform and took in their surroundings. The evening moonlight cast its soft shadows on the neighborhood streets. The whole town grew quiet as it settled down for the night.

So different from the world that they knew.

"Like something out of a Capra movie, ain't it?" commented Willie with a smirk.

Willie gave Spats a nudge and pointed his attention towards a nearby building.

Spats looked up to see the Rose & Harwood Savings and Trust, still closed for the holiday weekend. Spats nodded in agreement.

"Looks like we're in the right place."

CHAPTER FIFTEEN

BRENT sat outside on the veranda and enjoyed the warm night air. He'd spent so much time in the house these last few weeks, it felt good to just get outside. His body still ached from his injuries, but the pain had mostly subsided. And become tolerable enough that he required less medication.

The sun was going down, and it was getting dark out. It being Sunday night, most of the staff was gone. Worthington was in his room, reading the Good Book and doing his evening devotional.

Somehow, life was finding a sense of normalcy.

Brent held his grandfather's pocket watch. He watched the reflections of the dimming light as he moved it around in his hand. It was gold and ornate, a piece of superb craftsmanship from another era. No wonder Great Grandpa Dawson hadn't been able to sell it.

He opened it up and looked at the face. The larger set of hands told the time against a set of Roman numerals. At the bottom, a smaller set of hands told the seconds.

Worthington had talked about how an empire had been built on that watch. But as he looked it over, he realized something else. A family had been built on that watch, as well. It had brought his grandparents together. And was the cornerstone of the legacy that followed.

Somehow, he could still remember the first time he'd

seen it. Better days long past. Long before the incident. Before Grandma Kitty had passed away, even.

The watch had been a gift from Grandpa Nate, but his father had insisted on keeping it for him. "When you're older, Son."

Even thinking about it all these many years later, Brent could still hear his father's voice echo in the back of his mind.

SKIP MEADOWS grabbed the plate of steak and mashed potatoes from the order window almost before the Cook could ring the bell to signal that it was ready. Skip was young, in his mid 20s, with thick glasses and a tousle of brown hair beneath his paper hat. He wiped his hands on his apron and poured a cup of coffee. He quickly turned around and set it right in front of Mr. Larsen, who occupied his usual spot.

The 8:20 evening train had just arrived, so he expected to maybe pick up only a few more customers now that the dinner crowd was long gone.

Spats and Willie followed one of the passengers inside. They stood at the door as the other fellow quickly grabbed a booth by himself at the far end.

Like most diners, it was long and narrow, with the doors opening at the left end. Along the outer wall was a row of booths. On the opposite wall was a counter and stools, behind which was a window that connected to the kitchen. The place was mostly empty.

Still, Spats had no doubt he'd find the answers he'd come to get.

"Just grab a seat wherever you like, fellows," Skip instructed. "Be right with you."

Willie and Spats wasted no time and went straight to the counter. They pushed in between the mounted stools and leaned up against it. Willie gave Mr. Larsen a menacing look. He quickly got up and moved down a seat.

Willie nodded at Skip. "Hey, you look like a smart boy."

"Smart enough, I guess," Skip replied, clearly getting the insult. And smart enough not to argue back.

"Ain't too smart," Willie smirked, "otherwise you wouldn't

be working in a place like this."

"Say, what's the big idea?" Skip retorted.

Spats nudged Willie aside. "Lighten up, Willie. We're guests in this town. Need to be more hospitable."

"Hospi-what?" Willie asked.

"Just shut-up and wait by the door," Spats instructed. Willie shrugged and did as he was told.

Spats turned back to Skip with a menacing smile. "Sorry about my friend here, he's forgotten his manners. We just want to know where we can find Vicky Rose."

"What'd you want to see her about?" Skip asked anxiously.

"We're old friends from Terminal City," Spats told him. "Just passing through and wanted to pay our respects."

"Yeah, well," Skip answered, not entirely convinced. "Her father works at Rose & Harwood. It's just down the street."

By this point Spats had run out of both patience and decorum. Looked like Willie had it right from the start. He walked around the counter and sidled up close to Skip.

"Yeah, but they're closed Sundays, ain't they?" Spats replied. "So, why don't you be a smart boy and tell us where we can find her?"

AGNES SHAYNE paced anxiously across the kitchen floor as she looked up again at the clock. It was nearly 8:30 on a Sunday night. No word yet from her husband. He should have been home hours earlier. She did her best not to assume the worst.

She hustled back into the small, but comfortable living room where Bobby Junior played on the floor. It was nearly time for their radio program, *Mob Smashers*. They usually listened as a family. But that was before.

"When's Pa coming home, Ma?" Bobby Junior asked as he spun the chamber on his toy six-shooter.

Agnes put on a brave smile for her son. "Poppa's working dear, you know that."

"But he never used to work Sundays," Bobby Junior complained. "He didn't even come to church."

"I know, Dear," she said with more exasperation than she wanted to let on. "But you know, ever since your father made Detective, he's been a lot busier. He's got important work to do."

Just from the look on Bobby Junior's face, she could tell he didn't really believe it. Truth of the matter was, she didn't believe it, either.

VICKY cuddled up next to her sister on the front porch swing as they swayed back and forth. They watched their father light up his pipe as he sat in his usual chair. Outside on the lawn, the shadows slowly deepened and the fireflies twinkled in the night air.

If only their mother had been there. So many fond memories. If only reality hadn't intruded. A reality none of them ever expected.

Vicky was the first to notice the two men who walked up the street.

Their silhouettes looked eerily familiar. Especially the larger one with his bowler hat. His white spats caught the streetlights as they approached.

"Dad, Liz, you two need to go inside," she stated and sat upright. "Better yet, go out the back door to Mr. Haney's house and call the Sheriff."

Mr. Rose only managed a puzzled expression. "Victoria, what on earth...?"

Lizzie had more reason for concern. "Who are these people, Vick?"

"Nobody you want to meet, trust me," Vicky informed them with hushed anxiety. "Just do as I said."

Lizzie was too much like her sister to stand for that. "I'm not leaving you out here by yourself."

And before she could argue further, their father stood up and claimed his ground. "If anyone is to go inside, it'll be the two of you. I'm not about to leave you alone, either."

There was no point in arguing. Vicky just sat back in frightened exasperation. Mr. Rose sat back down and clenched his pipe. The three of them watched in dreaded anticipation until Spats and Willie finally reached the sidewalk.

Vicky was about to speak up when her father took out his pipe and greeted them as any neighbor would. "Nice night for a walk, eh? What can I do for you gentlemen?"

Spats stepped forward and looked straight at Vicky. He

was the picture of politeness, but still with the ever-present tone of a threat in his voice. "Evening, Sir. We've come to have a little chat with your daughter."

Edward Rose stood up from his chair and walked to the edge of the porch. "I don't believe I've had the honor of meeting you two gentlemen."

Willie glanced at Spats and shrugged. Spats stood there for a moment and took off his hat. "My apologies, good Sir. My name is Henry Green and this is my associate, George Stone."

Lizzie gave Vicky a knowing nudge. Mr. Rose looked at them skeptically. *Could have picked better aliases*, he thought.

"If you don't mind," Spats continued, "we've just come all the way from Terminal City. We have business that we wish to discuss with your daughter, Victoria."

Vicky got up and stood next to her father. She'd always known him as a stubborn man in poor health. But in this moment, she saw more strength in him than she ever dreamed possible.

Lizzie got up right behind her and joined them. Spats looked up, momentarily puzzled. For just a second, he wasn't sure which one was Vicky.

"Just how are you acquainted with my daughter, Mr. Green?"

WITH MASTER GREGOR seemingly on the mend and the house largely free of the other staff, Worthington at last had a few free moments to check the attic. He quietly made his way upstairs and turned on the light.

Once he had inventoried every dress, every blouse, every skirt, every hat, every pair of shoes, and every piece of jewelry, he was surprised by his findings. As expected, some items were missing. But others had been returned. And both cleaned and mended in the process.

Someone was definitely *borrowing* Mrs. Gregor's belongings.

VICKY sat down in the living room with Spats and Willie. This was the same room where they'd had the wake for her mother just a week earlier. The irony wasn't lost on her. She sincerely hoped that this wasn't a foretelling of things to come.

After a fair amount of prodding, she'd somehow convinced Lizzie and her father to wait in the kitchen. It was only after she insisted that she wasn't in any real danger. Which had been all the more difficult since she'd only minutes earlier tried to convince them to run out the back door.

Still, she hoped that if things started to go south, that at least one of them would have the good sense to call the Sheriff. More than likely, though, they'd both barge in, and it would just end in a bloodbath.

Despite this lingering doubt, she knew well that the key to dealing with these men was to show no fear. And to remind herself that *she* was the one who'd actually requested this meeting.

She just hadn't expected it to be in her parent's living room.

Vicky took the bull by the horns. "So, you wanted to talk to me. Let's talk."

Willie, for his part, wasn't sure what to make of all the doilies.

Spats just sat back and eyed her coolly. "My condolences to your family for your recent loss. I do hope you enjoyed the flowers."

For all she knew, he might've actually been sincere. But everything that came out of his mouth sounded like a threat. Twenty years in the Mob will do that to you.

Still, she wasn't about to be intimidated. At least on the outside. She just wished she could've taken some more pills beforehand.

"Yes, we did, thank you," she told him. For her part, she did her best to make every word sound sarcastic. "They were quite... lovely."

Despite her best efforts, he could still sense the fear in her voice. "Don't worry," he reassured her. "We only kill each other."

Willie let out a chuckle, then quickly stifled it. He was much better at being threatening.

"So," Spats began, "you wanted to ask me about the Ghost Man."

She inhaled sharply and collected her thoughts. Just a few short weeks ago he'd wanted to kill her. She was tempted to slap the tar out of that smug face of his. But that wasn't why he was there. If she wanted answers, she had to put her suffering aside.

"Who is he?" she asked.

"Wish I knew," Spats replied. "But since he tried to kill Big Jack, I assume he's working for someone."

Clearly, she'd already entertained that thought herself. "Did Whitey hire him? Or is he working for somebody else?"

"Your guess is as good as mine."

Vicky closed her eyes a moment and steeled her nerves. Try as she might, she couldn't avoid that night at the Asylum altogether. There was one burning question that remained. And one to which she knew he'd have the answer.

"Was he there that night at the Asylum? Is he the one who rescued me?"

Spats just sat back and smiled at her. "That's the *real* question now, isn't it? Can't say it's one I'm prepared to answer. I'll give it due consideration and let you know what I decide."

His evasion told her everything she needed to know.

Spats picked up his hat from the coffee table as they got up to leave. "My apologies, Miss Rose, for the unpleasantness of our previous encounters. Thank you to you and your family for a lovely evening."

Just as soon as they were gone, Lizzie and their father emerged from the kitchen. Still shaking from the encounter. Vicky, on the other hand, was not only relieved, but clearly determined.

"Are they gone?" Mr. Rose asked.

"Yeah, don't worry," Vicky reassured them. "Everything's fine. I don't need to worry about them anymore."

"How can you be so sure?" Lizzie wondered.

"Because," Vicky explained. "Now they've got somebody they fear a lot worse."

CHAPTER SIXTEEN

ELIAS THORPE relaxed behind the bar and picked up a copy of the neighborhood rag, *The Evening Hubbub*. It was nearly closing and the last of the evening stragglers had just left. He took a moment to flip through the pages before it was time to clean up, bobbing his head to the sweet sounds of smooth jazz that sang from their record player every night.

He and his wife, Flora, had run The Beehive for over twenty years and had resided in Bronzeville for most of their lives. They started out renting an apartment upstairs (where they still lived) and had eventually managed to buy the two-story building. With rent from the other three apartments, somehow they'd managed to make ends meet over the years.

It was two of their current tenants, however, that kept Mrs. Thorpe up nights. When she saw that her husband was reading *The Hubbub*, she just shook her head and remarked quietly, "Them two upstairs ought to be in it."

Elias could only shrug in frustration. They'd had this conversation several times already. And always in the same hushed voices. "Said they was gonna be gone by now. They ain't exactly the kind of men you can just kick out into the street."

"The one with the white hair is always trying to make jokes," she complained. "And they ain't funny. Not one bit."

"I know, I know," Elias agreed.

"You know them Italian boys been snooping around the neighborhood. Why don't you just go to the police? They'll be happy to find out where those two been hiding out all this time!"

"And what'ya think'll happen to us when word get loose that we ratted 'em out?" he countered. They would soon find out.

Elias was the first to hear the speeding black car as it raced from down the block. His immediate thought was for anyone out walking in the neighborhood. Even at that late hour. "Somebody's gonna get hit."

He didn't realize just how right he was. He walked around the bar just in time to see the car as it sped by. He even got a good look at the passenger.

And the grenade that was hurled through the front window.

DENNY could barely contain his excitement as Vicky stepped off the train and onto the platform at Union Station. It had been nearly two weeks since he'd seen her and he'd begun to wonder if she was actually coming back. He was even more excited when Vicky greeted him with a kiss. And thanked him for all that he had done while she was away.

She was followed by Lizzie, whom (he'd been pleased to learn) came back with her to help her get settled and find a new apartment. Lizzie had actually spent the summer in Terminal City during her college years. While she wasn't a local by any stretch, she did know her way around.

Denny had certainly proven himself invaluable. He'd picked up her car from the boarding house, washed it, and parked it at the *Crusader*. He gathered their luggage from the porter and refused any help getting it to the car (though he eventually had to relent and let Lizzie assist with one of her bags).

He'd even tried to pick up Vicky's belongings, but Mrs. Hershey wouldn't surrender them without a rent payment. He would have handled that, too, but he didn't have the money.

Previously, Vicky would have complained about such actions. And chafed at the thought of even encouraging that behavior. But she didn't have anyone else to call. And since their time together in Gibsonville, she'd become much more open to the typical actions of a courtship.

He excitedly suggested that they might "come over one night soon and have dinner with the folks." Lizzie agreed that it would be very nice, but Vicky wanted to get settled first.

"So where are you staying?" Denny asked as they made their way through the grand, illustrious station. "If you don't mind my asking."

His first thought had been to return the hospitality shown to him and invite both of them to stay at his family's house. But his mother had quickly dismissed that idea. First because they didn't have much room, but mostly on the grounds of propriety. Especially with Vicky being unmarried and Lizzie apart from her own spouse. Dinner would have to suffice.

"Hotel to-night, maybe a few nights," Vicky explained. "Probably the Sherman. Though I don't imagine we can afford that for too long."

"Don't worry," Lizzie reassured her. "I think we can manage." Denny got the distinct impression they'd had that conversation before.

"You could always room with Leonore," Denny teased playfully.

"We're not *that* desperate," Vicky shot back with a smile. "I'd rather sleep on the street."

Vicky liked that side of him. Especially over the fawning desperation he so easily displayed. It didn't come out much, but she so much preferred it when it did.

BRENT closed the book in his lap and took a moment to enjoy the morning sunlight that beamed through the many glass windows of the solarium. He was clean-shaven, fully dressed, and on the road to finding some peace. The near polar opposite of when he'd last been in that room.

He still had a long way to go, of course. The pain of losing Abbie was still fresh in his heart. And perhaps hurt far worse than the several bullet wounds across his torso. And would leave a much more lasting scar.

The sting of failure tortured him as well. So much so that he'd thought more than once about just throwing that mask and cloak (and the ring with it) into the furnace.

Yes, he'd been able to finally walk again. But it hadn't given him Abbie like he'd thought. And without her by his side, the price to which he'd so readily agreed now seemed much too high indeed.

And yet, after all of that, he'd somehow managed to find a glimmer of happiness. It could have just been as simple as feeling the warm light on his face. But it didn't take him long to find the true answer.

He'd already struck rock bottom. There'd been nowhere else to go but up.

"Can I get you anything, Sir?"

Brent looked up to find the young one standing in the doorway. With her doe-like eyes and youthful gaze, she looked like an angel standing there in the bright rays.

"No, I'm just fine...." He had to think for a moment. "Bridget. But thank you anyway."

"My pleasure, Sir," she curtsied with a smile before leaving. "So nice to see you well again, Sir."

He suspected that she might be carrying a torch for him. He also suspected that she wasn't the only one. As appealing a thought as that was, he also had to remind himself that she was also much too young.

Brent looked up again, this time to see Worthington appear in the doorway. The older gentleman looked physically weakened. His face was ghostly white.

"I'm afraid..." he could barely get the words out.

Brent sat up straight in his wheelchair. "What is it?"

Worthington had to clutch the doorway to keep his balance. It was all he could do to maintain his composure.

"I'm afraid there's been a terrible tragedy, Sir."

LEONORE stretched back in her chair and propped her long legs across her desk as she read the morning edition. She skipped the front page to review her own handiwork on the Society page. Bleeding headlines were not her forte and she preferred to keep it that way.

Speaking of bleeding headlines, she looked up to see a familiar face stroll into the office. But what really took her by surprise was that it was followed by another face that also looked strangely familiar. Though one that looked more grown-up. Yet also more... *homespun.*

"As I live and breathe," she reacted as she stood up, "there's two of them."

"Leonore, this is my sister, Lizzie," Vicky made the introductions with a smile that actually seemed genuine. Though her attention seemed more affixed to the vase of wilting flowers that sat on the corner of Leonore's desk. They'd clearly been there a good week at the very least.

As much as Leonore dreaded Vicky's return, in duplicate no less, she maintained a facade of camaraderie. After all, the two women before her had both recently lost their mother. She wasn't *that* cold-hearted.

"So pleased to meet you," Lizzie offered as they gently clasped hands. "I really enjoy your articles. Such an enlightening style."

"Nice that one of you reads them," Leonore smiled as she tried to determine whether or not that had been a compliment.

Yes, Lizzie thought to herself, Leonore was exactly as she'd been described.

"Who're the flowers from?" Vicky had to ask. "Charlie Hecht?"

"Actually, those are for you," Leonore explained. "They're from your *boyfriend.*"

"Denny?" Vicky reacted with confusion. "Why on earth would he send flowers here?"

"No," Leonore explained happily, "your *other* boyfriend."

Vicky looked at the card and quickly realized that this was not a conversation she wanted to have in front of her sister. It read, "With deepest condolences, Brent Gregor."

"Honestly, I hardly know him," Vicky immediately protested.

"Has Vicky told you about her little bond with Brent Gregor?" Leonore asked Lizzie with a mischievous leer. "She tried to get me to change a story — "

"That's enough, Leonore," Vicky quickly interrupted.

But this was too juicy for Leonore to let go. Her breadth of human kindness only ran so deep. "Hope you're not keeping secrets from your family, are you?" Leonore asked. *Oh, if she only knew.*

Lizzie leaned back with her arms crossed. "Oh, I've learned all sorts of interesting things these past two weeks."

Leonore was clearly intrigued. "Do tell!"

These two are getting along far too well, Vicky thought. This was not going at all like she'd expected. Or could even tolerate.

"That's enough out of both of you."

BRIDGET raced headlong into the laundry. She practically skidded to a stop on the tile floor and had to take a moment to catch her breath.

Mrs. Poole looked up with a start, wondering what in the devil all the commotion was about. Mollie and Elyse both immediately noticed that she was completely pale and crying.

"I just heard from Mr. Worthington the most terrible news!" Bridget sobbed.

Mrs. Poole hoisted her glasses up from their chain and struggled to put them on.

"What is it child?" she asked, finally able to get a better look at the girl.

"Mr. Coleman's been killed!" Bridget cried out.

CHAPTER SEVENTEEN

VICKY led Lizzie into the bustling City Room. Frank was hunkered down in his office busy working on the evening edition. The familiar clatter of typewriters echoed through the room.

Lizzie was a bit overwhelmed by the bustle of it all, but Vicky was right at home. Though perhaps not yet ready to jump back in with both feet.

Despite the frenzy of activity, they were met with warm greetings and a series of double-takes. "Hiya, Vick!" Perry shouted happily. "Welcome back!"

Lyons was sure he'd died and gone to Hell. "Oh my word, there's two of them." He immediately fished in his desk for a flask.

"Welcome back, Red!" Frank shouted, the look of surprise still evident on his face as he waved them into his office.

"Frank, this is my older sister, Lizzie," Vicky made the introductions.

"Really sorry about your loss," Frank consoled. "You two holding up okay?"

"Well as can be expected," Vicky replied. "One day as it comes."

After a few more minutes of consolation, Vicky was relieved to move on to other topics.

"You raised quite a ruckus before you left, Red," Frank shook his head.

"Hope I didn't bring on too much heat," Vicky offered, "and that I still have a job."

Frank scratched his chin and glanced at the calendar on his desk. "Doc said you had to sit out for two weeks, and it's been more than that. You need to check back in, of course, and if he gives you a clean bill of health, I don't see why not."

Vicky was elated. Then immediately skeptical. Of course. "You're not taking pity on me are you?"

Frank gave her a firm stare to show he meant business. "As long as you take it easy at first. *Then* we'll see about getting you back on the crime beat."

Vicky, true to form, was just about to debate the terms when Lizzie immediately stepped in and stopped her. "I'm here to make sure of that."

"You should listen to your sister more often," Frank informed her.

They were just on their way out the door when Vicky turned back around. "Might might want to call Betty, tell her to expect two more for dinner."

Then she added in hushed tones, "We need to talk where the walls don't have ears."

BEN SANDERS watched the long, black touring car from across street, which immediately piqued his curiosity. Cars like that never drove into Bronzeville. Not even someone from Lakeview Heights picking up their servants. They'd rather spring for a cab.

Whoever was in the car was certain to be there for the same reason he was. The gaping, burned out remains of The Beehive and the few apartments overhead.

The bar had been hit with a "pineapple" thrown from a speeding car the night before, just before closing. The explosion apparently struck a gas line, which took out much of the upper floor.

There had been five victims in total, all deceased. As a young negro man who'd lived the majority of his life in Bronzeville, three of them were people he would mourn deeply.

He'd known Mr. and Mrs. Thorpe long before they started

advertising in *The Hubbub*. He had many fond memories of ducking into their establishment in the late afternoon for a soda pop or piece of candy. And there wasn't a night when he didn't remember the sweet sounds of jazz spilling out onto the sidewalk and mixing with the moonlight.

He didn't know the older gentleman, Armstrong Coleman, all that well. But he was acquainted with his daughter, Mary. He also knew that Mr. Coleman had worked as a cook for one of the families in Lakeview Heights for many, many years. Which would certainly account for that car.

The remaining victims were two white men. Aside from the police, a rare and unusual sight in that part of town. Word on the street had already pegged them as Whitey O'Leary and Squint Mulligan. That they were wanted both by the cops and the Italian Mob told him everything he needed to know.

The place was still crawling with cops. Mostly to keep onlookers at bay, and to keep anyone else from getting hurt. You could still smell the gas from a block away.

The Detective in charge, Shayne, had recently been honored, which gave Sanders some degree of hope that the perpetrators might be brought to justice.

Considering who they likely were, that was doubtful. But also considering there was an interested party of some influence (as evidenced by the long black car), that certainly improved the odds.

Sanders spied a Police Officer he recognized. One who'd walked the beat in Bronzeville for a while. A muscular man with hints of grey in his thick mustache.

"Excuse me, Officer Billings, but would you mind telling me who's in that car?"

"Need you to back away, Sir," Billings directed politely. "Only the police and press are allowed in this area. Still trying to lock down a gas leak."

"I am the press actually," Sanders explained and quickly produced his pass. "Ben Sanders with *The Evening Hubbub*."

Billings' face quickly lit up with familiarity. He'd read the *Hubbub* many times. Its loose and colorful style was often more entertaining than the content. "Thought you only covered social events."

"You see many other reporters around here?" Sanders grinned.

Billings had to agree. Aside from that old stalwart Chester Lyons from the *Crusader*, the presence of news hounds had been noticeably scarce.

"Somebody's got to tell our story," Sanders explained. "We're expanding."

"That's Brent Gregor," Billings offered on the sly. "He was asking about one of the victims, Armstrong Coleman. But you didn't hear that from me."

"Absolutely not," Sanders reassured him with a friendly wave. The police were a welcome sight in Bronzeville. And he wanted to keep it that way.

LIZZIE handed Mrs. Hershey Vicky's final rent payment as they stood in the front hallway of the boarding house. She'd thought that the older woman would have at least invited her into the parlor, but that was not to be. "I'll send Mr. Morris by later this evening to get her things," Lizzie informed her.

"I think you should get her things now," Mrs. Hershey countered.

"Mrs. Hershey," Lizzie replied firmly in a tone usually reserved for her most troublesome pupils. "I just paid you through the end of the month, which is far more than you were owed. I think you can grant her a few additional hours."

Mrs. Hershey reacted with a huff. But quickly realized that she'd easily met her match in the stubbornness department. "You're just as strong-minded as your sister," she relented.

"My students will tell you even more so," Lizzie confirmed.

As she stepped off the front porch to leave, Lizzie noticed a dark tan coupe parked just down the street. She wasn't certain, but she thought she might have also seen it pull over when she arrived.

She kept on eye on them as she climbed back into Vicky's car. Each day seemed to illuminate a new detail or two about her younger sister's life in Terminal City. And based on what she'd learned already, she wasn't about to rule out the possibility of being followed.

DOROTHY MOORE, her husband, Reuben, and their young son, Reuben Jr., joined Brent Gregor in the living room of their downstairs neighbor's apartment. They would have used her own living quarters, but they resided on the third floor and the building had no elevator. As it was, Reuben Sr. and Jr. had both helped Worthington carry him up the stoop to the first floor.

Brent's eyes lit up just as soon as they met. "Little Dorothy?"

"Not so little any more, am I?" she replied with a heartbroken smile. Though he'd known Dorothy Coleman had gotten married and given her father a grandson, he still wasn't prepared for full reality of it.

She gave both Brent and Worthington the deepest of hugs before wiping her eyes and sitting down with her husband and son.

It had been years since he had last seen her. Back when she used to spend summers helping her father at the estate. Brent had thought she might have become a cook as well, but chose to pursue nursing instead.

She smiled at him with tear-filled eyes. "Mr. Gregor, I just can't thank you enough for coming all the way down here to see us."

Try as she might, she just couldn't contain the emotion. Reuben Sr. clutched his wife's hand and completed the thought.

"There just aren't words, Sir. Thank you very much."

Brent knew exactly how they felt. He'd been there himself, and at far too young an age. The pain in his heart still easily rivaled the pain he currently felt in his chest.

Brent did his best to console her. "I've known your father since the day I was born. He was a member of the family. As are all of you."

Brent found himself overcome with emotion as well. It took him quite by surprise. He did his best to hold it in. But what had truly hurt the most, even more than the pain of loss, was the sudden realization that this was partly his fault.

Worthington put a hand on his shoulder. No matter what occurred, he could always count on Worthington to be his pillar of strength.

He intended to do the same for them.

"I know that in these situations," he continued, "there can be a lot of expenses. I just want you to know, you don't have to worry about any of it. And anything else you need, just ask."

This time, there really weren't words. Dorothy was so overcome with emotion, she couldn't get a single word out. But the look in her eyes said more than her words ever could.

After they left, Brent instructed Worthington to set up an education fund for Reuben Jr. He intended to pay for the young boy to attend college when he came of age. Something he would inform Dorothy of later.

It would never replace the boy's grandfather, but it would certainly help guarantee his future.

Brent also inquired about the funeral expenses for the Thorpes, but was surprised to learn that those had already been covered. By Teddy Johnson.

BIG JACK raised a glass to Spats and Willie at the downstairs bar of the Four Diamonds. They'd been in this situation before, but after all the morning headlines, he was dead certain the outcome had been much different.

"To our old friend, Whitey. A worthy adversary. And to Squint, a loyal soldier. May they both rest in peace!"

They tipped back their wine glasses in honor of their fallen foes. "Salute!"

Big Jack rubbed his shoulder and sat down at one of the tables. He and Willie now had matching slings.

"Tell me about this reporter gal," Big Jack inquired as Spats and Willie joined him. "I hear she's back in town after her mother passed."

"Don't think we need to worry about her," Spats informed him. "Not yet, anyway. Like I told you, we had a little talk. It was very productive."

"She spill anything good about the Ghost Man?" Big Jack asked.

"She don't know any more than we do," Spats replied. "But she's curious. And that can be very valuable."

Big Jack took another sip and savored its flavor. It was a good Italian wine, shipped directly from Firenze.

"Frankly, I'm more worried about that copper, Shayne," Spats confessed.

"Maybe you need to lean on him some more," Big Jack suggested. "Remind him how things work in this town."

CHAPTER EIGHTEEN

MRS. AGNES SHAYNE sat anxiously in front of Vicky Rose in the basement archives of the *Daily Crusader*. It had taken everything she had to go down to the paper on her own. She was worried sick about being seen. And of word getting back to her husband.

Even after arriving she very nearly turned around and left. Especially after she asked to meet somewhere private and Miss Rose suggested they go down to the "morgue." She was tempted again when Vicky brusquely told the young man working there (who appeared to be sweet on her) to take a break and come back later, despite how terribly busy he was.

But once they finally sat down together, free of distraction, Miss Rose was an absolute jewel of sympathy and kindness.

"I really must apologize for the way I spoke to you before," Agnes began. "It was improper."

"No need," Vicky reassured her. "if I'd been in your shoes, I'd have done the exact same thing. Probably worse. Now what can I do to help you?"

Agnes sat quietly for a moment, hesitant to reveal her troubles. But in the end, she was more afraid to sit idly by and say nothing. And more afraid still of what that would bring.

"I'm just so worried about my husband," Agnes finally confessed. "I read your articles and... I don't know if that's what actually happened there, but it's the only thing that makes sense."

Her eyes welled up with tears. She fought to hold back the emotion and wiped her cheeks with a pink handkerchief.

Vicky leaned in closer and took the distraught woman's hands. "Just take your time, Mrs. Shayne."

Agnes did her best to compose herself and continue. "Something's eating him up inside. And I'm just afraid it's going to tear him apart. I really am."

Agnes looked up at her with a pleading gaze. "If you could just talk to him again. Just try, maybe you can help him."

Vicky sat there quietly for a moment. She wasn't really sure just what to say. Other than the truth.

"I'm afraid your husband doesn't want to talk to me, Mrs. Shayne. I've tried several times to see him and left numerous messages, but he's definitely been avoiding me."

"I know," Agnes acknowledged sadly. She sat there quietly for another long moment and collected her thoughts.

"There's this bar he goes to almost every night, McGillin's Tavern. Just a few blocks from our house. Comes home late with alcohol on his breath. I'm sure you'll find him there."

Agnes felt a sudden sense of guilt for what she'd just done. She'd betrayed her husband's trust.

But it was something she simply had to do. For his own good. Of that she was sure.

"He needs to tell someone the truth before it kills him."

CLYDE PIERSON stood up quickly from behind his desk and greeted Lizzie with flustered surprise. Other than being a little older, of course, he was just as she remembered him. Thick-bodied, unsure of himself, but very meticulous. His family had moved to Terminal City years earlier and made a good living from several apartment buildings. Which was exactly why she was there to see him.

"Mrs. Harper!" Clyde exclaimed. "Wh-what can I do for you?"

He'd always found her both appealing and intimidating and never knew quite how to react. Back in his school days, he usually just stared at the floor. She was glad to see that was no longer the case, but the barely masked look of terror was still unmistakable.

She shook his hand and did her best to put him at ease. "Good to see you again, Clyde. You've really done quite well for yourself. I'm actually in the market for an apartment. It's for my younger sister, Vicky. You remember her, don't you?"

"Yes, of course," he replied. Then he suddenly remembered something else far less pleasant. "And I was very sorry to hear about your mother."

Clyde actually had the elder Mrs. Rose for a teacher as well, and for much longer. It was impossible to grow up in Gibsonville and not have at least one Rose woman in the classroom.

He grabbed his pen and leather-bound notebook from where they'd been neatly arranged on the desk. For a brief moment, he felt like he was back in her classroom preparing to take notes. "Now, what did you have in mind?"

"Something with a private entrance, where she can come and go as she pleases. That's very important. Her previous landlord was far too nosy. Somewhere safe and in a good neighborhood, but not too expensive. And close to downtown, where she works."

"Well, that is *very* specific," Clyde reacted. Which was actually a welcome change. Most of his clients had no idea what they wanted, or at the very least couldn't agree.

"And a private telephone," Lizzie added.

He stopped short on that one. "Can it be a party line?"

Lizzie's sudden frown answered his question far quicker than her words. "Certainly not."

"Well, that is a tall order indeed," Clyde offered with a bewildered smile. He pushed up his glasses and quickly thumbed through a folder full of papers.

"I trust you'll be able to find something, Clyde," Lizzie told him. "I have the utmost faith in you."

He stopped short again. He'd heard that particular phrase far too many times in the classroom.

"This could take some time, but I promise to do my absolute best," he assured her.

"Of course, you will," she told him, still sounding very much like the teacher he remembered. "But the sooner you can find something, the better."

She handed him Vicky's card. "We're staying at the Sherman for right now. But you can always reach her at the paper. She writes for the *Daily Crusader*."

"Well, good heavens," he exclaimed. "I hadn't realized! I'll have to keep an eye out for her byline."

CHESTER LYONS walked into Leonore's office and immediately had the same adverse reaction Vicky experienced when she'd arrived. Everywhere he looked there were doilies, perfume, and flowers. *This ain't a newsroom*, he thought. *It's a garden party*.

Vicky was at her new desk, packing her things for her move back to the City Room. Lyons wasn't exactly thrilled to have her back, but he knew he'd get a lot further if he acted like he was. And expressed a little sympathy along the way.

"How you holding up, kid?" he asked as he sat down across from her. "Need any help carrying your stuff back?"

Vicky looked up at him with a firm glare. She might not have his years on the news beat, but she knew enough to see right through him.

"What'ya want, Chester?"

The jig was clearly up on that front, but he still kept the caring tone in his voice. "Look, I was over in Bronzeville this morning and happened to see your friend, Mr. Gregor, there..."

Vicky's expression quickly changed to one of irritation. Or at least it was more visible. "Why is it when every time somebody wants to talk to Brent Gregor, he's my best friend all of a sudden?"

"Well," Lyons explained, "you're the only one here who knows him."

"Barely," Vicky clarified. "I *barely* know him."

Lyons just ignored her protests and continued with his pitch. "Listen, as your mentor, I just thought you'd want to give him a call, maybe get a statement?"

Vicky's expression quickly changed to *incredulous*. "As my *mentor*? You've done nothing but give me hell since I got here."

She felt another headache coming on. She grabbed her purse and headed for the powder room. "Why don't you just call him yourself?" she asked on her way down the hall.

"Yeah, I already tried that," he called out after her.

LIZZIE stepped out of Clyde Pierson's office to find two gentlemen standing by Vicky's car. Despite their pinstripe suits and expensive shoes, they did not appear to be upstanding members of the community. The dark tan coupe that she'd seen throughout the day was parked right behind her.

She'd dealt with schoolyard bullies time and again and knew just how to handle them. But those bullies were usually far less intimidating. And unarmed.

She marched right up to both of them and looked them straight in the eye. "May I help you two gentlemen?"

Fingers replied, "Actually, Miss Rose — "

"Mrs. Harper," she corrected him. "Miss Rose is my sister. Were you sent to harass her or me? Because if you were sent to harass her, you have the wrong woman."

Lizzie doubted they would pick up on her double meaning, but it was there nonetheless. They were certainly thrown off guard by her confrontational response.

"We won't —"

"*Weren't*," she corrected him again. "We *weren't*," she repeated. We *won't* is incorrect."

This took both Fingers and Eggs aback. They were given the simple task to lean on a dame. Now all of a sudden it was like they were back in school with Sister Gertrude. This broad was a sight better and then some, but they still got the feeling that at any moment she could whip out a ruler and rap them both across the knuckles.

Fingers tried again, but this time from another angle. "I understand your *sister* needs a new place to live. Actually, we might be able to help you out a little."

"No need," she quickly replied. "I can abide just fine on my own, thank you. Now, if you're quite finished, I have things to do. Far more important than being harassed by you two layabouts."

Eggs instinctively put his hands in his pockets.

Fingers did his best to maintain his cool. "Well, if you change your mind, Ma'am, just let us know," he told her with an intimidating smile. "We ain't — *aren't* hard to find."

As they got back in their car and drove off, Lizzie realized they might need someone else in their corner. Someone more powerful and influential.

She looked up to see a Smithson & Gregor catalog store directly across the street.

WORTHINGTON assembled the entire staff in the servant's kitchen at the end of the day before they went home. But what took them all by surprise was the fact that Master Gregor was also in attendance. "I know that this has been a long and difficult day for each of us," Worthington began solemnly.

As he spoke, Brent quickly realized that he was the one from which they needed to hear. In his present state, it was all he could do to even face them. But he instead summoned the courage to do so, and lifted a hand to interrupt. "If I may, Worthington."

"Yes, of course, Sir," Worthington reacted with surprise. It was a reaction shared by everyone. Brent included.

Brent took a moment to collect his thoughts. Abbie was so much better at these things than he. Times like this, he wished she was there. But she wasn't. And it was time he learned to do such things on his own.

"I'm sure by now you've all heard the terrible news," Brent began softly. "Mr. Coleman has been in this house longer than I have. Longer than practically any of us. He was a part of... this family."

Brent had to pause. "Certainly as much as his own family. He will be loved. And greatly missed."

That was when the realization struck him. For so long, Brent felt that he had no family. His parents were gone, his grandfather left him behind, and then he'd even lost Abbie. But he never stopped to realize the value of those, other than Worthington, with whom he'd lived from day to day.

"I just want you to know," Brent continued. "how much I appreciate each and every one of you. Though I admit, I haven't always been very good at showing it."

Everyone shook their heads in polite disagreement. But they all, Brent included, knew it to be true.

"I'm not going to ask any of you to work to-morrow," he concluded. "Or even the next day for that matter. With pay, of course. Please take all the time that you need."

Brent kept a brave face as the entire staff thanked him profusely. Worthington would tell him later, and several times over, what a wonderful thing he had done.

It should have made him feel better. If even a little bit.

But the physical pain that still filled his body was a piercing reminder of just how badly he'd failed.

EVERYONE applauded as Frank's twin daughters, Audrey and Lillian, completed their final number and took their bows. Vicky couldn't help but cringe a little when she heard both Lizzie and Betty shout "Brava!" in unison. *School teachers to the end.*

"That was just lovely, girls," Lizzie beamed. "Absolutely wonderful."

"Thank you, Mrs. Harper," the twins responded simultaneously as Betty signaled for them to head upstairs.

"All right, off to bed, girls," Betty instructed. "I'll be up shortly."

Once the girls were safely out of earshot, Vicky immediately switched to the matter at hand. "You'll never guess who came to visit me in Gibsonville."

"Well, I already know about Denny," Frank teased.

"Yeah, well, that's another story," Vicky blushed. "But I'm talking about Vito Spats and Willie Potatoes."

Frank was stunned. "Spats went all the way to Gibsonville? Just to see you?"

"What on earth did he want?" Betty asked.

"Everything I know about the Man in Black," Vicky explained. "Wants me to find out who the guy is. Was on his best behavior the whole time. Couldn't have been more polite."

Lizzie scoffed in disagreement. "It was quite unnerving, believe me. Our poor father. He didn't sleep for days."

"Trust me, for Spats, that was polite," Vicky added. "I think this Ghost Man's got him spooked."

"So what else he tell you?" Frank asked, dying to know more.

"Nothing. Said he'd get back to me. Though he sent two of his boys to follow Lizzie around all day to-day."

"I'm rather certain they thought I was her," Lizzie added. "Didn't make me feel any safer, though."

Frank nodded in agreement. "You just be careful, Red. Both of you."

CHAPTER NINETEEN

BRENT wheeled himself into the kitchen and stopped to take it all in. His gaze followed every corner of the room. The dark tile floor, the deep sinks, the large bright windows, and the endless copper pots that hung over the large table in the center. It was as if Mr. Coleman had just stepped out. But was never coming back.

He had never seen it so empty before.

He was soon awash with memories of days long ago. When more than sunlight and echoes filled the room.

He remembered his boyhood and all the times he'd run into the kitchen. He'd go straight to the pantry and raid the cookie jar. Sometimes Mr. Coleman would have one waiting as soon as he heard Brent's little footsteps coming down the hallway.

He remembered the last Thanksgiving he celebrated with his parents. Of tasting the turkey that roasted in the large oven. He could still recall all the wonderful smells of that day. Of the stuffing, the yams, and all the wonderful pies that were set on the counter to cool.

But those days were long gone.

And so were the people that filled his memories. And just as before, he came back to the same conclusion. That it was all because of one man.

Big Jack.

Only now he had someone else to blame as well.

Himself.

Because one simple fact was inescapable. It was a realization that came back to him again and again.

Had he taken out Big Jack as he'd planned, Mr. Coleman would still be alive.

DOCTOR LEVINE took one look at Vicky and Lizzie and broke into a big smile. "Well, I don't have to ask how *you two* are related."

He turned off the lights in his lab and examined Vicky's latest X-ray on the radiograph viewer. He immediately nodded his head in approval. "Well, this is looking much better," he commented. "How are the headaches?"

"Still there," Vicky replied, "but not as painful. And not nearly as often."

"Excellent, excellent," he commented as he checked her pupils with the pen light. "I'd say those couple of weeks rest did you a world of good."

"So, does that mean she's ready to go back to work, Doctor?" Lizzie inquired.

"Yes, I do believe so," he confirmed and switched the lights back on. "But I do recommend that you take it easy at first. When you feel another headache coming on, just call it a day and get some rest."

"I promise," Vicky assured him.

Though both she and Lizzie knew that was easier said than done.

WORTHINGTON entered the servant's kitchen and was surprised to find Master Gregor there taking his breakfast. And pouring through the business section of the telephone directory.

While it was a welcome relief to see Brent up and busying himself in the early part of the day, Worthington was more than perplexed as to what this was about. He glanced down at the pages and saw that Brent was searching the automobile section.

"Are we replacing the vehicle that was lost, Sir?"

"As a matter of fact, yes," Brent replied. "I'm thinking we need something better, though. That can't be traced back here. And, preferably, bullet-proof."

He closed the directory in frustration and pushed it away. "But I've no idea where to find such a vehicle. Or even where to begin looking, to be honest."

Worthington pondered the situation for a moment. His better judgement told him to stay quiet. But he knew that if he didn't, considering what had already happened, it could mean the difference between life and death.

"Actually. Sir, I believe you already have one."

VICKY tugged at her patient ID bracelet as she and Lizzie passed through the main lobby on their way out of Terminal City General. They were almost to the registration desk when she saw Charlie Hecht pop inside the front entrance, take a quick gander, and pop right back out again.

Vicky's reporter's instincts quickly kicked in. "Something's going down here," she said.

Lizzie was perplexed. Many a pupil had regretted her well-honed powers of perception. But this time the truth had escaped her. "How did you figure that? That fellow at the door?"

"When Charlie Hecht walks by and doesn't offer so much as a whistle," Vicky explained, "something's up."

Vicky went straight to the elderly Nurse who worked the reception desk. "Excuse me, can you tell me if Nails — I mean, James McCarthy is being released to-day?"

"I'm sorry," the Nurse replied, trying unsuccessfully to play dumb. "But I really wouldn't know."

Her denial and pitiful attempt at lying was all the confirmation Vicky needed. "Thanks, Sweetheart," Vicky chirped. "You're such a jewel!"

Vicky grabbed Lizzie by the hand and tugged her down the hallway. "Come on, I bet they're trying to sneak him out the back alley."

As they hurriedly weaved their way down the pristine, white-tiled hallways, Lizzie soon realized that she'd just gotten a front row seat to watch her little sister at work. And the chance to keep a watchful eye on her at the same time.

They whirled around yet another corner and Vicky immediately spotted the double doors that led out to the alley.

She was just about to bolt through them with Lizzie in tow when they ran headlong into Nurse Pflegler. As the tall, no-nonsense Charge Nurse who worked that particular wing, she glowered down at the two of them with a stern, disapproving glare. Lizzie knew that look well. After all, she'd adopted it many times herself.

"And to where do you think you two are running off?" Nurse Pflegler barked. "I'm sorry, but only patients and hospital staff are allowed through this part of the hospital."

Vicky quickly showed her patient ID bracelet and was immediately glad she hadn't been able to remove it. "But I am a patient."

"Oh," Nurse Pflegler said, momentarily stunned.

Vicky hoped that she wouldn't ask just *where* they were going. Because she hadn't yet thought up an excuse for that one.

"Well then," Nurse Pflegler continued, "then I should ask you *please* not to run in the halls."

Lizzie had to wonder just how many times she'd said that very thing herself.

"Yes, Ma'am," Vicky said with as much contrition as she could muster. "So sorry."

As Nurse Pflegler left, she let out one last disapproving scoff to show that she meant business. Vicky tugged Lizzie through the double-doors and out into the alley normally used for deliveries.

They made it just in time to catch Nails McCarthy outside. His head low and handcuffed wrists raised to shield his face from the bathing glow of flashbulbs. The pretty young Nurse who pushed his wheelchair smiled and posed.

Vicky and Lizzie watched as two police officers helped him up and loaded him into the back of a black and white. Within minutes they drove off as the handful of the gathered news hounds chased after them on foot.

They were just about to head back inside when Charlie Hecht called out, "Hey Doll face! Welcome back!"

He and Gilbert both did a near double-take. "As I live and breathe, there's two of 'em!" Charlie exclaimed as he gave Gelbart a nudge.

Ben Gelbart quickly noticed the patient ID band on

Vicky's wrist. Charlie just as quickly noticed the ring on Lizzie's finger as he sized her up.

"Boys, this is is my sister, Lizzie," Vicky said as she made quick introductions.

"Really sorry to hear about your Ma," Gelbart offered as he gave Charlie a quick nudge with his elbow. "Sure hope you're feeling better, too."

"Yeah, right," Charlie chimed in, doing his best to sound sympathetic. "Absolutely."

Vicky was surprised to have seen only Nails, the young nurse, and the two policemen. "So, where was the mouthpiece? Thought for sure he'd be here to fight you boys off."

Dead silence. Instinct had kicked in once more and both of them remained tight-lipped. They weren't about to share a scoop, even though there was no chance of her leaving without it.

"Come on, have some sympathy for a gal," she appealed as she tugged at her hospital bracelet. "I'm hardly back on the job."

It didn't take long before Gelbart was the first to break. "Okay, O'Brien dropped him this week. Word on the street is he realized he couldn't win."

"They gonna delay the trial?" Vicky asked.

"Nah," Charlie added as he gave Lizzie his third or fourth once-over. "O'Brien put in a request, but the Judge refused. So unless Nails can find another lip in a heartbeat, he's gonna have to go to the public defender's office. You believe that?"

Actually, Vicky realized, she could.

This much was perfectly clear. The fix was in for Nails McCarthy.

WORTHINGTON returned to the servant's kitchen a short time later with a large stack of shipping manifests. Many, many years' worth. All of which had Terminal City as their final destination. He placed the stack in front of the young master.

Brent looked up at him curiously. "What's this?"

"Every last item that your grandfather has shipped home

from his travels," Worthington explained as he licked his thumb and flipped through the endless pages.

"Here," Worthington pointed out when he discovered the record in question.

Brent picked up the manifest and read it. His face quickly broke into a wide grin. Two years earlier, his grandfather had purchased a custom, black Mercedes touring car from a German general. Not only was it bullet-proof, but it was bomb-proof as well.

Brent couldn't believe his good fortune. "Where is it?"

"Crated up in one of the warehouses," Worthington explained. "Just like the hundreds of other items your grandfather has sent home."

Brent was elated to the point of disbelief. "Wonderful! I'll telephone Uncle Dick. Have him send the car straight over."

"If you don't mind my suggesting, Sir," Worthington quickly interrupted. "Might we request a large number of items, just to cover our tracks."

Brent quickly realized the value of his proposal. "Yes, of course. Good thinking, Worthington."

VICKY sauntered back into the police station with a renewed sense of purpose. She'd been a little unsure of herself getting back into the game, especially with Lizzie looking over her shoulder. But their experience at the hospital that morning had been just what she needed.

And with Lizzie back apartment hunting, she was finally on her own again.

"So, any more news on that masked phantom while I was gone?" she asked Desk Sergeant Coffey.

His face actually lit up when he saw her. "Oh, Miss Rose! Welcome back. So sorry to hear about your loss."

He was tempted to mention her own personal health as well, but wasn't sure how to broach the subject. So he just thought the better of it and left it alone.

"Thanks, Coffey. It's good to be back," she affirmed. "Helps take my mind off things. So, any news?"

"Ah, but no," he replied. "I'm afraid not."

That wasn't unexpected. "Yeah, didn't think so," she said

and tapped her nails on the desk.

"So, you back on the job now?" Coffey asked.

"Just easing into it," she told him. "Detective Shayne around by any chance?"

"No, Miss Rose," he answered with his usual half smile, "I'm afraid he hasn't come in yet."

"Yeah, didn't think so," she replied, tapping her nails again.

They stood there in awkward silence for a moment. Vicky was just about to leave when Coffey took pity on her. She was fine with pity. She could work with pity.

"But listen, I might have a tip for you, though," he offered. She was tempted to ask, *Let me guess, quit the paper and go find myself a husband?* But from the sympathetic tone of his voice, she could tell he was serious.

"Now, you didn't hear this from me," he began, "but just before that whole *altercation* between Nails and Detective Flynn, Nails stuffed a piece of paper in his mouth and tried to swallow it."

Now that definitely had her interest. And then some. "What was on it?"

Coffey leaned in close so as not to be overheard. "Sent it to the boys down at the lab to see if they could do anything with it. Still waiting on the report. But from what I heard, it might have been a phone number."

Vicky drummed her nails happily on the desk. "Thanks, Coffey! You're a real pal!"

CHAPTER TWENTY

LIZZIE pulled up to the Gregor Mansion in Vicky's car. It was her first visit to Lakeview Heights, but she did her best not to stare at the tremendous opulence that surrounded her. She pulled her hat down as the Guard approached. She knew that the likelihood of getting in on her own was slim, so she'd swiped Vicky's press pass that morning and trusted that she looked enough like her sister to fool the sentry.

"Good afternoon, Miss Rose," he greeted her as he checked her pass. "We weren't expecting you."

"So sorry to drop in unannounced," she confessed, "but I just arrived back in town and wanted to thank Mr. Gregor for the thoughtful bouquet."

It wasn't the best lie, and she wasn't the best liar, but she hoped that Vicky was a familiar enough face there that it would seem plausible enough.

"Not at all, Miss Rose," he answered. "It'll be just a minute."

She watched anxiously as he stepped back to the guard station and phoned the main house. With his back turned, she was unable to read his expression.

It was only a moment before he returned and happily and waved her through.

Well, that was interesting, she thought. Though she soon realized that she should have quizzed Vicky about the

Valet's name and other details before attempting this little mission.

But what was most clear was that Vicky and Mr. Gregor were certainly closer than her sister had let on.

What else is she hiding? Lizzie had to ask.

VICKY stopped outside the double doors of the Police Lab, unfastened the top button of her blouse, and fluffed her hair before going inside. She wasn't sure if this effort was even necessary, but she wasn't taking any chances.

"Excuse me," she said in her best breathy voice as she flagged down the first Lab Technician that looked her way. He was a thin, gangly fellow with horn-rimmed glasses and a really unfortunate haircut. His name badge was turned around backwards so that she couldn't read it. The overall resemblance to Denny was more than a little uncanny.

"Hi, c-can I help you?" His nervous disposition and reluctance to look her in the eye and elsewhere told her that he was just the man she needed.

"Oh, I sure hope so," she pleaded and leaned over the counter. "I'm here to pick up the report on the... James McCarthy case."

Thankfully, she'd managed to stop herself and get the name correct. Nicknames were listed under *Known Aliases*, not on official report titles.

"Oh," he reacted with surprise. And then didn't know what else to say.

"Detective Flynn wants it right away. He just keeps screaming about why he hasn't gotten it yet. I told him, 'I don't know.' So he says to me, he says, 'You get your little tush right down there, and don't come back until you get it! You hear?' So, here I am."

She smiled at him sweetly. He did his best to smile back. Then he watched nervously as she reached across the counter, took his police ID in her soft hand, and turned it around. "Donnie."

"Yes, well... I'm just so sorry," he stuttered and quickly backed away. And bumped into the cabinet behind him. "You see, nobody told me — It'll be just a minute."

"Thank you, Donnie," Vicky chirped as he disappeared

behind the towering shelves.

Impatient as she was, she had no choice but to wait. But she knew that every minute she spent there put her another minute closer to being recognized.

LIZZIE sat in the grand foyer and took in all of its splendor as she waited. The marble floors, the sweeping staircase, and even the suit of armor by the stairs. She noted a set of double doors nearby that looked securely locked. She could only imagine what was hidden on the other side.

She was soon met by a large, teddy bear of a man with a neatly trimmed beard and exceedingly polite demeanor. This had to be the Valet, she thought.

"Good afternoon, Miss Rose," he greeted her warmly. "Such a welcome surprise to see you again. Our deepest apologies for your loss."

Just as he took her hand, he seemed to notice something about her. Something different. Something *unfamiliar*.

All of which actually made things easier. For she had no intention of carrying the ruse any further.

She quickly introduced herself. "Formerly Miss Rose, actually. I'm Elizabeth Rose Harper, Vicky's older sister."

Worthington offered a relieved smile. They looked remarkably similar, but were certainly not twins. Though he found it interesting that he'd managed to meet both of them under false pretenses.

Lizzie waited hesitantly for his reaction. This would be when he either threw her out or welcomed her warmly. Preferably the latter.

He took her hand and offered a polite bow. "Pleased to make your acquaintance, Mrs. Harper. Bernard Worthington, at your service."

"I do apologize for the ruse, Mr. Worthington," Lizzie continued. "And especially for the intrusion. It's just that I was hoping to have a word with Mr. Gregor, if you wouldn't mind."

"And may I ask to what this is in regards?" Worthington queried with a curious eye.

"Yes, most certainly," she replied. "It's about my sister, actually."

VICKY nervously tapped her nails on the counter at the Police Lab until she realized how distracting it was. And that any undue attention would only help to break her cover.

After what seemed like an eternity, Donnie returned with a file folder clutched in his nervous hands. "So sorry to keep you waiting, Miss..." he stuttered, "I'm sorry, what was your name again?"

"Candy," she told him with a smile and a wink.

He swallowed hard and did his best to continue. "Yes, right. I mean, I've got it right here."

He opened the folder and showed her the report. She leaned over the counter to get both a better look and his undivided attention.

"I'm sorry this has taken so long," he confessed. "We tried everything, but I'm afraid we just weren't able to get the whole message."

He handed Vicky the folder. She immediately flipped it open and perused the three-page report. The first two were just a bunch of scientific gobbledygook. The last had the contents they'd managed to retrieve from the message. Just four numbers. "4239."

She flipped the report over to make sure there was nothing else. "So, this is all you got?"

"Yes, I'm afraid so," he admitted. "We thought it might be part of a phone number, a locker number, or even an address. There was more, but we just couldn't make it out."

Vicky tapped her nails on the counter again. Soon, she was lost in thought and had practically forgotten about her ruse. She tried to reason which of those possible solutions made the most sense. That's when it finally came to her.

"Hand me the telephone directory, will you?" she asked. He noticed she'd lost the breathiness in her voice, but was too shy to say anything about it.

No matter. He did just as he was told. She went straight to the business listings, flipped to the Bs, and then ran her finger down the page.

And there it was. The four digits were a perfect match.

RIVerside 4239. The Beehive in Bronzeville.

What a coincidence.

LIZZIE took a sip of her tea as she sat with Brent Gregor in the solarium. She noted that while the rest of the house was designed around grandeur and opulence, this room was more for relaxation and comfort.

He was different than she expected. Strikingly handsome, but frail. Reminded her of her father. Despite the warm summer temperature from the sunlight, he kept a blanket across his lap. She also noticed that he repeatedly paused and put a hand to his chest. She wondered if he had a weak heart. Also like her father.

But she hadn't previously known that he was in a wheelchair, which had momentarily taken her by surprise. Then after a moment, she vaguely remembered reading something about the tragedy years earlier.

He was very cordial, but seemed distracted. "I'm sorry, did I come at a bad time?" Lizzie had to ask. She set her teacup aside and sat up.

"No, not at all," Brent protested. Despite his welcoming smile, she could easily see the pain behind his eyes.

"We've also recently suffered a loss in our family," he revealed. "A senior member of our staff. The funeral is to-morrow, in fact."

Lizzie couldn't believe her unbelievably bad timing. She quickly realized the foolhardiness of her endeavor. Which she would have known had she done just a *minimal* amount of homework. And she a schoolteacher, of all people. She couldn't have been more embarrassed.

"Please forgive me," she offered as she got up quickly and straightened her skirt. "I'm just so terribly sorry. I can see myself out."

"Not at all," Brent countered with a soft laugh. "We could very much use a friendly smile. Please, have a seat."

"Now I understand why my sister speaks so highly of you," Lizzie offered.

"I'm afraid you have me at a loss," he admitted. "To be perfectly honest, I've only met Vicky on a few occasions. Our conversations were largely limited to her work for the newspaper."

"Of course," Lizzie replied. She suddenly realized that he was completely unaware that Vicky even had a sister.

Perhaps Vicky had been perfectly honest about the boundaries of their relationship after all.

"So tell me," he asked, "do you live in Terminal City?"

Judging by her dress, her speech, and wedding ring, he correctly surmised that she was married and lived elsewhere. Likely a small town a few hours away. She was educated, however. Perhaps even a schoolteacher.

"No, I'm visiting actually," she confirmed. "From Gibsonville, Missouri. Vicky doesn't even know I came by here, to be perfectly honest. I'm supposed to be on the hunt for a new apartment. I'm afraid her landlady is rather disagreeable."

"Perhaps I could be of assistance?" Brent offered.

"Oh no, I couldn't," Lizzie quickly replied, still a bit flustered from her embarrassment. "That's not at all what I came to see you about."

"Oh?"

She stumbled on just what to say. For it was at that moment when she realized the folly of her request. Here was a man in a wheelchair, physically weak and clearly in pain, and who'd barricaded himself behind large iron gates.

She had no other option but to proceed. But quickly tempered her expectations.

"Perhaps some advice, if you don't mind," she stammered. "It seems my sister has made some rather powerful enemies of late."

VITO SPATS stood in the doorway of Big Jack's kitchen. He observed as Estelle changed his bandages, mostly with her eyes closed. She wasn't ready to look at his wounds any time soon.

Big Jack just sat there and waited. Whether or not it hurt or was painless, no one could tell from his blank expression. It wasn't the first time he'd been shot and likely wouldn't be the last.

Once finished and with his arm in the sling, she patted the old Mob Boss on the back and kissed his forehead. He gave Estelle's shapely leg a squeeze. She let out a soft giggle and blushed. "Oh, Jack Darling!"

"So how's Cherry Nose?" Big Jack asked. "Still don't know

how he made it with seven slugs. Counting the other times I got hit, I'm still three slugs short of just making it even."

"Doing good," Spats confirmed as her fingered the brim of his hat. "Says they might send him home in another week."

Big Jack nodded in approval. "Pray on my mother's grave for a full recovery. I'll feel a lot safer when he's back behind the wheel."

Big Jack gave Estelle's leg another squeeze. "Listen, Sweetheart. Why don't you go out and buy yourself something nice, eh? Spats and I gotta talk business."

"Sure thing, Darling," she cooed dutifully.

Within moments she'd gathered her things and was gone. Only the whiff of her perfume stayed behind. Spats closed the door behind her.

"Have to tell you, Spats," Big Jack confessed, "if it hadn't been for your quick thinking, I don't know that I'd be sitting here to-day. Don't know how you saw it coming. But glad you did."

"Important thing is," Spats clutched the aging Capo's good shoulder, "them bullets didn't find their mark. Saints be praised."

Big Jack took a moment to catch his breath. As strong as he still was, Spats had never before seen the Mob Boss so weakened.

"Listen, Spats," Big Jack elucidated, "I've worked a lot of years, fought a lot of battles. Feel like I've learned a few things. Like how to know if you can trust someone. Or when you can't. Who's gonna take a bullet for you, and who's gonna put one in your back."

Had they not been alone in his house, Spats might have gotten nervous. Even so, he instinctively looked back towards the door. Back in the old days, after a speech like that, he'd already be gasping his last.

But, of course, the door was still closed. Willie was right outside in the living room. And Fingers and Eggs were out on the porch. Maybe in days past this would have been a threat. But not to-day. This was just an old man thinking about death.

Big Jack continued. "I just want you to know, something like that, it don't go unappreciated. When the time comes for me to step down, I know I can trust you to take care of things. I'm just asking you to be patient."

"Yeah, of course," Spats reassured him. "Long as it takes."

Spats understood perfectly. He understood how things were in the old days. And he well understood how things were then. But most of all, he understood exactly what Big Jack had requested.

He'd just asked Spats not to kill him.

CHAPTER TWENTY-ONE

VICKY settled back into her desk at the City Room. Finally. It had been weeks since she'd last sat in that chair and listened to the wonderful sounds of commotion and typewriters. It felt so good to at last be back, she just had to relish in the moment.

On the downside, her calendar was a little thin. Her one pressing engagement was for that night. A sure-to-be-awkward dinner with Denny's parents. And Lizzie. The very thought of it brought back a dull aching in her temples.

This was to be her first time meeting them. Not under ideal circumstances, by any means. She'd tried to cajole her way out of it, but he'd insisted. And after all he'd done for her lately, she couldn't very well say no. Besides, he'd already met *her* family.

She was pretty certain they'd like Lizzie better. Even if she was already married.

Better to focus on work.

The Nails McCarthy trial was set for first thing the following Monday, But even with her success at the hospital, she was woefully out of touch.

And despite the explosive, real story that she'd previously risked her life to pursue, she had nothing to show for it. The few leads she'd followed had turned up little. In the end, she'd only managed to make enemies. And very powerful ones indeed.

She glanced back through her notes to see if something, anything, stood out. She could try chatting up Dapper Sheridan again. Now that he'd been stewing in the cooler a few days, he might be more willing to spill something useful.

She grabbed her purse and was just about to head out the door when Perry Phillips called out to her. "Phone call, Vick! Line Three!"

Vicky picked up the phone and was more than surprised to hear Brent Gregor's voice. She quickly looked around to make sure Lyons wasn't in earshot. Thankfully, he hadn't yet made it into the office, as usual.

"Mr. Gregor!" she chirped as she relaxed back in her chair. The flowers he'd sent were nearly dead, but they'd still made the move back to her old desk.

She assumed he was calling her back. She'd tried to phone him two days earlier but was only able to leave a message with one of the maids. "I want to thank you again for the flowers. That was very thoughtful. They're quite lovely."

"My condolences to you and your family," he told her. "I wasn't sure where to send them and I'm afraid Leonore wasn't much help."

That's not surprising, Vicky grumbled to herself.

She was tempted to offer her own condolences regarding the bombing, but she didn't want him to think she was fishing for a story. So she just opted to let it pass.

"The reason for my call, actually," he continued, switching gears, "is that I understand you're in need of new living arrangements."

That took her by surprise. "How did you know?"

"Let's just say *a little bird told me*," he replied. "You're more than welcome to use my apartment in the city. Stay as long as you like."

Vicky was dumbfounded. She had no idea of just how to respond. After all, this was a man she hardly knew. And their acquaintanceship hadn't exactly begun under the best of circumstances. "Mr. Gregor, I couldn't take advantage —"

"It's no advantage at all," he countered. "You'd actually be doing me a favor. It's just sitting there empty."

She wracked her brain to figure out just who the *little bird* was. The obvious answer was Leonore. Clearly, they did speak to one another. The flowers were evidence of that. But why would Leonore mention Vicky's need for an apartment? That just seemed so unlike her.

"Mr. Gregor, I just couldn't — "

He wasn't about to give up so easily. "Just until you find another place of your own then? Please, I insist."

There was simply no getting out of it. This was a near repeat of her conversation with Denny regarding the family dinner. Only, the outcome was far more preferable.

"Yes," she finally relented. And in utter disbelief over her good fortune. "That would be just lovely. And unbelievably generous. I just can't thank you enough."

"Excellent," he replied, "what time shall we be there to pick you up?"

VICKY met Dapper Sheridan in the visitation room at the Terminal City Jail. Since it was a minimum security facility, they sat at a long table with just a foot-high wooden partition between them. A pair of deputies stood watch by the door.

After so many dead ends, she was hoping to get some answers. She did her best to pour on the feminine charm. "You'll help a gal out, won't you?"

Dapper wasn't about to take the bait. "Look here, Doll Face, I ain't no stoolie. I don't squeal on nobody. Not to the cops, not the D.A., and especially not to some dame reporter like you. Got me?"

Dapper tipped his hat at an angle. Just the way he'd seen Cagney do it a dozen of times in the pictures. Vicky quickly realized that it was going to take more than a friendly smile to get him to talk. She had to try a different tactic. It was go for broke or walk out empty-handed.

"Well, I don't know how you can do it," she chided him with a huff of frustration. "I just don't."

He squinted at her in confusion. "Do what?"

"Sit here like this," she chided him. "Whitey and Squint are being put in the ground to-day, and here you are hiding out in a jail cell because you're too yellow to be seen out on the streets."

"Oh yeah!" he snapped. "Whitey and Squint being put in the ground is *exactly* why I'm cooling my heels in this joint!"

She let out another deep sigh of frustration. "Look, I just need you to back me up on one thing. You can talk to me, or you can talk to Vito Spats. Was Nails armed or not?"

"Look here, Doll," Dapper argued. "I couldn't tell you nothing if I wanted to. Didn't see a thing."

"Yeah, that's what you all say," she smirked.

"Well, this time I'm telling you like it is," he asserted. "We was all in the outer room. There was only three people in that office. Nails, Flynn, and Shayne. On the square."

"Honest?" she asked, incredulous.

"Honest, I swear," he insisted. "You want the real truth? You gotta get it out of one of them."

MR. COLEMAN's funeral was a well-attended affair that, if nothing else, showed his daughter, Mary, just how much he was loved. In addition to Brent, Worthington, and the entire staff at Gregor Mansion, there were numerous guests from other estates in Lakeview Heights.

Nanny Miriam was there as well, and Brent was overwhelmed with joy to see her again. Aside from Worthington, she'd been more like family than anyone else he knew. She hugged him so tightly he winced. They both made a promise to visit soon.

Brent and Worthington were on their way back to the car when they were stopped by Ben Sanders. "Excuse me, Mr. Gregor?" he asked softly.

Worthington turned to address the dynamic young man who'd called out to them. "Yes?"

Sanders took off his bowler hat and bowed politely. "I'm sorry to bother you, Sir. Especially here. But if I could just have a minute of your time."

Brent looked at him curiously, but said nothing.

"The name's Ben Sanders. I'm the Editor, head reporter, and even the janitor at *The Evening Hubbub*."

Sanders took their puzzled silence as a need for clarification. "We're a newspaper. In Bronzeville. Mainly a social rag, but we're branching out. You see, the other papers don't really cover what goes on in our part of town."

Brent cautiously shook Sanders' hand. He was always wary of the press, Vicky included.

"Anyway, I didn't really have a question," Sanders continued. "I just wanted to thank you, Sir, for everything you're doing for the Johnsons. I understand you want be anonymous, but that one wasn't too hard to figure out. But don't worry, we won't print a word. Like I said, I just wanted to say thank you."

Sanders tipped his hat and backed away politely. This time it was Brent Gregor who stopped *him*.

"Just a minute, Mr. Sanders," he replied. "Worthington, would you give him my card?"

Worthington nodded, produced a card from his billfold, and handed it to the young man.

"I'd like to subscribe to this paper of yours," Brent revealed. "If you would, just send me a bill."

Sanders was bowled over from his good fortune, but wise enough to know that this was not the proper venue to display it. "Absolutely, Mr. Gregor. For you, I'll even hand deliver it. I do have to warn you though, it's a little different from what you're used to."

"Now you have me intrigued," Brent replied. "I look forward to reading it."

ACROSS TOWN, Whitey and Squint's shared procession was visibly less impressive than O'Boyle's. This was due to the fact that Whitey was a wanted cop killer and every single one of the pallbearers from O'Boyle's funeral were all either dead or sitting in jail.

As before, Vicky watched from the windows of the *Crusader* building along with Frank, Lyons, and the rest of the gang. Only this time she knew both the score and all of the players.

What really got to her, though, was that it only served as a stark reminder of her mother's funeral. But most especially that she hadn't the opportunity to say goodbye.

And that she had no one to blame but herself.

WORTHINGTON double-checked that the nearby grounds were clear and closed the large, barn-like doors of the garage. The automobile had long been the preferred mode of transportation when Gregor Mansion was built. But in a nod to tradition, the six-car garage (which was actually two separate buildings facing each other across a cobblestone courtyard) was designed to look like a pair of horse stables.

Brent clutched the arm rests on his wheelchair and closed his eyes. Worthington once again felt the sudden chill that always accompanied the use of his abilities. As Master Gregor's lifelong caretaker, he never once got accustomed to the miracle of Brent walking again.

Brent got up and moved through the myriad collection of large, wooden crates to reach his true objective. There in the back was a long, black Mercedes touring car. It could not have been more perfect.

Its previous owner had been a General in the Third Reich. And was designed to protect against any would-be assassin. The windows were tinted dark, the outside body was bulletproof, and the carriage underneath could easily withstand the blast of a grenade.

Grandpa Nate had become enamored with the automobile on a previous trip to Germany. Like many of his acquisitions, he'd decided then and there that he must have it. He made offer after offer until the General finally relented.

Brent found it odd that he would go to all the trouble of collecting these treasures, only to send them home in crates. Never to see them again.

"It's perfect," Brent remarked as he walked alongside the car. He ran his hand along the beautiful, sleek finish of the automobile's black exterior. An absolute chariot of beauty.

"We just have to remove these dreaded Nazi emblems and any other identifiable markings," Brent added. "Frankly, I'd much prefer to burn them."

Worthington, however, was deeply concerned in regards to another issue.

"Sir, what if your grandfather comes home to reclaim it?"

Brent's enthusiasm was suddenly dampened. "He didn't even come home for my mother's funeral. I don't think we have anything to worry about."

DENNY had already wrapped up for the day when Vicky appeared in the morgue. He could tell from her flustered expression that something had gone awry. "Denny!"

He just hoped she wasn't canceling on him. Especially at such a late hour. Though truth be told, that would have been her preference. But she couldn't do that to him. And there was no way Lizzie would let her.

"You're not canceling on me, are you?" he asked, just to make sure. There was that tone of desperation again that she found so unappealing.

"No, of course not," she reassured him, disappointed that the conversation had already gone in that direction. "We're just going to be a *little* late for dinner. Sorry to tell you at this hour, but I've been trying to get down here all day."

Her expression quickly turned from harried to elated. "You won't believe this, but Brent Gregor is letting me use his apartment until I find a new place to live!"

That certainly took him by surprise. Somehow he managed to stutter a reply. "Well, that's just... amazing. How did this happen?"

"I don't know," she attempted to explain, with little thought to how Denny might react. "We were just talking this morning — "

"Talking with Mr. Gregor?" Denny reacted.

"Yes, on the telephone," she explained. "It was about the flowers. Somehow, he'd heard that I need a new apartment. And anyway, he just offered to let me use his."

Vicky could tell from his confused expression that she needed to downplay her sudden good fortune. "It's just for a short while until I can find something else. Won't have to stay at the hotel all this time."

Denny did his best to sound excited for her. But on the whole, he just didn't know what to think. After all the times she'd pushed him away. And now she was moving into the apartment of someone she hardly knew?

"Well, that's just... wonderful."

VICKY confronted Lizzie when they met outside the *Crusader* building just after work. The last thing she wanted to do was spoil this incredible experience. But she just couldn't go without acknowledging her sister's meddling.

"So, you didn't tell me about your little visit to Lakeview Heights yesterday."

It hadn't taken too much for Vicky to figure out the identity of the "little bird." She knew it wasn't Leonore. So without considering any other details, she asked herself who *would* actually do such a thing.

"Had no idea it would result in this," Lizzie confessed. "I hardly even remember mentioning your housing situation."

"Well, apparently you did," Vicky retorted.

Lizzie gave her a concerned frown. "You didn't cancel on Denny, did you?"

"No, of course not," Vicky shot back, irritated that Lizzie and Denny both just automatically assumed that she would.

Before the conversation could get any more heated, Worthington pulled up in a long, black limousine. He hopped out of the driver's seat and offered a cordial greeting.

"Miss Rose, Mrs. Harper, so wonderful to see you both this evening.

Worthington opened the rear door. Vicky was about to get inside when she stopped momentarily, a look of disappointment on her face. The back seat was empty.

"Where's Mr. Gregor?"

"I'm afraid Master Gregor is unable to join us this evening," Worthington explained. "He sends his regrets."

"Oh," Vicky answered, clearly disappointed. "I was so looking forward to thanking him in person."

Worthington offered her a slight bow. "I shall be certain to relay your utmost appreciation, Miss Rose."

Then, in an instance of perfectly unfortunate timing, Denny drove past just as she climbed into the limousine.

VICKY and Lizzie stared up in awe when they arrived at Brent Gregor's apartment building, a twelve-story Italian Renaissance high-rise overlooking Harrison Park. Naturally, it was close to the Smithson & Gregor building, the Orpheum Theater, and the Museum of Art.

Worthington let them out at the main entrance, where

they were promptly met by Jennings, the resplendently uniformed doorman. He welcomed them by name. "Good evening Miss Rose, Mrs. Harper. We're so pleased to have you join us."

They took the elevator up to the 9th floor. Both Rose sisters were surprised to find that there were only two apartments there: 9W and 9E. The building was almost perfectly square with a courtyard in the middle. The apartments were L-shaped and positioned on opposite corners. Each had their own doorbell.

Worthington opened the door to 9E and gave them a brief tour. The first room was an elaborate entrance gallery which was easily longer than Mrs. Hershey's entire boarding house. The flooring had a checkerboard pattern of dark and light marble, and huge, ornate tapestries hung on each wall.

Vicky immediately found herself weak in the knees.

From there they passed into a richly furnished Reception room that was still twice the size of her apartment. To the right was a huge dining room with a long mahogany table and chandelier, a pantry for food preparation, a large kitchen, a service hall, and three "small," comparatively plain rooms for live-in staff. Again, the rooms for the staff were almost the size of her previous apartment.

To the left was the "smaller wing," with a well furnished living room, a library stocked full of books, and two large bedrooms, each with a private bath. Aside from the servant's quarters, virtually every room had a fireplace.

When they'd reached the Master Bedroom, Worthington informed her, "I took the liberty of having your things moved from the hotel."

Naturally, all of their belongings had been neatly put away in each of the bedrooms' walk-in closets. Vicky later discovered that Mr. Gregor had also settled their bill.

Finally, Worthington handed Vicky the key and added, "Someone from the staff will be in thrice a week to clean."

Vicky was beside herself and hardly knew what to say. Lizzie finally had to step in. "Mr. Worthington, this is just so wonderful. We can't even begin to thank you."

"Think nothing of it," he replied.

As appreciative as Vicky was, she well knew that there was no such thing as a free lunch. From what little she'd gathered of Mr. Gregor, he just didn't seem that type. But that was the thing. She *really* didn't know him.

She pulled Worthington aside and asked, "I can't thank you enough for all of this, Mr. Worthington. This is just *so* unbelievably generous. But I have to ask, he's not going to expect anything... *extra* in return, is he?"

Worthington gave her a reassuring smile. "No need to explain, Miss Rose. Master Gregor has his share of faults, but I can assure you, that is not one of them. He is and shall remain a gentleman."

Lizzie gave her sister a knowing look. "You can thank me now."

VICKY sat at a corner table and nursed her second drink at McGillin's. She'd managed to find one near the door that offered a great view of everyone who came in and out. She remarked that as bars went, it was kind of an upscale place. Certainly a lot better than O'Doule's, where Lyons and most of the cops hung out.

Her over-priced gin and tonic was no substitute for her double chocolates, but she really needed some alcohol after dinner with Denny's folks. She just hoped she didn't feel it too much in the morning.

Mrs. Morris had peppered her with plenty of questions about her cooking skills (none), plans for children (none), and plans to quit working (none). As she'd expected, they liked Lizzie more.

Vicky could only imagine what Mrs. Morris would think of her sitting alone in a bar half the night. She'd been there a good three hours already and, of course, had gotten plenty of attention.

She'd had to brush off at least four tipsy Romeos.

Lizzie had insisted that she come along for that very reason. But Vicky wouldn't hear of it. This is what she did for a living, she told her, and Lizzie would just have to get used to the idea. Though by that hour she was sure her sister was getting worried. And rightfully so.

It was getting late and, unfortunately, there hadn't been

one sign of Detective Shayne.

She was about to leave and went up to the bar to settle her tab. That's when she got a better look at a particular gal she'd noticed earlier.

She was an Irish girl, early twenties at best. Who flirted with a couple of young men. But what had gotten Vicky's attention was the young woman's dress.

It was old fashioned, but beautiful and clearly expensive. Not the sort of dress one usually saw in a place like that, especially. The same was true of her jewelry, a beautiful ivory brooch.

She looked like she'd been to an estate sale or raided her mother's closet.

The girl looked familiar. She'd seen her somewhere before.

Finally, one of the gentlemen stepped aside and Vicky got a better look. What's more, the girl noticed her, too. And looked straight back at her.

And her eyes grew wide with panic.

That's when Vicky remembered her.

CHAPTER TWENTY-TWO

VICKY stifled a yawn as she and Lizzie waited on the platform at Union Station. It was early Friday morning and Lizzie was booked on the early train back home to Gibsonville. "Sleep well last night?" Lizzie asked.

"A little too well," Vicky yawned again. "First time in weeks. Though I can't help feeling guilty about the whole thing. Can't wait for word to get around at the office. Leonore will never let me hear the end of it."

"Well, for that to be true, you'd have to actually *see* your benefactor," Lizzie suggested.

Vicky just shook her head in defeat. "Can't believe you actually masterminded this."

"Believe me, that was not my intention," Lizzie retorted. "But you have to admit, it was a rather beneficial consequence."

Vicky couldn't argue with that. Might even be worth the ridicule she'd endure at the office. And there was no downplaying her connection to Mr. Gregor now. Her return to Terminal City had *not* been uneventful. And while she was ready to get back on her own, she wasn't quite ready to let go, either.

"Sure you don't want to stick around for the trial?" Vicky asked, switching gears.

Lizzie gave her one of those wistful looks where Vicky knew exactly what she was thinking. "I wish I could. But

I need to get home and help take care of Father. I'm sure Bitsy's at her wits end by now."

Vicky nodded in understanding. Exactly what she knew her sister would say.

"Plus, I'd really like to see Will and the boys," Lizzie added. "Too much peace and quiet around here. I'll just have to read about it in the paper."

They heard the train whistle in the distance and both of them checked their watches. Right on time. And time, Vicky knew, for some last-minute sisterly advice.

"You've made some powerful enemies, Vick," Lizzie told her. "You need to be careful."

"Lord, you sound just like Frank," Vicky shot back.

"Yes," Lizzie nodded, "and for good reason. But I was going to add that you've also made some powerful friends. Don't forget that."

AS PER his morning routine, Worthington quietly entered Brent's bedroom with the breakfast tray. He set it down on the table and opened the curtains to let in just a bit of sunlight. He turned to the bed and was more than surprised to find it empty.

The wheelchair sat alone by the bed. But there was no chill in the air. That had him worried.

"Master Gregor?" he asked quietly.

He rushed straight to the Master Bath and peered inside. There was no sign of him there, either.

That had him even more worried.

DENNY checked his watch as he happily lumbered into the morgue. While the prior evening hadn't gone *exactly* as well as he'd hoped, he had finally succeeded in getting his parents to meet Vicky. That was Step 1. Getting his mother to warm up to her was Steps 2 through 700-something.

He was more than a little surprised to find Vicky already in his office, digging through his filing cabinets. "Just the gal I wanted to see! You're off to an early start this morning."

Vicky had a danish stuffed in her mouth and her nose buried in a file drawer. She waved and mumbled something that sounded like "good morning."

He bounced on his heels, barely able to contain himself. "Lizzie make her train okay?"

Vicky grunted in the affirmative.

Denny continued. "I'm sorry she had to leave already. You know, Mother really enjoyed meeting both of you last night. I thought the evening went rather well, considering."

Vicky's next grunt was decidedly less affirmative. Her attention, however, was still firmly affixed on the files. She pulled out a large folder, bit off a chunk of her danish, and set the remainder on top of the cabinet.

"Help you find anything?" he asked as he retrieved a couple of napkins. He handed one to her and gingerly placed the other under her pastry.

"I'm good," she answered with her mouth full as she licked her fingers and flipped through the clippings.

Denny watched anxiously and handed her another napkin. "Is that the Gregor file again?"

He'd happily helped her locate it before. But now that she was actually staying in the man's private apartment, he had to wonder if this was at all work-related. Perhaps a favor for her benefactor?

She didn't answer. He'd just backed away when she shouted, "Ha! Found it!"

"Found what?"

"The dress! Last night I saw this girl. She was wearing the most beautiful gown. But I swear it had to be from almost twenty years ago."

Denny was already confused. "Last night? Where was this?"

Vicky was too excited by her find and didn't bother with his questions. "She also wore the most exquisite ivory brooch. Way more expensive than anything she could afford, you know? Anyway, I *knew* I'd seen them before. Here!"

Like a magician pulling a rabbit from a hat, she plucked a photo out of the folder. It was of Sarah and Thomas Gregor, taken at a benefit some fifteen-odd years prior.

In the picture, Mrs. Gregor had on the exact same dress. And the *exact same brooch*.

LOUISA CROCETTI cheerfully opened the grand front door at her father's house to find Big Jack and Vito Spats. She greeted their visitors with a warm smile. As was their family custom, they only spoke Italian in their home.

"Zio Guiseppe, Signore Gennaro, benvenuto! Piacere vederti!"

She took one look at Big Jack's bandages and reacted with the appropriate concern. Her father preferred to believe that she was young and innocent. She preferred to let him.

"Zio Giuseppe, what happened?"

"Il mio bellissimo angelo!" Big Jack took her hand and kissed her on both cheeks. "Not to worry. "Just a little accident."

"I wish you a very speedy recovery," she offered as she led them to her father's office. "I'll let Papa know that you're here."

WORTHINGTON rushed into the garage and hurriedly locked the door behind him. As he'd feared, the lights were on and there was a distinct and familiar chill in the air.

"Master Gregor?" he asked as he worked his way around the collection of automobiles parked inside.

There he found his young charge, standing tall and admiring his his newest acquisition. Brent had removed every identifying emblem and filed them down. He'd removed the license plate and added dark curtains from one of the other vehicles.

And though he didn't admit this to Worthington until some time later, he'd even tested one of the doors to make sure it really was bulletproof. Just to be certain.

"Sir," Worthington reprimanded him, "shouldn't you be more careful wandering about? Someone could have seen you."

Brent just ignored his concern. He was too proud of his handiwork. "It's ready, Worthington. It's ready to go out."

Worthington shuddered at the thought. "Might I ask to what end, Sir?"

SALVATORE CROCETTI quietly closed the doors to his office. He fixed himself a drink before joining Big Jack and Spats in the large leather chairs.

"The trial starts first thing, Monday," Crocetti remarked. "I'm worried about that policeman. And how well he does on the witness stand."

"My Ace tells me not to worry," Big Jack assured them. "He's got it all under control. I'm more worried about that dame reporter. Not the first time she's stuck her nose where it don't belong. Asks too many questions. Just like that other news hound, Potter, a few years back."

"Yeah, but that Potter wasn't a dame," Crocetti commented. "And he wasn't a cop, either."

Spats didn't quite share their concern about Vicky. But he kept that opinion to himself.

"If we have to," Spats commented, we can find other ways to keep her quiet."

"You just make sure that Shayne keeps his yap shut and does what he's supposed to," Big Jack instructed.

"What about the dame?" Crocetti asked.

"Don't worry," Spats assured them both. "I'll keep an eye on her."

WORTHINGTON sat at the servant's table and poured a cup of hot tea before adding a splash of milk. What it really needed, he thought, was a tablespoon or two of gin. It was still early yet and had already proven to be quite the eventful morning.

Elyse stepped in, her head down, and closed the door behind her. "If you don't mind, I require a word with you, Sir. In private."

It was about to get more eventful still.

Worthington stood and motioned for her to join him. "What is it child?"

She kept her head low and sat down, ashamed to look him in the eye. "I'm afraid I've a confession to make, Sir. I'm the one who's been borrowing Mrs. Gregor's things."

Worthington looked back at her in stunned silence. Out of all the maids, she was the one he'd least suspected.

"I'd heard about them from the other girls," she continued.

"Curiosity got the best of me, I suppose. So one day I went up there to have a look for myself."

Worthington offered no response. He just sat and listened with a stern expression.

"Anyhow, I just thought it was such a shame to see all those beautiful gowns and no one ever gets to wear them. So I tried one on and for the first time in my life, it made me feel beautiful."

His continued silence pierced her like a dagger.

"I swear to you," she protested, "I never stole anything. You must believe me. I just borrowed them for a bit and put them right back. Even cleaned and patched them up."

She got up from the table. He followed suit and collected his thoughts.

"I'm terribly sorry," she offered. "I promise everything will be returned to its proper place. I take full responsibility."

His stern expression melted into one of sorrow. "My dear Elyse," he said softly, "I can't begin to express my disappointment."

She curtsied before him. "I'll collect my things then. It's been quite lovely working for you, Sir."

VICKY nervously tapped a pencil on her desk in the City Room. She probably would have annoyed everyone around her were it not drowned out by the ever-present sound of typewriters.

She was running out of time before the Nails McCarthy trial began first thing Monday. Despite a great tip from Shayne's own wife, she'd still been unable to track him down. But she did come away with an interesting bit of information and two solid marriage proposals.

She again stared at the photo of Thomas and Sarah Gregor. *Such a lovely couple*, she thought. *So happy in that photo, so alive. Such a terrible shame what happened afterwards.*

She'd just stuck the photo in a drawer when her phone rang. She was more than a little surprised to hear Louisa Crocetti on the line. And to hear the sounds of traffic in the background. She'd likely called from a pay phone.

"Why hello, Vicky," Louisa chirped. "I was just wondering

if you planned to attend the benefit at the Davenports to-night. They're raising money to aid the orphanage, you know. Such a wonderful cause. You're going to be there, aren't you?"

Vicky was smart enough to know that something else was going on. Though, at the moment, she couldn't imagine what it might be.

"Yes, yes," she assured her. "I'll definitely be there."

Louisa was elated. "Wonderful! It'll be so nice to have a friendly face there. See you then!"

Vicky hung up the phone and tapped her pencil on the desk again.

Looked like yet another late night. Only this time it wouldn't all be spent in a bar.

DETECTIVE SHAYNE worked his way down the embankment of the Wentworth Avenue Bridge. He didn't have to get far before the putrid smell of death hit him full in the face. It was a scent that was all too familiar.

A handful of Uniforms were already there to keep the lookie-loos at bay. Two of them leaned over the embankment tossing up their lunch.

Shayne stooped over to make his way under the bridge. A couple of hobos had spotted the body in the wee hours of the morning. They complained to the nearest beat cop first thing in the morning. They'd claimed that spot years ago and weren't about to share it with anyone. Dead or not.

Shayne bent down to get a closer look. Not that it would have done much good. The corpse had been in the river for a while. They'd have to depend on the boys in the lab.

Shayne worked his way back out from under the bridge to join the Rookies, who were all keeping their distance.

"Any idea who it is, Sir?" a fresh-faced Rookie asked him.

"Impossible to tell at this point," Shayne told him. "But I'm willing to bet even money it's Cherries Hogan."

Hogan had last been seen meeting up with his girlfriend at a borrowed apartment. Immediately afterwards, she began sporting a brand new mink coat.

Shayne had known it was only a matter of time before he'd turn up.

BRENT looked up in surprise as Vicky, already dressed in her flowing red gown for the party, elegantly made her way into the library. With her handbag she also carried a careworn hardback book, and set both of them on the lamp table next to her chair.

The dress was the same one that she'd worn to the Kennelly function. And while that was certainly frowned upon in the upper circles, he wouldn't have cared even if he'd known. He'd never before noticed just how beautiful she was.

"My heavens, I don't know what is more alluring. You, or that lovely gown," he finally managed to say. "To what do I owe the pleasure of such an exquisite vision?"

Vicky did her best to remain elegant as she sat down across from him. And resisted the temptation to hike up the front of her dress. Luckily, it managed to stay in place.

"Well, you know what they say," she told him. "I was *in the neighborhood.* I just wanted to thank you again for everything. But this time in person."

She'd thought about calling him regarding entry to the soirée at the Davenport's. That would certainly have been preferable to asking Leonore. But he'd done so much for already, she just couldn't impose further. It was easier just to sneak in. She didn't plan to be there very long anyway.

His expression suddenly changed to one of puzzlement. "You're not going to the Davenports to-night, are you? Don't tell me you're still writing for the Society Page?"

Vicky shrugged and gave a quick nod. She wasn't really at liberty to explain. "Something like that."

"Well," he proclaimed, "if I'd known what I was missing, I might have opted to go myself."

Vicky was surprised to find herself blushing. And anxious to change the subject. She wasn't sure if he was being sincere or just polite. And she was more than willing to just leave it at that.

"Like I said," she switched gears, "I just can't thank you enough for use of the apartment. It's just so... amazing and generous, I just don't know what all to say. But I promise to move out just as soon as I can find my own place."

He easily shrugged off her concern. "Not to worry, please.

You're welcome to stay as long as you need."

She reached back to the table where she'd set her purse. "Anyway, I wanted to bring you a little something. Just to say *thank you*. I wasn't sure what to get, but I know how much you like books. But then I had a hard time finding something I didn't think you'd already have."

She handed him the well-worn volume. The spine was cracked and the title long worn off. He opened the hardbound cover to read the title. *Around the World in Seventy-Two Days,* by Nellie Bly. Inside the front she'd written her name and the date in pencil.

Victoria Rose, 1920. She couldn't have been more than eight years old, he thought.

"I read it as a girl," she told him. My mother gave it to me."

Her eyes lit up as he carefully turned the yellowed pages. His did as well. It was exactly the sort of thing he'd most appreciate. Still, she was apprehensive about the choice of gift. Even more so after sitting there in his library, surrounded by thousands of volumes. "Please tell me you haven't read it, though to be honest I'll be quite stunned."

He was equally stunned. "Actually, I haven't."

Abbie had read it, of course. And had suggested it to him more than once. But he'd been understandably more interested in Bly's previous title, and never gotten around to this one. It seemed just then for good reason.

"It inspired me to become a reporter," she told him. "And made me want to go out and see the world. Well, still working on the second part."

Brent was stunned that she would give him something so valuable. "I couldn't possibly take this from you. Not a gift from your mother."

"Then consider it a loan," she told him.

He was practically speechless. "Thank you. I shall treat it with utmost care and return it post-haste."

"If that's your preference," she smiled. "But if you change your mind, it's yours to keep."

DETECTIVE SHAYNE lumbered down the sidewalk to McGillin's. It was early yet, but it had been a long day, and he needed a drink. Little did he know it was about to get longer still.

Willie Potatoes and Fingers Scarrone waited for him by the front door. They stepped out into the sidewalk to block his path.

Shayne huffed a quick shrug. Just one more thing to deal with. He thought Willie looked less intimidating with his arm still in a sling. Probably made it harder to get to his gun, too.

"Good evening, Detective," Willie greeted him with a smile."

"Alright, I'll play," Shayne replied. "What do you want?"

"What do say we go for a little ride?" Willie suggested. "Just want to have a little chat."

CHAPTER TWENTY-THREE

VICKY followed Worthington to the grand foyer and gave her dress another tug as they reached the front door. He graciously pretended not to notice.

"I do thank you for calling, Miss Rose," he told her. "I'm certain that your visit did much good for Master Gregor. We look forward to your return. You are most welcome any time."

Vicky was beyond grateful. Such a pleasant change from her evening with Denny's family.

"I just can't thank you enough for everything you've done for me," she replied. "There's no way I could ever repay you."

Vicky looked about conspiratorially as she took the photo from her purse. Then spoke to him in hushed tones so as not to be overheard.

"Actually, before I go, there's something important I need to tell you. It's about one of your maids."

THERE WAS dead silence in the back of the car. Fingers was behind the wheel while Willie kept Shayne company in the back seat. The hulking detective wasn't much for conversation himself, but for two guys who just wanted to chat, they weren't saying a peep.

Shayne took the opportunity to size them up. He knew their reputations and that they were both pretty tough.

Even after taking a bullet. But he'd fought tougher guys before and felt certain that if need be, he could handle them both, armed or not.

"So, you want to tell me where we're going?" Shayne asked.

"You'll see when we get there," Willie answered.

Shayne played along. "Thought you said you wanted to talk?"

Willie reassured him with a devious smile. "Don't worry about it, Detective. Just relax. We'll get there."

Shayne was smart enough to know this was all for show. Just to intimidate him.

But they couldn't have realized what he'd encountered down in the trenches during the War. He'd already been through a lot worse.

And then some.

VICKY wound her way through the Davenport Mansion in search of Louisa. The only thing she managed to find were a collection of puzzled looks. She wasn't sure if it was the dress or just her mere presence.

As luck would have it, she turned the corner into another room and found herself face-to-face with Leonore. And who was she chatting up? The hostess, Julia Davenport. The lovely young bride of Cecil Davenport IV.

Vicky was sure that Leonore's usual objects of feigned affection, Constance van Broman and distant cousin Gloria Lamonte, couldn't be far off.

Leonore immediately excused herself. She took Vicky by the arm and tugged her over to the side.

"What in the devil are you doing here? And wearing the *exact* same dress?"

That was clearly more of a crime than party crashing, Vicky realized.

"Don't worry about me," Vicky dismissed her. "I'm just here to meet a friend. Won't stick around long. Promise."

That's when the light bulb lit up over Leonore's head. She glanced over into the next room. There she was, the little Italian Princess, sitting all by her lonesome. As usual.

"Should have known you were joining your partner

in crime," Leonore smirked. "But don't think she'll get a single word in my column this time."

No wonder Mr. Gregor never goes to these things, Vicky thought. *He's the only sane one in the bunch.*

WILLIE POTATOES shoved his gun into Shayne's ribs as Fingers opened the car door. Shayne gave Willie an irritated look as he pondered whether or not to strangle him with his sling.

"Looks like we're here," Willie told him. "What do you say we get out and look around?"

Shayne didn't have to ask where. They'd passed through the great stone entrance gate on their way in. His eyes and ears had been assaulted by the smells and sounds of thousands of animals.

And the smell of death.

Second time in a day. Only this wasn't the rotted, lingering odor he'd experienced that morning. This was new and immediate. The smell of fresh blood filled in the air.

Terminal City, as its name suggested, was built on the railroads. And it's chief commodity from practically the day the first locomotive steamed into town was livestock. Before the trains went anywhere else, they went to the stockyards. Thousands of cattle, hogs, and sheep came through there every week. They came straight off the trains and sent down narrow chutes and directed into one of the hundreds of pens, all laid out in a perfect grid for as far as the eye could see.

There they were put up for sale and shipped out on the the very same trains on which they'd come in. But most of them ended up in the giant slaughterhouse that loomed behind them.

It was the perfect spot for Willie to make his point. For deep down inside, Willie Potatoes was a poet.

"You ever seen 'em slaughter an animal, Detective?" Willie asked. "I'm here to tell you, it ain't a pretty sight. They just knock 'em off, one after the other. Like an assembly line."

Shayne just stood there, stoic and silent. Careful to keep

both men within sight.

Willie gave a nod and they started up the long ramp up to the enormous butchery. It was a tall, wooden building that looked the length of a football field. The ramp was built wide and long for leading entire herds inside.

"Just wait till you see it," Willie informed him. "So much blood, it just runs like a river. But them cows and hogs, they don't know no better. They just get on the train, go for a little ride. No idea it's a one-way trip."

Once inside the huge building, Willie took great pride in pointing out the mechanisms of the "disassembly line." Such as the killing wheel that quickly hoisted hogs upside down and held them in place. Overhead meat hooks that ran on conveyor belts. Giant vats to boil hog hides for hair removal.

It would take the average farmer up to eight hours to butcher an animal. But here they could completely break down an entire hog in 35 minutes. It was a marvel of efficiency.

"You should bring your lovely wife and your boy down here for the tour one day," Willie beamed with amazement.

Then Willie gave him a friendly pat on the back. "You ever stop and think just where your food comes from, Detective?"

LOUISA led Vicky out of a pair of open French doors and onto the veranda. There was a lovely garden with a fountain and iron benches, all modeled in the style of a French chateau. Outside, they were able to relax a bit. She and Vicky both knew that the advantage of being disliked by everyone meant less chance of being overheard. Still, they were cautious and made certain that they didn't have company.

Louisa was also careful to keep her voice low. "I can't say too much, but I overheard a conversation where some people were talking about you. And it wasn't very nice. You should be careful."

Vicky had no problem guessing just whom she'd overheard. But she wasn't about to let this opportunity go by without pressing her for more information.

Louisa chose her words carefully. "Just that they think you ask too many questions. One of them promised to keep an eye on you."

Vicky was pretty sure she knew who that was, too. "Did they say anything else?" she asked.

Louisa thought for a moment. She was really hesitant to say more. But she knew that lives could easily be at stake. "They're really worried about the policeman. He might be in real danger. There was else something about an Ace, but they weren't sure that would be enough."

Vicky was puzzled. She hadn't heard anything about an Ace. Could this be about the Man in Black? That didn't make sense. If he was working with the Mob, why would he have tried to kill Big Jack?

Louisa was anxious to go. She'd already betrayed her father's trust and didn't want to say any more than necessary. But Vicky had just one more question.

"What about this Ace?" she pressed. "Is there anything you can tell me about it?"

"I don't remember exactly," Louisa told her. "Something to do with the policeman. Some kind of assurance. Please, just be careful."

FINGERS opened the car door again and Willie nudged Shayne to get out. This time they were standing back in front of the police precinct.

"Really glad we got a chance to have this talk," Willie told him as he stuffed a handful of bills into Shayne's shirt pocket. "When you get to McGillin's, be sure to have a few rounds on Big Jack."

It was all Shayne could do to not take both of them down right then and there. But he'd easily realized that they'd only wanted scare to him.

Willie patted Shayne on the arm. "See you around, Pal! We'll have to do this again sometime. Be sure to tell your lovely wife I said hello."

Shayne just stood there and gritted his teeth as they got back in the car and drove off. Within minutes they'd rounded the corner and were gone.

He didn't realize it, but Shayne wasn't alone. Detective

Lieutenant Flynn had watched the entire encounter from his third floor office window.

VICKY sipped a glass of orange juice as she carefully watched the clientele commune around the bar at McGillin's. She didn't need another night of drinking, especially dressed the way she was.

Somehow she'd managed to get her same table as before, despite it being a Friday night. Since most everyone there was crowded around the bar, she reasoned a table by the door was the least popular option. Unless you're a reporter on the lookout for someone.

Worried that she might miss him again, she hadn't taken the time to go home and change. Still in her luxurious red gown, she looked like she'd just escaped from a fancy dress ball. Which was more or less true.

Naturally, she got a lot more gentlemanly attention, too. There she was far less discreet about hiking up her dress and easily lost count of the numerous catcalls. And the pickup lines ranged from "Are you a runaway princess?" to "Are you a runaway bridesmaid?"

The sight of a beautiful woman in a bar wearing a low-cut, form-fitting red dress was just too enticing for any man. Drunk or sober.

And once again, there was no sign of Shayne.

While she watched and waited, she just sipped her orange juice and mulled over this whole Ace business. She tried to reason it out, starting with the obvious. *Ace in the whole, ace up your sleeve, flying ace.* She had no idea. And clearly needed more information.

In the end, she was only sure about one thing. This was definitely a new wrinkle.

She was just about to call it a night (again) when she noticed a large, hulking figure lumber in through the door. From the irritated look on his face she could tell something had prevented him from getting there sooner. And that particular something was still on his mind.

Probably not the best night to approach him, she thought. But she didn't have much choice. The trial was only days away and she was running out of time.

If she played her cards right, she might finally get some answers.

Vicky grabbed her purse and her drink and hustled up to the bar. Somehow she managed to squeeze in between him and the guy on the next stool. "You're a hard man to reach, Detective," she shouted above the noise.

He gave her a deeply puzzled look. She was much too well dressed to be a barfly. But there was something familiar about her. "Never thought you'd be the kind who avoids the press," she added.

That's when he figured it out. He just shook his head in frustration. "You just don't give up, do you? Anything to get my attention."

"Whatever it takes, Detective," she informed him. "Sooner you realize that about me, the better."

"Can't you just leave me alone?"

Shayne grabbed his glass and bottle of whiskey. Then barreled his way to the empty table by the door. There was no avoiding this conversation. But he wasn't about to have it where anyone could overhear.

She scooped up her train and followed right behind him. There was no using her feminine wiles with this one. Shayne operated on logic and gut instinct. And that was just what she'd give him.

"Look," she insisted, "You can deal with me now, or the Lord later."

He emptied his glass and quickly refilled it. "What difference does it make? Nails McCarthy had it coming a thousand times over. Never heard anybody complain when they plugged Dillinger."

"They're watching you," she informed him. "I heard it from a good source. They're watching us both."

Shayne slammed his glass on the table. Vicky was surprised it didn't break.

"Don't you think I know that?" he shouted.

Vicky moved the bottle further out of reach. There was no telling where his temper would take him. "I'm just trying to get to the truth, here. That's all. And I'm not the one who's having trouble sleeping at night."

He looked back at her with a stunned expression. She

quickly realized that hadn't been the best approach.

"How'd you know that?"

"Your wife told me," she confessed.

She thought for sure the glass would be shattered on that one. Instead, he got right up in her face and barked. The smell of whiskey unmistakable on his breath.

"You stay the hell away from my wife!"

"Just for the record," Vicky informed him as she gathered up her skirt to leave, "she's the one who came to see me. She doesn't want to lose you."

CHAPTER TWENTY-FOUR

THE TRIAL began first thing Monday morning.

Vicky took her seat in the back row of the press section. Naturally, all the prime spots were taken by Chester Lyons, Charlie Hecht, and the other usual suspects. Morty and Higgs sat with Vicky to keep her company.

It was her first time in the large, stately courtroom. The bench, jury box, and seating were all dark wood. The walls were a rich green with dark green columns and trim. Two grand, arched windows were on either side of the bench. Despite the growing number of spectators, the room was deathly quiet, save for a few whispers here and there.

Vicky casually looked about for any familiar faces. She was rather surprised to spot Brent Gregor and his Manservant, Mr. Worthington, seated on the opposite side. She immediately wondered why he was there. Especially since he was a known recluse. After all, she'd lived in his apartment for nearly a week and had only seen him at the mansion (which felt very odd indeed).

There was one face there that she didn't recognize. Unlike the rest of the press, he had to sit in the back of the courtroom. She later learned that his name was Ben Sanders, editor (and everything else) of *The Evening Hubbub*. And that he was there due to the bombing in Bronzeville.

She was even more surprised, however, to see Vito Spats

sitting on the back row. She'd thought for sure that the Mob wouldn't be caught within miles of this courtroom. He spotted her as well and tipped his bowler. She felt a sudden uneasiness in the pit of her stomach.

"What's he doing here?" she whispered to Morty.

"Making sure the verdict turns out like it's supposed to," the older newsman replied softly.

Higgs was just about to respond when Vicky beat him to it. "Pretty suspicious."

Higgs nodded towards the bench. "Same reason he's here."

Vicky looked up to see Chief LaSalle step out of the Judge's Chambers and take a seat up front.

ESTELLE MERCER slowly helped Big Jack into his white suit jacket and rewarded him with a kiss on the cheek. He was healing. But slowly.

She couldn't help but feel concerned. He'd always been so strong. And even though the worst had been luckily avoided, it was clear that the attack had weakened him.

"Why don't you just stay home again to-day, Darling?" she playfully suggested, careful to hide her actual motive.

Despite the tantalizing offer, he quickly shook his head in disagreement. "Spats and the boys been running things too long without me. Don't want them getting any ideas."

VICKY perched on the edge of her seat as a Police Officer pushed Nails, seated in a wheelchair, into the courtroom. She immediately had to wonder if his injuries were still that severe, or if it was just a sympathy ploy concocted by the Defense.

She glanced over to gauge Brent Gregor's reaction, but couldn't see him. Her view was blocked by Detectives Shayne and Flynn as they entered right behind Nails. The two decorated officers took their seats with the Prosecution.

"All rise!" the Bailiff shouted. "Court is now in session. The Honorable Judge H. Jacob Randolph presiding."

Vicky craned her neck as the elderly and respected Judge Randolph entered from his chambers and took the bench.

The Bailiff continued. "Your Honor, to-day's case is the

People vs. James McCarthy."

Judge Randolph carefully studied the docket and then peered over his glasses to address the D.A. "Doc, you ready to state your case?"

Doc Milford proudly clutched his suspenders and replied, "Yes, Jacob, we certainly are."

Judge Randolph then glanced to the Defense. "Young man, are you ready to state *your* case?"

Everyone in the courtroom was surprised when, instead of the young man at the defense table, it was the *young woman* who spoke up. "Yes, Your Honor, we are."

Her name was Helen Lockwood. She was thin and bookish, with her hair pulled back into a tight bun. Vicky knew the name, but had never met her in person. She actually worked in the public defender's office and typically handled prostitution cases. She managed to snag this one when McCarthy's previous attorney, the renowned H.H. O'Brien, dropped him as a client at the last minute. When it became astoundingly clear that he couldn't win.

The young gentleman by her side was actually her assistant. A law student who's father had gotten him a job for the summer.

Judge Randolph was clearly taken aback and stared at her for the longest moment. "Very well then," he replied, "let's begin, shall we?"

TOMMY CLAMS stepped out the front door of Big Jack's narrow, three-story brick home. The street was so quiet the only sounds were chirping birds and the neighborhood kids playing stickball. He had to wonder why Big Jack had such a modest place, while Spats was living it up at The Belmont. *Must have a lot of dough stashed in coffee cans,* he thought.

As Big Jack's latest driver, he didn't have much to worry about. Nails was still recovering, Whitey and Squint were both in a million pieces, and the rest of those yellow Irishmen were either in the ground or cooling their heels in the joint.

But his job was to keep Big Jack safe. He'd gotten the post while Cherry Nose was laid up. And he wasn't about to slack off. So he made double sure the coast was clear anyway. Even if it was just from kids on bicycles or squirrels finding nuts.

Estelle opened the door. She was quite a looker, that one. And dressed in a sheer negligee as she kissed Big Jack at the door.

Tommy was careful, too, and kept his eyes where they belonged.

He kept watch on the street as he opened the car door and helped the old man inside. And pretended not to notice how painful it was.

DETECTIVE FLYNN *accidentally* bumped his arm as he took the witness stand and was sworn in. He clutched it tightly (shockingly free of a sling despite the passage of time, Vicky thought) and winced in pain. The jurors and many in the audience murmured in sympathy.

"Nails took three bullets and nobody gives two shakes about him," Vicky commented.

Doc Milford again tugged his suspenders as he approached the witness stand.

"Detective Lieutenant Flynn," he began, "could you begin by telling me just how many years of dedicated service you've given to our fair city as an officer of the law? Please, take your time."

Flynn softly rubbed his arm as he responded, "Been a police officer almost twenty years now."

"A *decorated* police officer, is that right?" Doc Milford added. "As I recall, you were just recently promoted?"

"Yes, Doc," Flynn replied. "Just a few weeks ago, I was promoted to the position of Detective Lieutenant."

"And I'm if not mistaken," Doc Milford continued, "you were promoted as a *direct result* of your involvement of this *very* case. Is that also correct?"

"Yes, Doc, it is," Flynn confirmed.

Vicky locked her gaze on the Defense and wondered if they were going to raise even a single objection to Doc Milford's obvious grandstanding. The answer was clear. They weren't.

Doc Milford stepped back from the witness box and gazed

directly at the jury. "Detective Lieutenant Flynn, could you tell me, in your own words, what happened on the evening of June 24, Nineteen Hundred and Thirty-Six?"

Flynn calmly and convincingly regaled the court with the "official" version of the events that had transpired that night. He carefully explained how Nails had grabbed a pistol from the desk and fired at both him and then-Officer Shayne, striking Flynn in the arm before the brave Detective fired back in self-defense.

Vicky thought for sure the defense would tackle *these* points. How was this attempted murder of both officers if Nails only fired (supposedly) the gun once? How was it that Flynn, who'd just been shot, actually fired back? Why didn't Shayne fire in self-defense? Did Shayne even draw his weapon?

Of course, none of these questions were asked. And again, not a single objection was raised. It was all Vicky could do to not speak up. Thank goodness she had Morty there to keep her in her seat.

When it was over, Judge Randolph even thanked Flynn for his loyal years of service to the city. She felt another headache coming on.

EGGS MILANO stood guard outside the Four Diamonds with Fingers Scarrone. The two men watched the street in both directions as Tommy pulled up with Big Jack to let the boss out.

Eggs had wanted that job himself. He'd suggested it to Spats, but Spats just shrugged him off and gave it to Tommy. Eggs couldn't help but think it was because of his cousin. Paulie'd had that same job before until those Irish bastards Whitey and Monk bumped him off trying to take out Big Jack.

He and Fingers weren't supposed to leave their posts under any circumstances. But as he watched Big Jack grab his shoulder and struggle to get out of the car, he had to do something.

Fingers obviously thought it was the right idea, too. Because he helped.

The longer Big Jack was out on that sidewalk, the more vulnerable he was.

Eggs had never seen the Boss so weak before. And from only two slugs! Cherry Nose had taken seven. Sure, he wasn't dancing a jig just yet. But he was still kicking.

Fingers opened the front door and let Big Jack into the Four Diamonds. Tommy got back in the car, took it around back.

Both men let out a sigh of relief once Big Jack was safely inside.

And shrugged at each other in disbelief.

VICKY raced down the hallway, her heels echoing against the shiny tile floors. She was determined to speak to Brent Gregor before he left. "Mr. Gregor!" she called out as Worthington was about to wheel him outside. Two large Police Officers stood by the door to carry him down the steps.

"Miss Rose!" His face lit up as she rushed to greet him. "How pleasant to see you again."

"I just wanted to ask," she began, fishing for something to say, "what you think of the trial so far?"

His face quickly devolved into a frown. "I'm not exactly sure why I came, to be perfectly honest. I just hope people realize that there are more victims than those being discussed here to-day."

His words struck her like poetry. She quickly scribbled in her notebook. "Can I quote you on that?"

He thought it over for just a moment. "Yes, please do. Now, if you'll excuse me, I really must be going. I'm afraid I'm due some much needed rest."

"Yes, of course," she said and backed away. There was so much more she'd wanted to say. To thank him *again* for use of the apartment. And to ask what had happened with the maid.

Perhaps another day.

She was just about to return to the courtroom when he called out to her. "Oh, and thank you again for the book. I'm really quite enjoying it."

"You're welcome," she barely got the words out as they wheeled him out the door.

DAPPER SHERIDAN was brought in wearing his tailored suit and a pair of handcuffs. Vicky thought this was hardly necessary and again all just another part of the show trial this proceeding had become.

Vicky checked her watch. It was already well into the afternoon and Shayne had yet to take the stand. As soon as he was released from his shackles, Dapper was sworn in.

Shockingly enough, the Defense finally objected.

Miss Lockwood quickly stood up and made her case. Vicky wanted to cheer.

"Your Honor, this man has a long criminal history and is currently in police custody for a parole violation related to this very case," she stated firmly.

Judge Randolph immediately turned to the D.A. "What say you, Doc?"

"Your Honor," Doc Milford countered, "Mr. Sheridan, the gentleman in question, was at the scene of the crime and serves as a material witness. Any objections that the lovely Miss Lockwood has should have been raised prior to the start of this trial."

"Overruled," Judge Randolph stated with a quick bang of his gavel. "You may proceed."

Doc Milford grabbed his suspenders as Miss Lockwood sat back down in frustration.

"Mr. Sheridan," Doc Milford began with his usual bombast and eloquence, "tell me in your own words what happened on the evening of June 24th?"

A humbled and contrite Dapper dutifully recounted the same version of the story Flynn had provided earlier. Nearly word for word.

Vicky just shook her head in disgust. "He wasn't even in the room," she whispered to Morty.

As Dapper continued, the rear door of the courtroom opened quietly. That's when she received her biggest surprise thus far.

Detective Shayne also turned around as his wife, Agnes, and son, Bobby Junior, entered the courtroom and carefully made their way up to the front. They sat down right behind the good detective. Just in time for his testimony.

"This your doing?" Morty asked.

"Wish it was," Vicky replied.

THE BLACK SPECTRE moved silently up the rear staircase of the Four Diamonds with his guns ready. He reached the second floor landing and leaned up against the wall. As before, he kept to the shadows and remained completely unseen.

The door was ajar. He peered through and drifted down the hallway towards the same gambling hall he'd infiltrated previously.

This time was drastically different, however.

There were no guests. No revelers. And no city officials.

And save for the two men in the back alley (which he'd easily eluded), he hadn't seen a single guard.

That had him deeply puzzled.

CHAPTER TWENTY-FIVE

DETECTIVE SHAYNE stood in the witness box and placed his large right hand on the Bible. He looked straight at Agnes and Bobby Junior as the Bailiff repeated the oath.

"Do you solemnly swear that you will tell the truth, the whole truth, and nothing but the truth, so help you God?"

"Yes, I swear," Shayne answered firmly.

He sat down uncomfortably as Doc Milford approached the Bench. "Detective Shayne, if you don't mind my asking, how long have you been with the police department?"

Shayne shifted in his seat and stared straight at Bobby Junior. "Twelve years, eight months."

"And this is not your first time to be decorated is it, Detective?" Doc Milford asked proudly.

"No, Sir," Shayne mumbled.

"If you don't mind speaking up, Detective," Doc Milford chuckled. "My hearing's not as good as it once was."

"Sorry, Sir," Shayne spoke up. "No, this is not the first time, Sir."

Shayne twisted awkwardly in the witness stand as Doc Milford regaled the jury with the heroic tale of how Shayne "ran headlong into a *barrage* of gunfire" to rescue three children.

Shayne attempted to dispute the use of the word "barrage" and his "near death" from being shot, but he was the only one who did. The Defense stayed silent through Milford's entire grandstanding performance.

Vito Spats sat up straight on the back row and adjusted his bowler. Despite his efforts to be noticed, he was already impossible to miss.

Doc Milford eventually moved on to the day in question. Instead of having Shayne recount the events in his own words, as the well-spoken Flynn had done, Doc Milford just asked him a series of pointed questions. The plan, Vicky noted, was to just have him corroborate Flynn's version of events with a simple yes or no. And then get him off the stand as quickly as possible.

"Detective Shayne, on the evening of June 24th, did you accompany Detective Lieutenant Flynn to the office of James McCarthy with the intention of learning the whereabouts of Edward O'Leary?"

"Yes."

"Detective Shayne, did you and Detective Flynn then enter said office and encounter the defendant, James McCarthy?"

Vicky moved again to the edge of her seat. They were making this as easy as possible for Shayne to cooperate. She noticed, however, that the detective never once looked at the D.A. His gaze was firmly locked on the faces of his wife and young son.

"Detective Shayne," Milford continued, "did you see James McCarthy draw his weapon from the desk drawer and fire it at Detective Flynn, striking him in the arm?"

Shayne clenched his teeth and sat there silent as a stone edifice. His gaze firmly affixed on his admiring child.

"Detective Shayne," Doc Milford repeated, releasing his suspenders. "Remember now, Sir, you are *under oath*. Did you *see* James McCarthy shoot and injure Detective Flynn?"

"No," Shayne retorted firmly. "No, I did *not*."

THE BLACK SPECTRE retraced his path through the large doors and into the spacious gambling room. Big Jack's office, where he expected to find the notorious mobster, was just in the back.

The casino was a picture of contrasts from his first visit.

The lights all out, the tables quiet, and the room devoid of people.

There was only one sign of life. A sliver of light coming from the slightly ajar office door.

The Spectre hadn't noticed the pineapple motif when he was there before. Carved into the doors and wooden trim. Repeated in the wallpaper. The symbol for hospitality.

He was about to move to the office when he spotted one more. A ceramic pineapple that had previously been on the mantle.

Only now it was smashed on the floor below.

JUDGE RANDOLPH shouted and banged his gavel repeatedly. "Order! Order in this court!"

Doc Milford did his best to rescue the situation. "Thank you, Your Honor. Now, Detective Shayne, in your sworn testimony before this trial, you clearly stated that you *saw the defendant* shoot Detective Flynn."

Milford paced a moment to let that sink in. Shayne tugged uncomfortably at his collar. His gaze still firmly locked on his family.

"Are you now saying," Milford continued, "that in all the commotion and under threat against your *own* life, you didn't actually *see* the defendant shoot Detective Flynn?"

Shayne had reached his breaking point. "No. It didn't happen that way at all," he replied.

The courtroom erupted again.

Vicky jumped to her feet along with everyone else. Her first instinct was to bolt for the telephones in the lobby and call in the story. Which is exactly what Charlie and Lyons did. But there was no way she was going to miss what followed.

And her byline would be all the better for it.

No amount of banging from the Judge could calm the assembled down this time. Detective Shayne stood up proudly and addressed his son directly. Consequences be damned.

"I'm sorry, but I took an oath to defend the law. And I took an oath to tell the truth just now. I can't sit up here in front of God, my wife, my boy, and the good people of this city and *not* tell the truth. The whole truth. The *actual* truth."

The attorneys on both sides just stood there in stunned silence.

Agnes Shayne was both shocked and relieved.

Bobby Junior stood up straight. His little face beamed with pride.

"It wasn't self defense," Detective Shayne stated.

"Nails McCarthy was unarmed."

THE BLACK SPECTRE moved silently towards Big Jack's office. He peered through the doorway.

Just as he expected, the old Mafioso was slumped over at his desk. That's why the building was so empty.

The Spectre went inside for closer observation.

Big Jack, still resplendent in his bright, white suit, had just eaten his last meal. Literally.

He'd collapsed face down in a large bowl of linguine and clams.

The corpse looked fresh. It hadn't been long.

He quickly surmised that Big Jack had been murdered by someone he knew and trusted. His desk faced the door. There was little room behind it.

Yet he'd died from three gunshots to the back of the head.

JUDGE RANDOLPH banged his gavel again as Doc Milford screamed his objections. All of which were to no avail.

Miss Lockwood couldn't believe what she was hearing. Or that she had actually won her case. She was tempted to interject, but the normally quiet Shayne was doing just fine on his own.

"Detective Flynn shot Nails McCarthy three times in cold blood! Finally, he turned the gun on himself to make it look like there was a struggle. That big promotion was just to keep me quiet. Then he threatened my career. Even threatened my family! Just to get me to lie about it."

Agnes Shayne tried to cover Junior's ears, but was unable to block out her husband's booming voice.

"Nails McCarthy is guilty of a lot of things," Shayne concluded. "And he probably deserves to spend the rest of his life in prison. But he's not guilty of this."

"Who threatened your family?" Miss Lockwood called out.

"The Mob," Shayne answered forcefully. "Detective Flynn made a deal with the Mob!"

Flynn pointed at Shayne with his injured arm and spat angrily, "You'll burn in hell for this!"

"Shayne better watch his back leaving this courtroom," Morty commented.

Vito Spats just sat there quietly for another moment. Then tipped his hat to the people next to him and left.

Chief LaSalle did the same.

THE CROWD spilled out of the courtroom like a bursting dam. The few reporters that remained forced their way through the masses in hopes of getting to a phone. Most everyone else just wanted to get out so that they could tell someone, anyone, what they'd just witnessed.

Shayne told Agnes and Bobby Junior to stay put. She tried to pull little Bobby to the side, but they were swept out into the hallway with the rest of the clamoring horde.

Higgs actually ducked into the Judge's chambers and got through to the *Standard* before he was caught. Higgs bragged later that he gave the Judge a sob story about not being able to compete "with those young whipper snappers," so Randolph had pity and let him stay on the line.

Morty was the only reporter who just stayed put and jotted down his story right where he sat. When it was all over, he casually walked out of the nearly empty courtroom and down the street to the *Standard*.

Flynn practically led the charge of those pushing their way out. He even toppled a reporter or two. After Shayne's explosive testimony, he wasn't about to stick around to see what happened next. Especially if it involved his arrest.

Which is exactly why Vicky stayed on his heels. She well knew that with all the players involved in this sordid tale, there was little chance Flynn would make it out free of handcuffs. Or worse.

Detective Lieutenant Flynn was almost to the door when Vicky spotted a familiar face in the crowd. She didn't know him well, but she'd seen him enough to know his name. And like the rest of his ilk, it wasn't easily forgotten.

Besides, he was the only one pushing his way *into* the courthouse.

Vicky screamed, "Gun!"

But it was too late.

Fingers was too close to his prey. And it was impossible to hear her over the cacophony of voices that filled the hallway and then some.

But everyone heard the gunshots.

There were three loud pops. One right after the other. Fingers had stuck his pistol into Flynn's gut and pulled the trigger.

If there'd been any more, they were easily drowned out by the endless sound of screams as people dropped to the floor.

Had he done the same and scrambled out with the rest of the crowd, he might have lived. That very well might have even been the plan.

But instinct told Fingers to run.

And after the life he'd led, that instinct was just too hard to ignore.

He'd almost reached the doorway when a barrage of Police gunfire took him down from all sides. Followed by an explosion of even more screams.

He had to have known it was a one-way ride.

Especially since he'd just gunned down one of their own in a building full of Cops. Dirty or not.

When the last echoes of gunfire had died out, Vicky finally felt safe enough to look up. Many still remained huddled down until the Police reassured everyone repeatedly that it was safe.

Only then was there an accounting of the dead.

The cries of pain immediately told her that others had been hit. A few from ricochets. Others from direct hits.

Vicky clutched her forehead. The loud echo of the gunfire against the marble surfaces still pounded inside her head.

She looked up to see a man standing over her.

Ben Sanders offered her a hand and helped her up. "You okay, Miss Rose?"

She had to check her person just to make sure. "Yes, I think so. Thank you."

Shayne rushed through the hallway, did his best to step around those that were scattered all over the floor. Glanced hurriedly at each face as he passed.

He called out frantically, but received no answer.

"Agnes! Bobby!"

Vicky quickly searched about. But she didn't see them, either.

Suddenly, Shayne stopped short in his tracks. His face turned ghostly white.

He crumbled to the floor in cries of pain.

All that he held dear in the world had suddenly and horribly been taken from him.

EPILOGUE

THE NEXT several days saw funerals both large and small.

Big Jack's funeral more than rivaled that of Dean O'Boyle just two months earlier. Once again, Vicky, Frank, and the rest of the newsroom watched from the windows of *The Daily Crusader*. The parade stretched for blocks on end with the most ornate and expensive casket the city had ever seen. And as with O'Boyle and the bosses before him, every flower shop in the city worked overtime to create floral arrangements of unprecedented achievement.

Smaller than Big Jack's but still quite impressive was the funeral for Detective Lieutenant Michael Flynn. The procession past City Hall and Police Headquarters was given escort and honors for their fallen brother. At the graveside service, he was given a twenty-one gun salute and his wife, Ethel, was presented with his badge and hat, both suitably framed. The revelations from the trial were swept under the rug and quickly forgotten. Nothing like getting gunned down on the job to make people forget.

The day prior, Detective Shayne had a modest, quiet funeral for both Agnes and Bobby Junior. Despite a fair amount of ill will towards him in the department, none of his fellow officers wished upon him anything close to the unspeakable tragedy he'd experienced. Accordingly, his brothers in blue provided a police escort and were well represented among the mourners. They even dipped into the "widows and orphans fund" to help with the funeral expenses.

Chief LaSalle, however, did not attend.

Agnes' family attended from Ohio, as well as their friends from both church and the neighborhood. Including a few Shayne didn't recognize. One in particular offered her condolences afterwards. She introduced herself as Mrs. Sally Poole. She'd known Agnes many years earlier when they'd both worked as maids for the Gregor family. From one tragedy to another.

Fingers Scarrone was buried in a pauper's grave on the outside of town. The plots were owned by the county and usually reserved for executed prisoners.

THE FOLLOWING week, Vicky found herself once again outside the Belmont. The glittering jewel of the city, the faint scars from all the bullet holes barely visible. She found it so very fitting.

This time however, she was given the red carpet treatment. The middle-aged Doorman immediately opened the front entrance and happily ushered her inside. "Good to see you again, Miss Rose. Right this way."

Likewise, Big Joey also greeted her warmly just as soon as she entered the grand lobby. "Welcome, Miss Rose. If you'll follow me."

The crowds quickly parted as he lead her across the lobby. A private elevator waited for them at the end of the bank.

EDNA HEMMINGS followed Mr. Worthington into the grand foyer of the Gregor Mansion and marveled at the opulent surroundings. Even as a young negro woman who'd grown up in rural Virginia, she was no stranger to the fine restaurants of New York City and Paris. But this was easily the largest home she had ever entered. And even more astonishing was that it was for just one man.

Once Mr. Worthington had dispensed with the greetings and pleasantries, he began to cover the rules of the house. And there were many. The majority of which resulted in dismissal if broken.

"We do not touch the Master's belongings unless

required to do so," he instructed. "I cannot emphasize this point enough. Most especially in regards to Mrs. Gregor's wardrobe and jewelry, which are stored in the attic. You are not to enter the attic under any circumstances whatsoever unless instructed otherwise. Or you will be dismissed. Understood?"

"Yes, Sir," she answered dutifully.

They soon reached a set of closed doors. "This is the Master's Study. These doors are to remain locked at all times. No one, and I mean no one, is permitted to enter. Understood?"

He offered no explanation. But none was necessary. She well knew that this was why it was called the *Murder Mansion*. Even more importantly, she knew not to say a word about it.

"Yes, Sir," she replied.

Pleased with their progress thus far, Mr. Worthington stood tall and straightened his waistcoat. "Very good. Now, if you shall follow me to the kitchen, I should like to introduce you to the rest of the staff."

VICKY sat down anxiously in front of Vito Spats in the living room of his luxurious suite. She casually looked around to take in the opulence that surrounded her. It reminded her of Brent Gregor's apartment, though not nearly as spacious. In the past, she'd always eyed such living spaces with envy. And even though it wasn't her own, on this occasion she actually had something better. She had to chuckle at the thought.

But what surprised her even more was her lack of fear. Even with Willie Potatoes standing guard at the door. Even surrounded on all sides by armed killers.

She'd faced that already. And in her parents' home of all places. But what steeled her nerves even more was the fact that, this time, she was an invited guest.

Vito Spats had summoned her there. Not met on the street and forced into a car as was their custom, but with a formal invitation. An phone call requesting her presence. The only caveat was that she not bring a notebook or recording device of any kind.

Spats sat back and tapped his pinky-ringed finger on the lamp table next to his large, dark leather chair. He offered her a smile that looked at once both devious and welcoming.

She was anxious, yes, but anxious for answers. And now it looked like she might actually get them. To what end, she had no idea.

"I've given your request a lot of thought, Miss Rose," he explained. "And truth be told, I'm gonna help you. Tell you everything I know. No strings attached."

She eyed him skeptically.

Why would he do that? She had nothing to offer in return. And the Mob wasn't exactly known for their charity. Not when it came to information. Spats had something else up his sleeve. She was sure of it.

But she wasn't about to let any of that get in her way.

"The Man in Black," she posited. "Is *he* the one who rescued me at the Asylum?"

"Yes," he told her.

She had to let that sink in for a moment. After all these many weeks. After all the skepticism she'd faced. Even from herself. She'd finally confirmed it.

Assuming he wasn't lying, of course.

"Why? Why was he even there?"

"I've honestly no idea," Spats replied.

But just when she thought every answer would lead to a tacit denial, he offered what he *did* actually know.

She sat there in utter amazement as he detailed everything he and his men had encountered that night. How the Ghost Man had faced off against the Orderlies. Broken one's arm, choked another, and given one a concussion. How he'd faced off against Ned, gotten scared, and had actually tried to run away.

She couldn't believe what she was hearing. Especially the last part about the Ghost Man running away.

Again, with the assumption that he was telling the truth.

Willie couldn't believe what he was hearing, either. *Spats was spilling everything. And to a reporter, no less! A hell of a looker, yeah. But still a reporter.* As much as it pained him, though, he knew enough to be a good soldier and kept his yap shut.

"Who called the Fire Department?" she asked.

"Couldn't say," he replied.

She'd originally assumed it was Denny, but he'd strongly denied it. She could only assume it was one of the Nurses. But why, she had no idea.

She was tempted to ask about the Ace that Louisa had mentioned, but there was no way to broach the subject without likely compromising her source.

Better to leave that one for another day.

For her next question, she opted to try something more open-ended. "What can you tell me about the hit on Big Jack?"

Vicky sat back in wide-eyed silence as Spats spared not a single detail. How Big Jack had just brought Salvatore Crocetti upstairs. And that both Chief LaSalle and Mayor Barker were there playing Blackjack.

She nodded knowingly. Surprised, but not surprised. Willie just shook his head in disbelief.

Spats then told her how he felt a strange chill (*That was interesting*). Just before the lights went out —

"Wait a minute," she asked. "You say the lights went out?"

"Yeah," he confirmed. "Just like at the Asylum."

That was even more interesting, she thought. Though again, she had no idea why.

Finally, he told her how the Ghost Man had opened fire, struck Big Jack in the shoulder, and was hit several times before he made his escape. How they'd followed him to an alley, seen the trail of blood, and rained dozens of rounds upon his automobile before he disappeared.

"To where?" she asked. "Did you find him?"

"No," he answered, the anger and disappointment clear in his voice. "Whoever he is, someone is helping him."

This time she was certain he was telling the truth. Everything he told her squared exactly with what she already knew. Both from Charlie Hecht and conversations in the City Room.

"Who do you think it is?" she asked. "The North Side?"

"That was my original thought, yes," he confessed. "But since then, I've come to doubt it. No specific reason, mind you. Just my gut's telling me different."

That was when she noticed that he'd only referred to himself in the entire conversation. And that except in regards to the shooting at the Four Diamonds, he'd *never once* mentioned Big Jack.

"Well, one thing's for certain," she concluded. "He's certainly not working for you."

MOLLIE stepped into the servant's kitchen and found Mr. Worthington fixing a pot of tea. She tried to read his expression, but as was his usual, he remained a closed book.

"Close the door, please," he instructed her. That was all she needed to realize that their conversation was not about to go well. He invited her to sit down.

"As you know," he stated, "Elyse confessed to *borrowing* Mrs. Gregor's dresses and jewelry. And for that, she was dismissed."

"Yes, Sir," Mollie answered with her head low.

Worthington glared at her knowingly, but otherwise showed no emotion. "But she's not the guilty party, is she?"

"No Sir, she's not."

"Very well," Worthington stated as he got to his feet. "Gather your things. Your services are no longer required."

"Yes, Sir," Mollie answered through tear-filled eyes. "I understand, Sir."

She looked back at Mr. Worthington, but he offered no sympathy. She could only bow her head in shame.

That's all she ever was. A servant. All she could have ever hoped to be. And now she no longer had that.

WITH VICKY GONE, Willie was finally able to voice his confusion. He paced about anxiously. Both unsure of what to say or where to begin. But being Spats' right hand, he knew he had the leeway to say something.

"Spats, no disrespect," Willie stuttered. "But I swear, I don't understand. You told her *everything*. I mean, for a minute there, I thought you was gonna confess to stealing milk money in the second grade. And what I really can't figure is, we got *nothing* in return."

Spats just sat back and smiled at his underboss. "That's where you're wrong, Willie. We got plenty. I got Miss Rose working for *me* now."

Willie tried to make sense of it, but couldn't. "How you figure that?"

"She's like a bloodhound," he explained. "I've given her everything she needs to put her on the scent. And I promise you, she won't stop. Not until she finds out who this Ghost Man really is."

Willie finally had a better grasp, but still wasn't convinced. "But what if she don't tell you? I mean, she just took down our *top nut* at the police department!"

"Exactly," Spats reassured him.

WORTHINGTON hurried through the grand house in search of Master Gregor. His first stop, of course, was the solarium. He was more than a little surprised to not only find it unoccupied, but Master Gregor's book was discarded upon the lamp table.

He followed an open door to discover him outside on the rear veranda. Just sitting in his chair. Enjoying the warm summer breeze, the chirping of the birds, and the fountains so carefully maintained by Mr. Oldstead.

The young master looked at long last content. Finally at peace for the first time in his entire adult life.

The trusted Valet so didn't want to spoil it. But he was afraid that he must.

"Master Gregor," Worthington hesitantly interrupted. "So sorry to bother you, Sir. But a telegram has just arrived. I'm afraid it's from Paris."

Brent knew as well as Worthington that a cable from the City of Light could only bring bad news. But certainly not unexpected.

Brent showed no emotion. "Is it from Anna?"

"Yes, Sir," the older gentleman confirmed. "I'm afraid so."

Worthington handed the small yellow Western Union envelope to Brent. The young master eyed it carefully. He didn't have to open it. He knew exactly what message it contained. There was little reason for her to contact him otherwise. And he knew exactly what the coming days held in store.

He would have liked to say this didn't exactly happen at a good time. But when do they ever? Truth be told, it was just as good a time as any.

Because the fact of the matter was, and as cold as it sounded, it was a part of his life that had actually died away many years earlier.

Worse still, it had happened when he was only a child. And in the most desperate time of his young life. And that was something he'd never been able to forgive.

"Shall I open it for you, Sir?" Worthington asked.

Brent looked at the older man with appreciation. The one person who'd always been there for him. Always willing to soften the blows.

"No, but thank you, Worthington," he replied.

Brent tore open the small envelope and read its contents. He let it fall to his lap.

It was just as he'd suspected.

"Grandpa Nate died."

END.

READ THE FIRST EXCITING CHAPTER!

An ambitious reporter looking for her big break. A millionaire recluse looking for a cure. Can they survive a violent, corrupt city?

Vicky Rose is a reporter stuck in the City Hall beat, but she knows she's destined to cover crime. She sees her chance at a big break when the mayor is murdered in his office.

Reclusive millionaire Brent Gregor has been trapped in a wheelchair since the night a home intruder killed his father. Now, the only thing he cares about is being able to walk again.

The mayor's murder reeks of mob violence, but all the evidence points to someone else. Vicky knows the only hope of finding the truth rests in Gregor's hands, but he's unwilling to help until the one person who might be able to cure him changes his mind....

www.blackhoodpress.com

READ THE PREVIOUS EXCITING CHAPTER!

A crusading reporter out to prove her worth. A burgeoning hero in denial about his.

When a Mob Boss is gunned down by police, Daily Crusader reporter Vicky Rose is the only one who suspects he was unarmed. Desperate to justify her promotion to the crime beat, her search for the truth leads her into a cesspool of corruption deeper than she ever imagined.

Brent Gregor, his existence as The Black Spectre still a deeply-held secret, only wants to use his newfound powers to win back what he has lost. And to take revenge on those who took it from him.

Both face unexpected consequences that could cost them their lives. And both have to decide if what they wanted was actually worth the price.

www.blackhoodpress.com

About the Author

Roger Alford grew up on a steady diet of *Star Wars* and Jim Henson. After discovering old time radio and movie serials in college, he realized he'd been born in the wrong decade. His Internet videos, which include the popular mash-ups *The Twilight Zone: Planet of the Apes* and *Raiders of the Lost Ark: The Serial*, have been featured on ABC News, CNN, Inside Edition, plus multiple books and newspapers. When he's not plotting the latest adventures of The Black Spectre or brushing up on Mafia history, he's traveling the country and eating in great restaurants with his wife and family.

INDIA:
22-1-13-3-26-22-16 25-17-18-18-19-22
5-17-18 18-17-17 13-9-17-14-19
18-17 18-3-19 18-22-15-18-3